Twisted Lives

Ali Spooner

Affinity
eBook Press
NZ
2014

Twisted Lives
©2014 by Ali Spooner

Affinity E-Book Press NZ LTD.
Canterbury, New Zealand

1st Edition

ISBN: 978-1-927282-92-2

Editor: Ruth Stanley

Cover Irish Dragon Designs

Acknowledgements

I would like to thank Affinity Ebook Press, my publisher, and staff for giving me the opportunity to publish this work. I would also like to thank Terry Baker, whose wonderful reviews have inspired me to do more with my writing. To my readers, thank you for supporting me and providing feedback on my stories.

Dedication

I would like to dedicate this book to my readers. Thank you for the wonderful feedback and continued encouragement to keep writing. Without your support, none of this could be possible.

Table of Contents

Chapter One

The tape measure in her hand reeled in as Alex Graves shook her head. "This just won't do, Glen," she said to her site supervisor. "This beam is off a good two inches and will have to be reset."

"Yes, ma'am," Glen said, obviously disappointed. "I'll get right on it."

"Why don't you and the boys reset the beam, then head out for the weekend," Alex suggested as she placed a comforting hand on Glen's shoulder. "We've all put in a hard week and deserve a break."

Alex was a tough boss who demanded perfection from her crew, but Glen was truly thankful that she'd chosen him as her right hand. Over the four years he had worked for Alex, she had taught him more than his previous employers had in ten years. She sometimes drove him crazy, but her demand for quality made her one of the most sought after contractors in the state.

"You go ahead and we'll do the reset and lock up," Glen said as he and Alex walked toward the door.

Alex reached into her pocket and withdrew a fifty-dollar bill. "Take the crew over to Brewster's, the first round's on me."

"Thanks, boss!" Glen's grin lit up the room. Her genuine care and concern for her workers was another reason Glen loved working with Alex.

He watched as she walked to her truck and climbed inside. It was rare for someone of her age to have achieved such success, and the fact that she was a woman in a male dominated field added to the accomplishment. So many of the things she did reminded him of her father, who had taken a chance on a lanky high school kid years ago and put him to work.

Glen knew Alex's success came from a childhood spent with her father. Alex's mom, Ann, had died in a freak auto accident when Alex was ten years old and being an only child, she spent all of her free time with her father. By her early teens, Alex was completing small projects under the watchful eye of her father who tutored her in every aspect of construction. Her father, now deceased, had inspired her love of building.

An overachiever, Alex had graduated top of her class from Georgia Tech with a structural engineering degree. She was proud her father had lived long enough to see the completion of her first custom home. His face glowed with pride when he inspected her first solo project, and even with his critical eye for detail, he found it very difficult to find anything in the structure to criticize.

✝

Alex walked out to her truck, a ten-year-old Chevy she just couldn't bear to part with. She could well afford to purchase a new vehicle, but her reliable old truck was a welcomed relief after a long day. The still powerful engine roared to life and Alex smiled her appreciation for the aging vehicle. Shifting into drive, she drove slowly past the project for one last glance before heading home. The offset beam was just a minor glitch; overall Alex was pleased with the progress made during the week.

Content, she pulled onto the drive that would lead her back down the mountain and to an early start on a relaxing weekend. There was enough sunlight left to allow a circuit around the lake in her canoe so she could test the performance of a new fly she had tied the night before. Along with building things, Alex had developed a love of fly-fishing in her youth and enjoyed the challenge of the trout in her spring-fed lake. After the battle of bringing the fish to the canoe, Alex would gently remove the hook and release the fish to battle again another day.

As she pulled onto the paved road, her body began to relax. The fresh country air coming through the windows blew her shoulder-length dark hair around the edges of her face. Alex pulled on a pair of sunglasses to block the late afternoon sun streaming through the windshield. A smile grew on her face as she turned on the radio to her favorite country station and sang along until she neared the turnoff to her home. Almost adjacent to her driveway was a small, older model Honda Accord parked beside the road, the hood raised and steam billowing from underneath.

Alex slowed and pulled off the road, parking behind the disabled vehicle. She settled her sunglasses on top of her head and began walking slowly up to the car. Alex noted the backseat packed tightly with clothing and other personal belongings. As she strolled past the driver's side of the car, she glanced inside to see a small dark-haired child asleep in the passenger's seat. Alex continued walking and caught her first glimpse of the driver hidden by the upraised hood of the car. Her eyes began their exploration at the gleaming white tennis shoes and followed the line of the tight-fitting Levi's to the woman's tiny waist. A stream of colorful words reached Alex's ears as the woman cursed her bad luck and waved a hand at the steam escaping the obviously damaged motor. She found herself smiling at the woman talking to the car. Her blond hair had fallen into her face and when she tossed her head to clear her vision, she found Alex smiling at her.

Mesmerized by the deepest blue eyes she had ever seen, Alex stood frozen and found she'd lost her ability to speak. Her heart raced in her chest as the woman straightened and wiped the hair back from her face.

"I am so glad to finally see someone else on this road," the young woman said. "I haven't seen another vehicle for almost an hour." She breathed a sigh of relief. She looked directly into Alex's dark eyes and felt the smile that lingered in them. The warmth that flowed from the woman's eyes burned directly through her chest to surround her heart.

Alex cleared her throat, afraid her voice had abandoned her for good. "Looks like you could use some help here," Alex said when she finally managed to speak, thankful that her voice didn't squeal with the sudden surge of excitement she was feeling at the sight of the beautiful stranger. Alex tore her eyes away from the woman and peered underneath the hood. "Nothing like stating the obvious here, Alex," she mumbled to herself.

"We were cruising right along and all of a sudden the engine died. I was barely able to get it off the road before the momentum stopped it here."

Alex looked closely into the face of the woman and noted the yellow tint of fading bruises on the woman's cheek before tearing her eyes away again to look at the smoldering engine. Alex could still smell the smoke that wafted from under the hood. Instinctively she reached for the dipstick, and as she feared, the engine was bone dry, not a drop of oil registering on the stick. "Umm, when was the last time you added some oil?" Alex asked. She could tell from the startled look on the woman's face that vehicle maintenance was not one of her strong points.

"I hate to be the bearer of bad news, ma'am, but it looks like you may have burnt up your motor." The woman frowned and her eyes filled with tears at Alex's assessment. "It's going to be impossible to tell for sure, though, until a mechanic can tow her in and give it a good once-over," Alex said, hoping to communicate a glimmer of hope to the young woman.

Alex's attempt failed miserably. The overwhelmed woman broke into tears and buried her face in her hands. Alex could think of no other action to calm the distraught woman so she wrapped her arms around the beautiful stranger and held her until her sobs subsided and she regained her composure. The warmth of the beautiful woman pressed against her body reminded Alex how comforting it was to hold someone close and managed a smile when the woman looked up at her.

"I'm sorry for turning into a blubbering idiot," the woman said, looking up into Alex's eyes but not pulling away from the physical comfort of Alex's long arms. "My name is Bet, and the munchkin in the passenger seat is my daughter, Kylie." She finally disengaged from Alex's embrace to point toward the sleeping child.

A chill overtook Alex as Bet pulled away from her and she fought off the shiver threatening to slide down her spine. "My name is Alex. I noticed from your car plates that you are from Alabama. What are the two of you doing up here alone?"

"That's a long story," Bet said as stepped to the driver's side of the car to check on her still sleeping child. Alex could feel the pain the woman was carrying with her fade as she looked at the sleeping child.

"Well, it's going to be at least Monday before a mechanic can look at your car, ma'am," Alex said. "The only mechanic in town has Falcon season tickets and he takes his wife into Atlanta every weekend they play at home."

"At least tell me there is a motel in town."

"As a matter of fact there is one," Alex said, "not that I would recommend it, though."

"Well, aren't you just a ray of sunshine." Bet immediately recognized the sarcastic tone she had used. "I'm so sorry."

Alex laughed. "Not a problem, I get that kind of remark from strange women all the time." Bet smiled at Alex's witty remark and Alex felt her heart skip a beat.

"I do have a solution to your problem, though," Alex said, once again with a serious face. "I have a home about a mile up that drive with plenty of space for two guests and I have no plans for the weekend other than a little fishing. Besides, if you haven't noticed, you are in the middle of nowhere out here and the closest town is a twenty-minute drive," she added.

"I really hate to impose on you, but it does seem like my options are pretty much nil at this point."

"Great, it's settled then. Show me which bags you need and I will grab them while you collect your little munchkin."

Bet reached inside to pop the trunk and said, "The two in the trunk," then walked around to wake her sleeping daughter.

Alex slowly and quietly lowered the hood and then walked around to retrieve the bags from the trunk, placing them in the bed of the truck. Bet walked toward her carrying the dark-haired child, who was rubbing her sleepy eyes. When she reached Alex's side, the child looked up at her with those same deep blue eyes. "Hiya," she said. "What's your name?"

"Alex. What's yours?"

"I'm Kylie, and I'm four." She held up four fingers.

Alex chuckled at the small child as she reached to open the door for Bet and Kylie, closing it behind them when they had settled in the truck.

"Where are we going, Mommy?" Kylie asked as Alex slipped in behind the wheel and cranked up the truck.

"We are going to spend the weekend with Alex. Our car got sick and it will be a few days before it is well again," she explained.

"Okay, Mommy." Kylie snuggled into Bet's chest. "Do you have a little girl," Kylie asked innocently.

"No, but I do have a dog named Max and he is four also, if that counts," Alex replied.

Kylie's eyes lit up at the mention of a dog and Alex knew that Max would have a new best friend. Max her four-year-old black Lab, was fantastic with kids and would enjoy a new playmate.

"Wow, is that your place," Bet asked as Alex's home came into view on the side of the mountain.

"Home sweet home," Alex said as she continued up the drive.

"It's so beautiful," Bet said in awe of the cabin set so naturally into the surrounding woods.

"Thanks, I built it myself," Alex said. Stunned, Bet gave her an appraising look.

"Look, Mommy, a lake too," Kylie squealed in delight.

"That must be Max," Bet said as the young Lab raced up to meet them, a soggy tennis ball in his mouth.

"One and the same," Alex replied as she killed the motor on the truck.

Bet and Kylie eased out of the truck and were immediately welcomed by Max, who woofed his welcome around a mouthful of tennis ball.

"Sit, Max," Alex instructed. Max obediently dropped to his seat, the ball rolling between his feet.

Kylie squirmed out of Bet's arms onto the ground, and was greeted by wet, sloppy kisses from Max as she hugged his neck. She squealed with pleasure.

"I think that is enough for now Max," Alex said as she bent down to pick up the tennis ball and hurled it as far as she could into the lake. "Go get it, boy." Max streaked to the lake, leaping into the water and swimming frantically toward the ball. Alex grabbed one of the bags and helped Bet carry them onto the porch. Max was just reaching the ball when they set the bags down on the porch and turned to watch him swim back to shore and shake himself dry before bringing the ball to Alex on the porch. "Good boy," she praised as he released the ball into Alex's hand.

Alex opened the door and Kylie instinctively placed her hand on Max's collar, letting the big dog lead her into the house. Laughing at the sight, Bet followed her daughter inside. Alex smiled when a peal of laughter rang throughout the house and it suddenly dawned on her what was missing from her home. The giggles and chatter of mother and daughter gave the house warmth and Alex reveled in the sweet sound.

While Max gave the tottering Kylie a tour of the downstairs, Alex and Bet carried the bags upstairs to two adjoining rooms. "Let me show you around," Alex said after dropping the bags off. Bet followed her down the hallway to a stairway to a loft.

"This is beautiful," Bet said of the wide-open area that overlooked the entire first floor and served as Alex's bedroom. Alex led her to a French door that opened onto a small deck that spanned the full length of the house. The view of the tree-covered mountain from the deck was amazing and Bet stood mesmerized by it until the sound of Kylie's laughter brought her back to earth.

Walking to the edge of the loft Bet and Alex peeked down to see Max and Kylie wrestling on the rug in front of the stone fireplace, Max's woofs accenting Kylie's giggles as they played together.

"When was the last time you two had a meal?" Alex asked.

"We had lunch about twelve thirty, but to be honest, I'm starved."

"Let me grab a quick shower and I'll see what I can throw together," Alex said. "Make yourself at home and I'll be right out." Alex disappeared into the bathroom and Bet heard the shower turn on.

✝

Bet descended the stairs and walked through the kitchen that was equipped with stainless steel appliances. A dream kitchen she thought as she opened a fully stocked pantry and freezer. Bet continued her tour of the lower level, locating what could only be

Alex's office with a nearly full glass wall opening onto a view of the valley. Sighing deeply, Bet felt some of the tension she had been carrying since leaving Alabama dissipate. She returned to the living room to join Max and Kylie, sinking into a comfortable, deep leather chair to watch them play. Relaxing into the chair, she allowed her eyes to close. Several minutes later, she woke up to silence. Kylie and Max had stopped playing and she turned to find Kylie sitting on the kitchen counter talking quietly with Alex as she prepared a meal. Bet watched as Kylie and Alex talked comfortably together as Alex's hands formed homemade burgers and bacon sizzled on the open griddle.

"We are having bacon cheeseburgers, Mommy," Kylie called out when she noticed her Mom was awake.

"Sounds yummy," Bet said. "Sorry, I must be more tired than I thought."

"Not a problem. Kylie is assisting me in creating cheeseburgers in paradise," Alex said, causing Bet to smile brilliantly.

"What can I do to help?"

"The oil should be ready if you want to cook the fries while we finish the burgers and set the table," Alex said as she sent Kylie off toward the table carrying utensils. "Sure hope you gals like sweet tea or milk, because that's all I have to offer for drinks."

"Tea for me, please, and milk for your assistant," Bet requested as she watched them set the table.

"Two iced teas and a milk coming up then," Alex said as she handed condiments for Kylie to set on the table. "Such a good helper I have here." Kylie beamed at Alex's praise. Alex lifted Kylie onto the counter to continue watching as she and Bet finished preparing the meal.

Bet drained the fries and set them on the table as Alex melted the cheese over the thick slices of bacon atop the burgers. She placed burgers on a plate and left a fourth to cool for Max, who patiently waited for his treat.

As they sat at the table, Kylie took Bet's hand and reached for Alex's. "Do you mind if Kylie says grace?" Bet asked.

"Not at all." Alex took Kylie's small hand in hers and reached for Bet's to complete their small circle.

Bowing their heads, Kylie started her prayer. "Dear God, thank you for this cheeseburger and for our new friends, Alex and Max. Thank you for Mommy and for sending us to our new home. Amen."

"Amen," Alex said as she reached for a burger and placed it on Kylie's open bun before taking another and passing the plate to Bet, whose eyes were wide from shock over Kylie's last comment.

She wasn't sure how she would explain to her daughter that this was not their new home, but she would find a way tomorrow to let her know they were just visiting.

Alex, quite cognizant of Kylie's statement, refrained from commenting, but an idea was beginning to form in the back of her mind. She watched as Bet helped a struggling Kylie create her burger then cut it into manageable portions for her small hands. They both ate hearty meals and Alex wondered when they last had full stomachs.

Earlier, while Bet napped, Kylie had told Alex that her daddy was mean to both she and her mommy and Mommy had promised that they would find a new home safely away from him. She told Alex how they had crept out of the house while her daddy was sleeping on the couch.

Even without Kylie's revelations, Alex had deduced from the fading bruises that Bet was fleeing from an abusive partner. It took an incredibly courageous person to pack up what they could and escape from harm. Alex was sure Bet was an extremely strong person. She would keep Kylie's secrets to herself and allow Bet to fill in the blanks when she felt comfortable talking.

After the threesome finished their meal, Alex gave Kylie a chopped up hamburger to feed to her new friend Max while she and Bet picked up the kitchen. The supper chores done, Max and Kylie moved to play in the living room, and Bet asked if it would be okay if she took a shower. Alex showed her where things were located then returned downstairs to take a comfortable seat.

Max and Kylie romped and wrestled until both were exhausted. Bet had not returned downstairs as of yet, so Kylie climbed up in Alex's lap and with heavy eyes wrapped her arms around Alex's neck and fell asleep. Max sat next to them and put his head on Alex's knee, watching over Kylie as she slept.

"Do you want me to take her," Bet asked as she walked down the stairs in shorts and a T-shirt and saw Kylie asleep in Alex's arms, a scene that appeared all too natural for someone they had just met.

"No, she's fine for now. Let her sleep a few minutes and then you can take her up for the night," Alex replied. "It's been a long time since I've held a little one while they slept and I forgot how good it feels."

"It's a very natural look for you." Bet said with a warm smile.

"She seems like such a good kid. You have done a good job raising her."

"She has definitely been the highlight of my life."

Kylie sighed at that moment and snuggled further into Alex's neck. "I have never seen her take to someone like she has to you. Usually she is pretty bashful around new people, but you wouldn't think that the way she's snuggled into you," Bet said with a grin. "How about carrying her upstairs and I will tuck her in for the night?"

"All right." Alex carefully climbed the stairs with Kylie in her arms. Bet pulled back the covers and Alex laid the child gently on the bed. "I am going to take Max out while you finish up here," Alex said as she slipped quietly from the room.

Downstairs, Max headed for the door, followed into the darkness by Alex. Max trotted off across the yard and Alex reached into a small box and pulled out a pack of cigarettes. She had smoked for years after college but had quit except for her one smoke of the evening before going off to bed. She lit the cigarette and inhaled deeply, taking a seat on the porch steps as she listened for Max running through the woods. She watched the fireflies as they sparkled and danced on the front lawn as she enjoyed her solitary smoke.

†

The door opened and Bet stepped out just as Alex exhaled a puff of smoke. "Do you have another one of those?" Bet asked. "I sure could use one about now."

"Inside the box beside the door," she said, pointing.

Bet lit up and joined Alex on the step. "Oh my, that tastes good," Bet said as she took a draw off the cigarette.

"I only allow myself one a night," Alex said, as Bet got comfortable on the step beside her.

"It's so beautiful and quiet here. I can't tell you how many years it has been since I have seen fireflies," she said. "I've never seen them in Mobile."

Taking advantage of the small bit of information, Alex asked, "Is that where you two are from?"

Bet took a long draw from the cigarette and exhaled loudly as she braced herself for the coming conversation. "Yes, Kylie and I are from Mobile. I have been married to her father for five years and finally got to the point that I couldn't take another beating," she said in one long breath. "I decided that we would both be safer and happier far away from him, so last night when he started drinking, I slipped a sleeping pill into his drink. When he finally passed out from the combination of the drug and liquor, I packed what I could into the Honda, carried a sleeping Kylie out to the car and left. I made one stop at an ATM to clear out my account and to call my supervisor at the hospital to let her know what was going on."

"Are you a nurse?" Alex asked.

"Yes, I have been an RN for almost five years."

"That is really great."

"What do you do for a living?" Bet asked.

"I own a small construction company and I specialize in building custom homes here in the mountains."

"If this place is any indication of your work, I bet you are in high demand."

"I stay busy," Alex admitted. "We generally build eight to ten homes a year."

"Well you certainly have a talent," Bet said. "This place is a dream home."

"I try to design a home around the owner's personality, and this one fits me to a T," Alex said. "The open, airy design gives me the creative freedom to think and the lighting to draw deep into the night if the inspiration strikes."

"I would like to have a home like this for Kylie someday," Bet said with a tone of determination in her voice.

"What are your plans," Alex asked, "if you don't mind me prying?"

"To be perfectly honest, I'm not sure what my plans are. When I cranked up the car my only objective was to get as far away from Brian as I could, so I pointed the car north and drove. Six hours later, just north of Birmingham, I pulled into a rest stop to get some sleep. When I awoke four hours later, Kylie was quietly playing with her toys. We found a nice little diner for an early breakfast and headed east to Georgia. Kylie began getting restless after a few hours so we stopped and bought a sandwich and chips for a picnic lunch at a nearby park. We ate and she played for about an hour before we continued our journey. Three hours later I found myself broke down at your driveway and here we are," Bet said, her voice cracking with uncertainty.

"I plan on obtaining a license wherever we land and resume nursing as soon as possible," Bet added.

"How long would it take to get a Georgia license?" Alex asked out of curiosity.

"Usually thirty to forty-five days," Bet answered. "Until then I can get something to hold us over."

Bet shivered and Alex realized almost an hour had passed since they started talking. "It's getting cool, are you ready to go in?"

"I think that's a good idea," Bet said, hugging her body for warmth.

Alex whistled for Max and was startled when he rose from the darkness a mere three feet from where they had been sitting. Neither of the women had seen the black dog lay down as he joined them. His stealth and dark fur allowed him to listen to their conversation as they sat together on the steps.

Alex took their cigarette butts and dropped them into a can on the porch.

"Thanks for the cigarette and all your hospitality," Bet said.

"It has been a pleasure having you two here. Max is a great friend, but most of the time he's not much of a talker," Alex teased.

"Seriously, though, I don't know what I would have done if you hadn't rescued us today. To be honest," Bet said, "I don't even have a clue where we are right now."

"Well, that's an easy one to answer. You are presently in Graves Cove, population one woman and one dog," she said with a chuckle. Max woofed when he heard *dog*, as if it were his cue to make a statement.

Both women laughed at his response and Alex reached to open the door. Bet stopped her movement by placing her arms around Alex's neck and kissing her on the cheek. Startled by the embrace and the feel of Bet's hard nipples as they pressed into her Alex hesitated only briefly in returning the embrace. The darkness of the porch hid the flush on Alex's cheeks as she enjoyed the comfort of the physical contact.

Max trotted through the open door followed closely by Bet and Alex. "Is there anything you need tonight?" Alex asked.

"No, I think you have done plenty for us today."

"I am going to lock up and head to bed then," Alex said, feeling suddenly weary.

"Goodnight then and thanks again for everything."

✝

Alex refilled Max's water bowl and checked the locks on the doors before heading to the stairs. Max bounded up the stairs ahead of her and waited at the landing, then led her up the final steps to the loft. The soft glow of the bedside lamp welcomed her and she stripped out of her clothes and slid beneath the covers onto cool, clean sheets. She reached and turned off the light, listening as Bet shuffled around the bedroom for a few minutes before climbing into bed with Kylie. Max took up his familiar spot beside Alex's bed and all was quiet in the house.

Alex slept for several hours before she woke to the sound of Max's claws on the hardwood floor. She listened as Max descended the loft steps and walked into the guest bedroom to check on Kylie and Bet. Alex heard Bet whisper to him, "We are all right, boy," and then she heard the soft clicking of his claws as he climbed back up to the loft.

A smile grew on Alex's face as she heard Max lay down and she thought all is right in this house tonight. With that comforting thought bouncing through her head, Alex returned to a deep, restful sleep.

✝

When Brian Stewart awakened from his drunken stupor, accentuated by the sleeping pills Bet had slipped into his drink, he released his rage on his empty home. Pictures and decorations that Bet had been so eager to dress their home with were smashed and small pieces of furniture lay shattered like matchsticks throughout the house, all victims of his anger. He had torn through the house to their bedroom and found a large hole in the closet where her clothing had been. Several pieces of clothing were scattered across the bed. He figured she either couldn't fit them in her suitcase or was too rushed to take them all. When he sank down on the bed his eyes fell on a piece of paper laying on the table beside the bed. Bet's hastily written note only further fueled his rage, and he sat on their bed and ripped apart the clothing Bet left behind.

Vowing to return his wife and child to their proper home, Brian quelled his rage long enough to call Bet's family and a few close friends in an effort to track her down. Bet's mother and her friends were unable or unwilling to give Brian any useful information, and after several calls, he slammed the phone down on the receiver.

Brian had paced the floor trying to figure out a course of action when his hangover-blurred eyes focused on the kitchen table. His wallet sat beside an overturned beer bottle and a thought occurred to him. He reached inside his wallet to find a card with a password to a program that he installed months earlier that would track Bet's car. He downloaded the program on his phone and waited for the information to update.

Brian smiled when he looked at his phone to see that his wife and child had made it at least to Georgia. He hastily packed a small bag and headed out to his truck. Headed north, Brian was confident that he would soon track down his wife and child.

Brian drove beyond the fall of darkness before turning into a rest stop for some sleep. As irony would have it, Brian pulled into a parking spot mere feet away from where Bet and Kylie had slept hours earlier.

Chapter Two

Shortly after dawn, Alex awoke to the aroma of coffee brewing. She could hear the sizzle of bacon as it began to fry on the griddle. Rising from bed and stepping into a pair of sweats and a T-shirt, Alex looked down from the loft to see Bet cooking while Max and Kylie played together in the living room.

Max was the first to notice Alex's arrival, woofing his welcome to his companion. "Good morning, Alex," Kylie said with her sweet, little voice.

"Good morning everyone," Alex said with a smile.

"How do you take your coffee," Bet asked.

"Light and sweet, just like I like my woman," Alex replied without thinking. Her response had become so standard with her construction crew that it just came out naturally.

Bet chuckled at her response and prepared a cup of coffee with two sugars and a splash of cream. Handing the cup to Alex, she noticed the flush of embarrassment that graced Alex's cheeks. "Light and sweet enough for you?" she asked. Alex's blush turned redder.

Alex took the offered cup and turned to head for the door. "Need to go out, Max?" she asked, hearing Bet's chuckle behind her. Max trotted to the door followed by Kylie. Alex held the door open for the two of them and followed them out to the porch. Sitting on the porch steps, she enjoyed the coolness of the crisp morning and watched the two youngsters at play as she sipped her coffee.

She heard the door open behind her and felt Bet sit beside her, coffee cup in hand. Kylie squealed with laughter every time Max brought the tennis ball to her for a throw and waited patiently for her wind up.

"Those two are quite a pair aren't they," Alex said.

"Yes, they are," Bet said as she sipped her coffee. "Hungry? I found the last of the bacon and some pancake mix if that sounds good to you."

"Beautiful," Alex said. "I haven't had pancakes in ages."

"Let me get started on some pancakes then," Bet said as she rose from the step.

"You need any help?" Alex asked.

"Thanks, but I can manage. Why don't you stay and watch the kids and let me cook for us."

"That I can do," Alex said before taking another sip of coffee. "By the way, Max and I usually spend Saturday morning out on the lake. Would you and Kylie like to join us this morning?"

"Kylie would love it, but I think I will stay behind and do some thinking, if you don't mind. Try to figure out what I am going to do," Bet said.

"No problem at all," Alex responded though she was disappointed Bet wouldn't be joining them. She watched Bet return to the house to finish breakfast and then turned to find Max charging at her.

"Easy boy," she said. The dog skidded to a halt right in front of her and dropped his tennis ball at her feet. Alex set her coffee cup down on the step and bent to retrieve the ball. She hurled the ball as far as she could and Max zoomed off after it. Alex walked out to where Kylie was standing, cheering Max on.

"Would you like to go fishing with Max and me this morning?" Alex asked.

Kylie looked up at her, eyes glittering with excitement. "Fishing! I have never been fishing before!"

"Can you be quiet and sit really still?"

"Yes, ma'am," Kylie responded.

"Well, you have to be quiet or the fish will hear us coming," Alex whispered.

"I can do it," Kylie whispered back.

Max returned and dropped the soggy ball in Kylie's hand, indicating it was her turn to toss it for him. With a giant windup, Kylie reared back and threw the ball twenty feet. Max rushed after it, catching it on the second bounce.

"Good boy," Kylie said when Max brought the ball back and delivered it to Alex.

"Max, you want to go fishing?" Alex asked. The big dog answered with a deep woof, dancing in circles with his excitement, making them both laugh. "I guess we have a fishing trip planned then." Alex lobbed the ball toward the lake. "Let's go wash up for breakfast." Alex said as she turned toward the house. Kylie ran up and slipped her hand inside Alex's as they walked back to the house. Alex's heart smiled as she shortened her stride to walk hand in hand with Kylie.

Bet walked out onto the porch and smiled at Alex and Kylie. "I was just coming to get you three," she said, careful to include Max. "Wash your hands and let's eat." She held the door open.

Alex held Kylie up to the sink in the bathroom so the small child could wash her hands and then handed her a towel before washing her own. *I should come up with a stool for Kylie*, Alex thought without a second's hesitation as she hung the towel back on the rack.

"We are going fishing," Kylie announced as soon as she climbed onto the dining room chair.

"Is that so?" Bet said with mock surprise at Kylie's revelation. "You know you have to be still and quiet to catch fish."

"I know, Mom, Alex already told me," Kylie replied. "I promised her I wouldn't scare the fish." Kylie stuffed a bite of pancake into her mouth.

Bet smiled at her daughter's happiness and shared the smile with Alex as she passed her the syrup. Alex instantly felt warmed to the very core at the sight of Bet's smile and blushed slightly as Bet's eyes met hers, holding her spellbound for several seconds.

"Maybe after we go fishing we can come back in for a quick sandwich and then we will ride into town to pick up some groceries," Alex suggested. "What would you two like for dinner?"

"Spaghetti," Kylie said.

"Kylie loves my spaghetti," Bet said with a grin.

"Spaghetti it is then."

Max finished the pancakes Bet had put in his bowl and walked over to the front door, sitting down to wait for their fishing trip. "Almost done, Max," Alex said as her companion waited patiently.

"You two go ahead," Bet said, "I will pick up the dishes."

Kylie was just waiting for her mom to say that. She rushed to join Max sitting at the door.

"Guess I'm the one holding us up." Alex took her last bite of pancakes, chewing as she stood up and grinned at Bet. Grabbing two bottles of water from the fridge Alex said, in her best Arnold imitation, "We'll be back."

Bet laughed at Alex's antics. "You guys have fun," she said as Max and Kylie disappeared out the door ahead of Alex.

†

Kylie and Max rushed toward the dock and Alex had to practically run to catch up with them. She put Kylie in the middle seat of the canoe and Max eased in, settling in front of her. Alex placed the water in a small compartment and reached up to retrieve her fly rod and tackle box from the storage box on the pier. Amid all the excitement, Alex had forgotten to pick up the new fly she had tied, but she knew there would be many other opportunities to try it out. She sat down on the rear seat and untied the canoe from the dock. Picking up the paddle, she moved them out into the lake. Max turned around and sat facing Kylie, placing his big black head in her small lap. Her fingers automatically started stroking his head as they paddled across the lake.

Alex owned a wide-bottom canoe so there was very little risk of tipping, but Kylie kept her promise of sitting still. Alex paddled parallel to the shore then set down the paddle and picked up her fly rod. She checked the fly on the line and spit on it for luck then sent her first cast toward the shore, guiding the line over and back, above Kylie's head until she had the proper length to make her cast. Alex had barely turned sideways on her seat when the first fish struck the fly.

The suddenness of the strike startled Kylie and she cried out, quickly covering her mouth with her hands to quiet herself.

Alex chuckled at Kylie's behavior and whispered, "That's okay we have already caught him."

19

Kylie smiled her relief and watched as Alex fought the fish to the side of the canoe and then lifted the fighting fish into it. The trout flopped around on the floor until Alex trapped him with her hands.

Kylie watched closely as Alex carefully removed the hook from the side of the fish's mouth. "Does that hurt him," Kylie asked with a look of great concern on her face.

"Not really," Alex said, explaining how it was best to hook a fish like that to keep from hurting them.

Kylie leaned toward the side as Alex placed the fish back into the water and moved him through the water to make sure he was ready to swim. "Are you ready to watch him take off?" Alex asked.

"Yes," Kylie said.

"Okay, then count to three for me."

"One, two, three," Kylie said, and Alex released the fish, which flapped his tail against the canoe before swimming off.

Kylie laughed at the fish and Alex joined in, laughing as well. Not to be outdone, Max barked, one of the few times he would use his full voice to announce his approval.

"Are you ready to catch one?" Alex asked Kylie.

Kylie's eyes grew wide at the question. "Do you really think I can, Alex?"

"I'm sure of it," Alex said. She motioned for Kylie to join her on the seat. "I'll help you with the first one."

Kylie sat sideways on the bench seat between Alex's straddled legs and watched as she lifted the fly. "Your turn," Alex said. Kylie spit on the fly for luck just as she had observed Alex doing.

Alex chuckled and started the cast, Kylie watching her very intently. As the fly settled onto the water, Alex handed the rod to Kylie. Kylie gripped the rod tightly. They both leaned forward to watch the fly float silently across the water. "When you see the fish strike at the fly you need to pull up on the rod like this." Alex placed her hand on the rod and pulled upward. "That is called setting the hook," Alex explained to an engrossed Kylie.

"Got it," Kylie said with confidence as she stared at the fly.

Alex could see a ripple in the water and whispered, "Get ready." They watched as a large rainbow struck at the fly and Kylie instinctively jerked, setting the hook. "Okay, now that you have him hooked you need to bring him in," Alex said. "You see this little handle?"

Kylie nodded and Alex instructed her to start turning the handle slowly to reel in the fish.

Kylie had trouble holding both the reel and rod in her small hands, so Alex held the rod and guided the fish while Kylie turned the crank. It took several minutes for Kylie to reel the fish in.

"Wow, you got yourself a whopper," Alex said and once again Kylie squealed her excitement.

†

Bet had finished clearing the kitchen and was sitting on the porch when she heard Kylie's squeal. She raised a hand above her eyes to block the sun and looked out across the lake. She saw Kylie grab the line and lift the fish as high as she could. Bet wished for a camera to capture the glee on her daughter's face as she caught her first fish, squealing with excitement.

Kylie certainly seemed happy here, happier than Bet could ever remember seeing her in her short life. The events of the day were beginning to take on a fairy tale element. Bet smiled and hoped it would be a happy conclusion.

Back in the canoe, Alex had captured the dangling fish and removed the hook. Kylie started counting when Alex put the fish into the water and seconds later her first catch swam away. Kylie's eyes glowed with excitement as she looked up to Alex and Alex knew a new fisherwoman had been born.

"Fantastic job," Alex praised Kylie. "Are you ready for another?"

Kylie shook with excitement as she nodded her head. Alex realized she had just found her fishing partner. Alex paddled a few strokes to get them moving again before casting out the next line.

Kylie caught six more fish before Alex thought it was time to give the fish a break. Reaching behind them, she opened their bottles of water, handing one to Kylie. Taking the cue, Max moved to the front of the canoe and lowered his head to get a drink of his own.

They sat in silence for a few minutes, sipping their water and floating across the calm lake. Alex asked, "Kylie, how would you like for you and your mom to live here?"

"I like it here a lot," Kylie admitted as she scooted closer to Alex. "It feels like home." Alex was shocked at such a mature comment coming from such a young child. She looked back toward the house to keep Kylie from seeing the tears as they rolled down her cheeks.

Alex knew then what she had to do. Somehow, she would come up with a plan to convince Bet that she and Kylie should stay with her. Alex was certain Bet could get a job at the small local hospital that constantly struggled to compete with the larger cities for nurses. There was plenty of room in the house and they could provide the companionship Alex now knew she was lacking.

Alex stroked in silence toward the dock as she worked out a plan in her head. Max brought her back to reality with his whines from the front of the canoe where he awaited her permission to leap from the canoe to swim to shore.

"Go ahead, boy," Alex said, and he took flight from the front of the canoe, racing them to the shore.

Alex lifted Kylie onto the dock and she immediately took off running toward the house to find her mother. Alex could hear her excited chatter as she told her mother about her fishing adventure. Alex secured the canoe and stowed her fishing gear before she started the walk toward the house. Max met her at the end of the dock and danced around excitedly as she climbed the small hill.

When Alex reached the porch and looked into Bet's eyes, she could see the tears in them as her young daughter continued her tale. "You have got a natural fisherwoman on your hands," she said, sitting down on the top step, resting her back against a support post to face Bet and Kylie. "Fish will shake with fear when they see Kylie coming at them."

"Did the great fisherwomen work up an appetite?" Bet asked Kylie.

"Yes, ma'am," Kylie said. "Do we have any bologna?"

Alex grinned. Bologna was her favorite lunchmeat and there was always at least one pack in the refrigerator.

"I do believe we are in luck, Kylie," Bet said. "If I had to guess, I would say bologna is Alex's favorite too."

Kylie looked at Alex in disbelief. "Yes, ma'am, I love bologna too," she said to the beaming child. "I like my Ruffles inside the sandwich, though."

"Now that is too weird, that is exactly how Kylie eats hers," Bet said. "Mayo?"

"Wouldn't have it any other way."

"Well, let's go fix some bologna sandwiches then," Bet said to Kylie as she stood up from the rocking chair. Alex started to rise but Bet said, "Sit still, I believe we can handle this project."

Alex looked at Max who once again was patiently sitting in front of her. "Oh Max, what to do, what to do?" she asked of her silent companion. Hearing the uncertainty in Alex's voice, Max moved forward and placed his head in her lap. Alex patted Max on the head and then took his large head in her hands. Looking directly into his yellow eyes, Alex asked, "Where do we go from here, my friend?" Max thumped his tail on the steps but offered no further advice.

Alex stood and walked over to the outdoor faucet to wash the slobber from her hands. As she climbed back onto the porch, Kylie pushed the door open and emerged from the house carrying a large glass of iced tea.

"Here you go, Alex." Kylie handed Alex the large glass.

"Thank you, Kylie." Alex took a sip then placed the glass on the porch railing. She pulled up two milk crates next to the rocking chairs, making a seat for Kylie and a table for the sandwiches.

Kylie took her seat and Alex sat in one of the rockers as they waited for Bet to bring the sandwiches. Kylie looked up to Alex who asked, "Hungry?"

"Yes, ma'am," Kylie replied. "I'm thirsty too."

Alex handed the glass of tea to the small child and watched as she took a big drink. "That's good," she said as she handed the glass back to Alex. "Thanks," she added as an afterthought.

Bet had found a serving tray, which she had loaded down with a platter of sandwiches, a pitcher of tea, and two smaller glasses. "Here we go," Bet announced as she carefully placed the tray on the milk crate table.

Bet handed a half sandwich to Kylie along with a napkin. "Thanks, Mom," Kylie said before biting into the sandwich, the Ruffles crunching loudly.

Alex smiled and picked up a half sandwich and took a large bite. "Never knew fishing could work up such an appetite," she said to Bet, nodding toward Kylie who was halfway through her first sandwich.

"She has a good appetite and will eat anything I cook," Bet said. "Kylie isn't a picky eater like some children, so I feel I've been blessed."

"Truly blessed," Alex said as she ate her sandwich and watched Kylie.

The large stack of sandwiches slowly disappeared as they finished the meal in silence. Taking the last bite of her sandwich, Alex asked, "Are you two ready to head into town?"

"Ready when you are," Bet responded.

"Let me take the tray back in and grab my keys and I'll be ready."

"Kylie, would you go upstairs and grab my purse for me, please," Bet asked.

"Yes, ma'am." Kylie ran ahead to open the door for Alex.

Alex set the tray on the kitchen counter and went to the office to get her keys. She waited for Kylie at the front door then locked it behind them.

Kylie handed Bet her purse and ran down the steps, followed closely by Max. The pair made a beeline toward the truck. Alex called out to them. "We won't take the truck to town today." She pointed toward a small garage. They walked to the building and Alex opened the door to reveal a sleek, black Subaru Outback.

"Very nice," Bet said.

"Thanks. My going-to-town vehicle," she said with a grin.

Bet belted Kylie into the backseat before joining Alex up front. Alex rolled down her window and instructed Max to "stay" before they drove out onto the driveway. Back at the paved road, Alex turned left and pulled in behind the Honda. Bet looked at Alex with curiosity.

"Kylie needs her car seat so she doesn't break her neck trying to see out."

Bet grinned and went to the Honda to remove the car seat. Minutes later she had Kylie securely fastened in. "There, that has to be better," she said as she kissed Kylie's forehead.

"Thanks, Mom," Kylie said as Bet climbed back into the front seat. Alex grinned and pulled back onto the road.

Alex drove the winding road with ease, pointing out the few local landmarks she could. When they approached a four-way stop, a sign posted at the intersection, pointed toward Atlanta, 150 miles away.

Turning right and driving for another ten minutes brought them to the outskirts of a small town. Alex pulled into the parking lot of a garage and left a note pinned to the door asking the owner to come out first thing Monday morning to tow Bet's car into town for evaluation.

They passed by a small school and Alex explained that K through 12 attended the same school, but proudly stated it had one of the highest education ratings in the state. She pointed out several small businesses and the two diners in town.

No golden arches or other fast-food joints had invaded the small town as of yet, a sight that pleased Bet.

Alex slowly rolled by the County Hospital, which was one of the biggest buildings in the county. "It's small, but surprisingly modern."

"Looks fairly new too," Bet said.

"It's only eight years old."

They pulled into the parking lot of the grocery store and headed inside. Kylie took Bet's hand as soon as she got out of the car and when Alex walked beside them, she reached up and placed her hand in Alex's large paw. Bet looked over at Alex and smiled at the shocked look on Alex's face. Alex glanced up and returned the smile then strolled proudly into the small grocery.

Sad to release Kylie's hand for even a moment, Alex went to retrieve a shopping cart. When she returned, Kylie reached up for her hand again, her dark blue eyes glowing with excitement.

Alex guided them down each of the aisles as they picked out supplies for their spaghetti dinner. Alex and Kylie picked out some snack items, after receiving Bet's nod of approval. Alex couldn't resist grabbing a bag of large marshmallows and tossing them into the cart. After dinner tonight, she would light a campfire down by the lake and they could roast some marshmallows.

When they reached Alex's driveway on the trip home, Bet asked Alex to stop by her car so she could get another of their bags. Then reaching the house, they unloaded the car, and Alex drove it back into the garage as Bet and Kylie put the groceries away. Max appeared from the woods and walked back into the house with Alex and went straight to Kylie, who hugged the big dog's neck.

"If you can get things started in here, Max and I will finish up some chores outside," Alex said.

"I'll be fine so you go right ahead," Bet said.

Kylie looked at her mom. "Can I go with Alex?"

Bet looked at Alex who nodded her head. "Yes, you can, but after dinner I want you to take a bath."

"Yes, ma'am," Kylie said as she ran over to Alex and grabbed her hand.

Together they walked down to the fire ring. Alex smoothed out the ashes from the last fire then went to the garage and found three lawn chairs. Kylie took the smallest of the three as Alex carried the others to the fire ring.

"You know what we need to do next?" Alex asked Kylie.

"No, ma'am," Kylie replied with a curious look.

"We need to find some wood if we are going to have a campfire. Do you think you could help Max and I find some?"

"Yes, ma'am." Kylie grinned.

They walked around the house picking up fallen branches making a rather sizeable pile in no time. Alex included a few logs from her fireplace woodpile and showed Kylie how to lay a campfire.

"We need to pull the water hose down here too, so we can make sure the fire gets put out well," she said. "Wait here and I'll bring it down."

"I can get it." Kylie ran back up to the house and picked up the end of the hose, pulling it as she walked.

Alex smiled as she watched the child tugging on the hose, but allowed her to complete the task by herself. "Thanks," she said when Kylie arrived.

They finished just as the sun was going down, and once again Kylie placed her hand in Alex's as they walked back to the house.

Bet had just finished setting the table as they entered the house. "Better wash up."

"Hang on a second, Kylie." Alex disappeared into a small storeroom off the kitchen. She returned with a small plastic stool and carried it into the downstairs bath, setting it down in front of the sink. "Try that on for size, Kylie," she said with a grin.

Kylie climbed up on the stool, which was the perfect height for her to be able to wash her hands independently.

Alex washed her hands and they shared a towel for drying. Kylie climbed down from the stool, and moved it against the wall away from the sink and out of the grownups' way.

Bet had served up portions of spaghetti and salad. She poured glasses of tea for her and Alex and a glass of milk for Kylie before joining them at the table.

Kylie reached over for her mom's hand and stretched her little arm across the table to reach for Alex. Alex placed her hand in Kylie's and completed the circle by accepting the soft hand Bet offered.

Bowing her head and squeezing her eyes closed, Kylie said, "Dear God, thank you for the spaghetti we are about to eat and thank you for a fun day. Thanks for a Mom who loves me and thank you for bringing us to Alex," she added. "Oh yeah," she continued, "thank you for Max, my new best friend. Amen."

"Amen," Alex and Bet said in unison.

At the sound of his name, Max thumped his tail against the hardwood floor.

"This is great," Alex complimented Bet as she reached for a slice of garlic toast.

"Very yummy, Mom," Kylie agreed.

After they finished their meals, the three of them cleaned the kitchen. Max gladly chowed down on the leftovers as the dishes were loaded into the dishwasher.

"Let's go get our baths and then we can join Alex down by the fire," Bet said to Kylie.

✝

Alex watched the pair climb the stairs then went to the mantel to locate her pocketknife. During their search for wood, she had collected three sticks that, with a little trimming, would be perfect for roasting marshmallows. Picking up the bag of marshmallows, Alex walked out onto the porch, stopping by the small box to get her nightly cigarette then pocketing the lighter before walking to the fire pit.

After lighting the fire, Alex sat in one of the chairs and picked up the first of the sticks for trimming. Working carefully to shave off the rough edges and carving sharp points on the ends, Alex prepared the sticks. Taking a final drag off the cigarette, she dropped the butt into the crackling fire.

Sitting back in the chair, Alex watched the fireflies light up the night with their yellow-green glow. Lost in the quiet serenity of the early evening, Alex did not realize Bet and Kylie had joined her until Max woofed to announce their presence.

"Feel better?"

"That shower is heavenly," Bet replied as she sat next to Alex.

"Are you ready to roast some marshmallows?" Alex asked Kylie.

"Will you show me how?"

"Sure thing." Alex ripped open the bag of marshmallows and picked up a stick. "All you have to do is spear the marshmallow onto the stick and then hold it over the flame like this." Kylie's eyes grew wide as the marshmallow burst into flame. "You have to be careful with this part," Alex said as she brought the flaming marshmallow to her mouth and softly blew the flame out. Alex bit into the crispy marshmallow as Kylie broke into giggles. "I'll make you a deal. You roast them and I will blow them out for you." She skewered a marshmallow on a stick and handed it to Kylie. "Here you go," she said to a very excited little girl.

Bet and Alex watched as Kylie leaned forward in her chair to extend the stick over the flame. Within seconds, the marshmallow burst into flame and Kylie carefully handed the stick to Alex, who, as promised, blew out the flame.

"This one is yours Mommy," Kylie said as she took the stick from Alex and pointed the sticky treat at Bet.

Bet pulled the gooey marshmallow off the stick. She popped it into her mouth and moaned as the sugar hit her taste buds. "Very yummy, Kylie."

Kylie nearly poked Alex in the face as she whirled around so Alex could reload her stick. Alex pushed a marshmallow onto the stick and Kylie placed it over the flames. They repeated this process for nearly an hour, taking turns eating the sticky treats until they could eat no more. Even Max shared in a few of the sugary morsels then licked his lips for a half hour trying to get all the sticky sugar off his muzzle.

Totally stuffed, they sat back in their chairs and watched the fireflies dance across the night. Kylie's eyes grew heavy and she crawled up into Bet's lap to snuggle. Within a half an hour, she was dozing comfortably in her mother's arms.

"She's getting heavy," Bet whispered after a while. "I am going to tuck her in." She stood and carefully walked to the house.

Alex picked up the water hose and began dousing the glowing embers. Once she was satisfied the fire was extinguished she walked back up to the porch and replaced the hose. Pulling another cigarette out of her box and lighting it she sat down on the steps to enjoy her smoke.

A couple of minutes later Bet walked onto the porch and lit a cigarette, joining Alex on the steps. Her thigh brushed Alex's as she sat close to her. "Thank you for a wonderful day," Bet said. "I don't believe I have ever seen Kylie this happy."

"What about you? Are you happy as well?"

"How could I not be? In less than twenty-four hours you have given us more unconditional love than we've had in years."

Alex could see tears making Bet's eyes shine. "Are you happy enough to stay?"

Bet burst into tears, scaring Alex, who thought she had made a terrible mistake. "I'm sorry, I shouldn't have asked that of you, but having you, and Kylie here has been terrific."

"Oh Alex, you sweet, sweet woman, you have nothing to apologize for. You have made both of us feel so welcome; it is truly like coming home. I would love to take you up on your offer," she said, instantly relieving Alex's worries.

"I was thinking earlier today, that it would be easy for you to get on at the hospital. They are constantly in search of nurses and we can get Kylie registered for school."

Bet smiled at her suggestions.

"Guess you will need to talk it over with Kylie first."

"Yeah, right, it will take a nanosecond for Kylie to agree to live here with you and Max," Bet said with a chuckle. "If you hadn't already noticed, she has chosen you for a second Mom."

"Are you okay with that?" Alex asked.

"I can think of no one better to teach Kylie how to fish and camp," Bet replied. "And no better partner to help me raise her."

Alex felt a jolt of electricity pass through her body when Bet used the word "partner"—a thought that both excited and terrified her at once.

Alex felt Bet shiver and asked, "Are you cold?"

"Just a chill," Bet said as she leaned closer to Alex.

Alex wrapped an arm around Bet's shoulder to share her body heat and simply said, "Welcome home."

They sat together for a few minutes, enjoying the silence of the still night and the comfort of one another's body. As the temperature dropped, Alex finally suggested they head up to bed. Entering the house, Alex locked up for the evening and climbed the stairs with Bet.

Stopping outside her bedroom door, Bet turned and hugged Alex close. The warm, comforting feeling of Bet in her arms was nearly more than Alex could bear. She struggled with her desire to kiss Bet and nearly fainted when Bet stood up on her tiptoes and kissed Alex on the cheek.

"Good night," she whispered, and then slipped into her bedroom.

Alex climbed the stairs to the loft and quickly shed her smoke-filled clothes, tossing them into a hamper as she headed for the shower.

The warmth of the shower caressed her skin as it washed away the remnants of the campfire. Alex toweled off and slipped naked between the cool sheets. Lying there in the quiet darkness, Alex's thoughts returned to the feeling of Bet wrapped in her arms. She fantasized of going beyond a friendly hug and Alex felt the moisture bloom between her thighs. With those thoughts bouncing through her brain, Alex dreamed of Bet.

†

Bet snuggled in next to her sleeping daughter and wondered what would happen if she were lying next to Alex. She had never been with another woman, but there had been women that she felt a certain attraction to. Bet had never admitted it could be more than simple attraction. With Alex, it was different, and she couldn't deny she was rapidly falling in love with her. The mere touch of her body made Bet's heart race, and more than once she had felt a surge of dampness grow between her legs. Alex had a way of looking at her that made her want to give her all to this woman, a feeling that confused and excited her at the same time. She could hear the shower running and fell asleep with thoughts of running her hands over Alex's naked skin.

Chapter Three

When Alex awoke the next morning she found Bet sitting on the edge of her bed, watching her sleep. Alex had tossed the covers off during the early morning hours, and her body was exposed from the waist up. She moved to cover her nakedness, but Bet blocked her hand.

"Don't on my account. You are absolutely beautiful, Alex," Bet softly said.

Alex relaxed as Bet's eyes caressed her skin. She felt the lingering dampness between her thighs reawaken. Bet was wearing a thin nightshirt and Alex could see her erect nipples as they strained against the thin cotton. "What time is it?" Alex asked to break the silence.

"Almost five."

"Too early to be up on a Sunday morning."

"Mind if I join you then?"

Alex lifted the covers and rolled onto her side to make room. Bet pulled the shirt over her head and lay down, scooting backward until she found Alex's warm body.

Alex's hard nipples pressed into the soft skin of Bet's back and Alex was sure Bet would feel the dampness between her legs as she spooned her body into Alex. Bet reached behind to find Alex's hand and pulled her close, placing Alex's hand on her warm belly.

Alex held her breath until she could no longer hold it then slowly exhaled into Bet's soft hair as she snuggled in to her. "Relax," Bet said as she closed her eyes and drifted off to sleep, wrapped in the comfort of Alex's embrace. Eventually Alex did relax and the slow rhythmic breathing of the beautiful woman sleeping in her arms finally lulled her to sleep.

✝

When Alex awoke three hours later, she was once again alone in her bed. Had she dreamed that Bet had come to her she wondered as she rolled onto her back. She listened for sounds below, but the house remained quiet, the only sound the soft ticking of her alarm clock.

Alex sat up in bed then turned to place her feet on the floor. Her feet touched the soft cotton nightshirt lying beside the bed, which confirmed she had not been dreaming. She bent down to pick up the shirt and buried her face in the shirt. She could still smell the faint scent of Bet in the worn fabric.

Falling for a straight woman is not a good thing. Alex couldn't resist taking one more smell of the shirt before she left the bed. She walked into the bathroom and turned on the shower in hopes the warm water would soothe her aching body, but the ache Alex was experiencing was not one she could easily wash away.

Alex had not had a lover for more than two years. Sharon had been her partner for over a year until the attraction of Atlanta overwhelmed the quiet little house on the lake, and she took off in search of high adventure. When Alex had visited her in Atlanta a few times, the distance and change in Sharon was more than she could bear so they had agreed to end their relationship.

Alex grabbed a towel as she stepped out of the shower onto a thick rug and began drying off. Out of the corner of her eye, she glimpsed movement and turned back toward the bedroom.

"Good morning," Bet said as she offered Alex the cup of coffee. "Light, and sweet, just like you like your woman."

Alex instinctively moved to cover her nakedness with the towel, but Bet did not simply set the cup down and walk away. Instead, she set the cup down on the vanity and leaned against the bathroom doorframe, watching Alex.

Never shy, Alex decided that if Bet wanted a view, she would surely give her one. She turned away from Bet to dry her back and then faced her again to dry her front. "How did you sleep last night?" Alex asked rather coyly.

"I slept wonderfully, and you?" Bet replied, stepping farther into the bathroom.

"Like a rock," Alex managed to say as she watched Bet's hand grasp the corner of the towel and wipe down her body from the base of her neck down between her small breasts.

"You missed a spot," Bet said as she dropped the end of the towel.

"Thanks," Alex stammered. The gentle caress of Bet's touch was pure torture but Alex wished it would go on forever.

Leaning against the doorframe again, Bet noticed Alex's rock-hard nipples. She smiled at the obvious effect she was having on Alex.

Suddenly unsure under Bet's gaze, Alex slipped on a pair of cutoff shorts and pulled a sports bra over her head, quickly followed by an old T-shirt. She reached for the coffee cup and leaned back against the vanity, taking a sip.

"Is Kylie up yet?" Alex asked.

"She and Max have been outside playing for almost an hour," Bet replied as she took a step closer to Alex.

Dear God, don't let her touch me right now. Senses fully armed Alex watched as Bet's hand reached up and gently moved a lock of damp hair that had fallen into her eyes. Bet's fingertips traced their way down Alex's cheek to her soft lips.

Bet had never kissed another woman but her desire to kiss Alex vanquished any apprehension. Bet leaned toward Alex, covering her lips softly, slowly kissing her. Wanting to take the kiss further Bet's tongue gently parted Alex's lips and probed sweetly into her mouth. Placing her hands on Alex's shoulders, pulling her close for a deeper kiss, Bet felt Alex's heart racing in her chest. When she could no longer breathe, Bet broke the kiss, her bright blue eyes smiling up at Alex.

Stepping back, Bet said, "Come on down and I'll get you some breakfast." She turned and walked from the bathroom leaving a breathless Alex clutching the vanity for support.

†

"We had toast and cereal," Bet said as she watched Alex climb down from the loft a few minutes later. "I can make you something hot if you prefer."

I'm hot enough already thank you. "Toast and cereal will do just fine," she said as she walked into the kitchen, coffee cup in hand.

"Can I fill you up," Bet asked, reaching for the coffeepot.

"I'd love that," Alex replied as she handed her the cup. *Oh, the ways I could think of for you to fill me up.*

Alex reached for a bowl and filled it with cereal as Bet refilled her coffee. Bet dropped two slices of bread into the toaster as Alex poured milk over her cereal. "I haven't had Captain Crunch in ages," Alex said, taking a bite of the crunchy cereal.

"Kylie's favorite." Bet buttered the toast and brought it over to Alex.

They stood at the counter, looking out the window, watching Kylie and Max play. "They make quite the pair don't they?" Alex asked as she looked toward Bet.

Bet grinned as she leaned into Alex and licked off a drop of milk that had fallen onto Alex's chin. Without missing a beat, Bet said, "Just like old friends."

Alex felt her knees go weak and knew if she didn't put some space between them soon she would explode from the sexual tension.

Dumping her bowl into the sink, Alex fled. "I'm going to go check the mail." Alex went out the door. Kylie and Max flocked to her as soon as she stepped off the porch at full stride.

"Where're you going?" Kylie asked.

"To check the mail."

"Can I go too?"

"It's a long walk. You better go ask your mom."

Kylie ran into the house, returning seconds later. "Mom said I could go if you wanted me to," Kylie said with a grin.

There was no way Alex could disappoint Kylie. "All right, let's go." The mailbox was nearly a mile away, but Kylie did well keeping up with Alex and Max. The coolness of the morning felt good on Alex's heated skin and she slowed her frantic pace.

"Mom said you asked us to stay, Alex. Can we really live here with you and Max?"

"For as long as you want," Alex replied as Kylie slipped her hand into hers.

"Great," she said with a huge smile.

Now all she had to do was to come up with a plan for dealing with her feelings for Bet.

Alex did not want Bet to feel obligated to have a sexual relationship as part of the agreement for her and Kylie to move in. She also didn't want her heart broken by a straight woman who just wanted to experiment. If there was going to be a relationship between them Alex wanted it based on mutual attraction, instead of unspoken feelings of indebtedness.

Alex thought back to the kiss they had shared in the bathroom barely an hour earlier. There certainly appeared to be a look of genuine attraction in Bet's eyes. She couldn't deny she'd enjoyed the sensations that flowed through her body like a current of electricity every time Bet touched her or looked deep inside her with those blue eyes.

Alex returned from the stupor of her thoughts when Kylie tugged on her arm. She had spied a doe with her fawn and was eagerly trying to point them out to Alex.

"Look!" Alex strained to see where Kylie was pointing.

"I see them," Alex whispered.

Max woofed and startled the doe who bolted back into the dense forest, followed closely by her fawn.

"Shush, Max," Alex scolded, but it was already too late. All Alex could see was the white of the mother's tail as she disappeared into the camouflage of the forest.

The moment was gone so Alex and Kylie continued on to the mailbox. "Sit, Max," Alex instructed the obedient dog. He promptly dropped to the drive and watched as Kylie and Alex walked the remaining few yards to the mailbox.

Alex lifted Kylie up to the box and pulled open the door. Kylie reached in and pulled out the small bundle of letters, which she handed to Alex after she was back on the ground. Alex flipped through the bundle that was mostly junk mail. Hardly worth the long walk, but Alex needed the distraction from her feelings for Bet so she was glad she had forgotten to get the mail yesterday when they came home from town. Alex looked across the road to check on Bet's car. "Guess we should bring the truck down later to unload the car," Alex said.

"I can help," Kylie said as she took Alex's hand and they started the long walk back up to the house. The return trip was steeper and about a third of the way home Kylie started to tire.

"You want a piggyback ride," Alex offered.

"Yes, please." Kylie climbed onto Alex's back as she knelt down.

"Here, you can hold onto these." Alex handed Kylie the mail.

Alex walked carefully up the remainder of the drive and put Kylie back on the ground. "How about taking the mail into the house for me?"

She watched Kylie walk toward the house then she and Max headed for the dock. Kicking off her shoes, Alex walked the length of the pier and sat down on the end of the dock, her feet dangling in the cool water. The mornings had begun to cool down, but the days continued to be warm enough for a swim. "Maybe today," Alex said aloud as she lay back on the dock. Max lay down beside her and the pair dozed in the warm sun.

A trickle of sweat rolling down her side woke Alex from her nap. Kylie was sitting beside Max, her hand buried in the soft fur at the scruff of his neck. She was talking to him quietly as Alex peeked through partially opened eyes. Stretching slowly, Alex sat up on the end of the dock and asked Kylie, "How long have I been napping?"

"Not long."

Alex looked down at her watch and saw that nearly an hour had passed. "Can you swim, Kylie?"

"Mom says like a fish," Kylie said proudly.

"Well, let's take the truck down and unload the car and then come back and go for a swim."

"Cool!"

Alex stood and together they walked back to the house. This time Alex wasn't surprised when Kylie reached up and took her hand. She smiled as they walked and chatted.

When they entered the house Alex could smell a cake baking, a smell that hadn't graced her house in a long, long time. Bet was putting away clean dishes as she unloaded the dishwasher.

"Kylie and I thought we would take the truck down and bring up the rest of your stuff," Alex said. "When we get done, we thought we might all go for a swim, if that's okay."

"Sounds good. Would you mind if I stayed behind until the cake finishes baking?"

"I think Kylie and I can handle the car," Alex said. "Chocolate icing?"

"Nothing but," Bet said with a grin.

"Can't wait." Alex picked up the truck keys. "Ready, Kylie?"

"Yes, ma'am." She headed out the door.

"Be back soon," Alex said with a smile.

Alex had barely started down the drive when she realized she hadn't gotten Bet's keys. Putting the truck in reverse, she backed up the drive until she could turn the truck around. As she pulled up to the house, Bet came out the door and walked to the driver's side.

"I imagine these would help," Bet said, dangling the keys as her hand came to rest on the arm Alex had draped out the window.

Alex's skin tingled under her touch and she blushed slightly. "Yes, ma'am, they would," Alex said as her eyes locked with Bet's. She reached for the keys and felt blue eyes penetrating down to her soul.

"Let's try this again," Alex said as she put the truck in gear. As she pulled away, she looked into the side mirror to find Bet smiling.

Alex pulled up behind the car. Telling Max to stay, she and Kylie climbed down from the truck and Alex used the keys to open the trunk. She located a small bag that Kylie could handle then pulled out the larger bags. They carried the first load to the truck and returned for a second. Cleaning out the trunk, Alex unlocked the car and Kylie scooted in to hand her the small plastic bags out of the packed backseat. Alex then placed her in the bed of the truck and handed the bags up to her. They walked back to the car together and inspected it closely.

"Are we all done?" Alex asked.

"I think that is all of it," Kylie responded. They walked back to the truck and Kylie climbed back in, welcomed by Max with a sloppy kiss.

Alex looked back at the meager belongings and realized how difficult it must have been to leave so much of their lives behind during their escape. Alex vowed to replace whatever she could as quickly as possible as she climbed into the truck and drove back to the house.

Bet joined them as they began to unload the truck and helped them carry the bags up the stairs to the bedrooms. When they had finished, Bet turned to Kylie. "Why don't we find your bathing suit and you and Alex can go for a swim while I put our stuff away?"

"You sure you don't need some help?" Alex asked.

"No, ma'am, you two have done a lot already, so I will take over from here."

"All right then, I am going to go put on my suit. I'll be waiting for you on the porch when you get ready," she told Kylie.

"I'll hurry." Kylie was already searching through a bag for her suit.

Alex climbed up into the loft and located a modest one-piece swimsuit. She slipped it on and pulled her T-shirt back on before going to the linen closet to grab a couple of towels. Alex pulled out two and then went back for another with hopes that Bet would join them later.

Alex walked out to the porch and sat in a rocker waiting for Kylie to join her. The day had indeed turned out warm and Alex was eager to hit the water.

Max was the first to hear Kylie's approach and ran to the door to meet her. Bet had located a pair of floaties, too, and had blown them up and slipped them over her little fish's arms before sending her down the stairs.

"Let's do it," Alex said when she saw Kylie and bent down to pick up the towels before they walked out onto the dock. Max had picked up his tennis ball and dropped it at Alex's feet as she stood at the end of the dock. Alex picked it up, throwing it as far as she could into the lake. Max flew down the pier and sailed out into the water then began swimming toward the floating ball. Kylie's giggles filled the air with a magical sound. Alex draped their towels over the railing and asked, "Do we take the plunge, or do you want to ease into the water?"

Kylie answered by taking off at full speed and jumping off the end of the dock, barely making a splash as she hit the water. Alex's laughter rang across the lake as she pulled her shirt over her head and ran down the pier performing a perfect ten cannonball as she hit the water. She surfaced and swam toward Kylie who was bobbing up and down in the wake of her dive. Shortly afterward Max joined them, with a mouthful of tennis ball. Alex took the ball from him and threw it toward the shore into the shallow water.

Kylie kicked her feet and slowly floated toward Max, and Alex floated on her back until they reached a depth where she could stand. As soon as Kylie realized Alex was standing, she immediately asked her to flip her off her shoulders.

Alex knelt in the water and Kylie climbed to a standing position on her shoulders. Bobbing slowly in the water, Alex and Kylie counted to three before Alex launched Kylie through the air. It wasn't exactly a flip but Kylie squealed with laughter as she swam back to Alex.

They repeated this sequence for about a half hour before Kylie tired. They swam over to the ladder and crawled back up onto the dock. Max swam to shore and shook the water from his coat then trotted down to join Kylie and Alex as they lay at the end of the dock breathing hard.

Alex was certain her muscles would be sore Monday when she returned to work. Even though she was in good shape, she knew she'd worked muscles playing with Kylie she hadn't worked in quite a while, but the fun she was having made it all worthwhile.

As they lay on their backs, Alex looked up into the fluffy, white clouds and pointed out doughnuts and various other shapes with Kylie. "May I join you two?" Bet said from somewhere behind them.

"Hi, Mommy," Kylie said with a smile as Bet lay down between Kylie and Alex. Bet had put on a bright blue bikini, which really made her eyes stand out. A light dusting of soft blond hairs formed a trail down her abdomen and covered the bronze skin of her stomach.

Alex struggled with the temptation of reaching over and tracing that trail to its terminus. Instead, she turned on her side to get a better look at Bet. "Get all settled in?"

"Yep, got everything put away, frosted the cake, and laid out some chicken breasts for dinner," Bet replied in one breath.

"Time for a break then," Alex said. Alex stood and walked toward the garage. She emerged several minutes later rolling a huge inner tube down the hill toward the dock. She dropped the inner tube into the water and held it in place while Bet crawled into it, stretching her legs across the warm rubber. Alex then handed Kylie down to Bet and asked, "Is there room for one more?"

"I think we could squeeze you in," Bet said as she rested Kylie on her lap.

Alex moved the tube over to the ladder and carefully crawled down onto it. Bet positioned Kylie between them, wedging the small child securely in the middle.

"All set?" Alex asked.

"Yes, ma'am," Kylie said. Alex used her foot to push them away from the dock and out into the lake.

Alex's left arm stretched above Bet's head and Bet repositioned to rest her head there. Alex used her right arm as a paddle to set them afloat on the water. Alex rested her head on the inner tube and relaxed as they floated across the calm waters.

They floated peacefully around the lake for an hour before Kylie started to wiggle. Alex paddled them back toward the dock and when they were in shallow water, she picked Kylie up in her arms and helped her to stand up in her hands. Kylie squealed with laughter as Alex counted slowly to three and then sent her flying across the water. Kylie came back up giggling.

"You're really good with Kylie," Bet said as she snuggled closer to Alex.

"She's a lot of fun," Alex said with a smile.

"Watching the two of you at play makes me smile. You know, you share so many familiar features, Kylie could pass for your child," Bet remarked.

Alex hadn't realized just how true Bet's statement was as she watched the happy child swimming with Max. Max had allowed her to grab onto his collar and was slowly pulling her to shore, her laughter echoing along the water.

"I'd be proud to have a child like Kylie in my life."

"I think she is there already," Bet said as she worked her hands under Alex and flipped her off the tube into the water.

Alex surfaced, sputtering. "Oh, no you didn't just flip me!"

Kylie, who was now standing close to shore, turned toward the commotion. "Yes, she did Alex," Kylie said, clapping for her mother.

"Time for you to get wet then." Alex overturned the large inner tube into the cool water.

It was Bet's turn to come up sputtering. Alex couldn't help notice the erect nipples poking out at her. "Are you a bit nippily?" she asked with a wicked grin on her face.

"A little cooler than I had anticipated, but still very pleasurable," Bet said.

"Very nice." Alex turned and pushed the inner tube toward the shore.

Bet jumped toward Alex and grabbed her shoulders in an attempt to dunk Alex. Alex stood solid, easily deflecting the smaller woman's attack. Bet wrapped her legs around Alex's waist hoping to gain an advantage, but Alex hooked her arms under Bet's knees, trapping her, and dove backward into the water.

Kylie bent over laughing as she realized Bet's plan had backfired. "She got you good, Mommy," was all she could say before the giggles overtook her again.

Alex stood up, arms stretched toward the sky, and cried out, "Winner and still queen of the lake."

Bet laughed at Alex's antics as she moved in for a second attempt. Alex easily overpowered the more aggressive woman but did enjoy wrestling with her, their bodies entwined together as they struggled.

Finally exhausted, Bet raised her hands in surrender. Alex reached for her hand and together they walked toward Kylie who was sitting on the small beach still breathing hard from her laughter. Max rushed up to Alex, ball in mouth for a throw. Alex hurled the ball out into the lake and Max dove into the lake for a long swim. Kylie, Bet, and Alex watched Max as they sat quietly on the beach.

"I'm hungry, Mom," Kylie said.

"Me too," Alex said. "How about we cook up some hot dogs for lunch?"

"Are you coming too, Mommy?"

"I think I will take a shower while you two cook."

Alex swam out to retrieve the inner tube and tossed it up on the dock before climbing the ladder. She grabbed their towels and met up with Bet and Kylie at the end of the pier. Bet wrapped a doubled towel around Kylie and then wrapped a towel around her waist. Hand in hand, they walked back to the house closely followed by Max.

Bet went upstairs to shower while Alex and Kylie washed their hands and headed to the kitchen to cook lunch. Alex filled a pot of water and placed it on the burner to boil. "Will you hand me the pack of hot dogs from the fridge?"

Kylie pulled hard on the refrigerator door and when she finally tugged it open reached in and retrieved the hot dogs.

"What do you like on your hot dogs?" Alex asked.

"Mayonnaise, ketchup, and pickle relish."

"Pretty close to me," Alex said. "I usually hold off on the relish though and sometimes I add onions."

"Eww," Kylie said. "Those things stink."

"Yes, they do, but they sure can taste good from time to time." Alex dropped the hot dogs in the water and walked to the fridge to get the condiments. She went to the pantry and returned with a pack of buns, paper plates, and napkins, then set them on the end of the counter next to the condiments. Alex bent down and picked Kylie up, placing her on the counter next to the sink. She leaned on the counter next to Kylie and together they watched the water, waiting for it to begin to boil.

"A watched pot never boils," Bet said as she walked down the stairs.

"We weren't watching the pot. We are waiting for the dogs to bark," Alex said with a wink to Kylie. Max barked on cue then stretched out on the rug in front of the fireplace and cocked his head at Alex. Kylie looked at Alex in surprise and all three broke into a fit of laughter.

Bet walked into the kitchen and placed her hand on Alex's shoulder while pretending to listen for the barking dogs. "Kylie, after lunch you need to take a bath and then lay down for a nap. I am going to massage Alex's shoulders and then we will nap too."

"Mommy gives good massages," Kylie said to Alex.

"I bet she does," Alex said to Kylie. "Hey, did you hear that? Listen."

Kylie strained to hear the sounds coming from the pot of boiling water and could finally hear the hissing sound coming from the hot dogs as the ends burst open. "Sounds more like a cat to me," Kylie stated very seriously.

Alex could barely contain her laughter. "You know, you are right, but hot cats just don't sound as good."

Alex took the pot and carefully drained the water into the sink. Bet had already placed opened buns on the paper plates and Alex put a hot dog in each one. "Off to the table with you," Alex said, putting Kylie back down on the floor.

Kylie sat down at the table and watched as Bet prepared her hot dog.

"May we splurge with a soda?" Alex asked Bet.

"Sure, why not."

Alex pulled three chilled cans out of the fridge. She popped the top on one and sat it on the table for Kylie.

Bet placed Kylie's hot dog down in front of her. "Do you want me to cut it in half for you?"

"Yes, please." Kylie then took a portion of the hot dog in her small hand, raising it to her mouth for a bite.

"So hungry you can't wait for us," Bet chided her young daughter.

"Sorry, Mom," Kylie said after she swallowed. "It looked so good, I just couldn't wait."

So young, but clever enough to know just what to say, Alex thought as she sat down at the table. "They do look good." Alex bit into her hot dog. "Tastes good too," she said as a drop of ketchup oozed out of the bun and onto the corner of her mouth. Alex wiped the corner of her mouth with a napkin and then looked at Bet who was watching her with a wicked grin on her face.

As they ate lunch, Kylie's eyes got heavier and heavier. Alex felt that after a warm bath, the tired child would go right off to sleep. Once they finished, Bet told Kylie, "Go on up and get your pajamas out and I will be up in just a minute after we pick up the kitchen."

"Yes, Mommy." Kylie slowly crawled up the stairs.

Alex closed up the condiments and carried them to the fridge as Bet tossed the used napkins and plates into the garbage. "Why don't you take a hot shower and then lay down on the bed," Bet suggested. "I know if Kylie is that sleepy, she must have given you a good workout. Let me get her bathed and down for a nap and I'll be in to give you that massage."

"Okay, see you in a bit," Alex replied a bit nervously as she wiped off the table and counter.

Kylie was sitting on the edge of the bed as Bet entered the room. "Are you ready for a bath, sweetie?"

Kylie followed her mom into the bathroom. Bet unwound the towel from around Kylie and peeled off the slightly damp suit as they waited for the tub to fill. Kylie stepped into the warm water and sat down in the tub. Bet wet her hair with a plastic cup and then lathered her dark curls, massaging her daughter's scalp. Kylie tilted her head as Bet rinsed her hair and Bet hoped she could finish off the bath before Kylie went out on her. Bet quickly bathed Kylie's body then wrapped a soft towel around her young daughter. Patting her dry, she helped her put on her pajamas and then turned back the covers on the bed.

Kylie climbed into the bed and Bet pulled the covers up. Kylie looked up at Bet and with a sleepy voice said, "I love you, Mommy."

"I love you too, Kylie." Bet bent down to kiss her daughter's forehead. "Sweet dreams honey," she added, but Kylie was already fast asleep.

Bet returned to the bathroom to brush her hair and teeth before climbing to Alex's loft.

Chapter Four

Alex enjoyed the pulsing of the water against her tired shoulders. She hated to admit it, but Kylie had given her a good workout and she probably would be sore tomorrow. She stepped out of the shower and after drying off and brushing her damp curls and teeth went to lie facedown on the bed.

Bet walked into Alex's room and saw her lying naked on the bed, lightly dozing. She smiled to herself and walked into Alex's bathroom. Finding some lotion, Bet quietly crept onto the bed, her eyes roaming over Alex's body from head to toe. She poured lotion into her palms, rubbing them together to warm the lotion and then moved to straddle Alex's hips. Gently lowering her body onto Alex's, she leaned forward to place her hands on her shoulders. As her fingers touched Alex's skin, she felt her tense slightly. "Relax," she whispered as her hands began to knead her shoulders.

"How can I relax when I have a beautiful woman sitting on top of me?"

"Very easily I hope." Bet's hands worked the knotted muscles of Alex's strong shoulders.

"Feels good," Alex purred and felt herself relaxing under the gentle pressure of Bet's hands.

Bet smoothed the fragrant lotion down Alex's back, working her way slowly down her body. Alex remained suspiciously quiet and Bet wondered if she had drifted off to sleep. *That would be disappointing.*

As Bet worked her way down across her hips and onto the deep muscles of her thighs soft moans let her know that Alex was definitely still awake. Bet slipped off the bed and took Alex's right calf in her hands, massaging it deeply. Bet poured more lotion into her hands, sat on the edge of the bed, taking Alex's right foot in her hands, massaging the warm lotion deep into her muscles.

"That feels really good," Alex said. She was really enjoying Bet's attention and her body was pulsing with excitement.

Bet worked her way up Alex's left leg and then crawled up beside her on the bed. "Roll over," she whispered softly.

Alex rolled over and Bet could see the desire burning in her dark eyes. Bet softly caressed Alex's face and worked her way down her neck. Alex's erect nipples screamed for attention as Bet's soft hands stroked her arms and chest.

Bet looked into Alex's eyes as her hand gently cupped Alex's breast. Alex closed her eyes and moaned as Bet's fingers softly brushed across her nipple. Bet leaned into Alex and gently parted her lips with her tongue, probing into Alex's mouth as she continued teasing her nipple. Alex returned her kiss and buried her hand in Bet's hair, pulling her down for a deeper kiss.

Bet's hand slowly stroked down Alex's body as their kiss became more passionate. Her hand came to rest between Alex's thighs. She could feel the damp curls press into her palm as she cupped Alex's mound with a gentle squeeze.

Alex moaned deeply into Bet's mouth, her body trembled as Bet's hand remained stationary. Bet broke the kiss and looked directly into Alex's eyes. "I want to make love with you, Alex."

"We need to get you out of those clothes," Alex said with a grin.

Bet stood and slipped quietly out of her clothes. She turned and smiled bashfully at Alex. Her eyes shone with excitement as she looked at Alex. "I've never been with another woman before, so I have no clue what I'm doing. You will have to show me the way."

Alex reached for her, pulling Bet on the bed and rolling her onto her back then moving on top of her, kissing her deeply. She felt Bet's wetness blend with hers as she slowly rolled her hips into Bet and her hands began to explore Bet's body.

Alex broke the kiss. She softly kissed down Bet's cheek before burying her face in Bet's neck. Her teeth nibbled on Bet's neck and her moans grew louder, echoing in the loft. Alex slipped down further between Bet's legs and felt the heat of her wetness as it coated her stomach. Alex took Bet's supple breasts in her hands and planted soft kisses all over them, intentionally bypassing Bet's swollen nipples. Alex could feel the tremors in Bet's body as she lowered her mouth to suckle Bet's left breast, her left hand rubbing softly over Bet's right nipple.

Alex listened to Bet's breathing increase as she suckled more firmly on her breast. The fingers of her hand rolled the nipple of her other breast and Bet arched her back, pressing her breasts deeper into Alex's mouth and hand.

"That feels so good, Alex," Bet said between gasps. She buried her hands in Alex's curls as she pulled her close. Alex's teeth continued to nibble the tender, sensitive flesh of Bet's nipple and she felt Bet's body explode in an intense orgasm. She continued her nibbles, alternating between breasts as Bet's body convulsed with spasms of pleasure.

"Are you okay?" Alex softly whispered.

"Oh, my God, yes, Alex, so please don't stop," Bet pleaded.

Her hands cupped Bet's breasts, stimulating her nipples as her mouth licked a slow trail down Bet's body. The tip of her tongue slowly swirled around Bet's navel as her warm breath teased her skin. Alex could feel Bet rocking her hips as she kissed her way farther down her body.

Alex slid fully between Bet's spread thighs. Bet's body trembled with anticipation as Alex's fingers played in the soft, soaked curls nestled there.

Alex used the tips of her fingers to part Bet's lips gently, caressing the velvety smooth muscles underneath as she explored the opening of her new lover's body. Bet shook with each stroke of Alex's fingers as they gently probed her wetness. Alex looked into Bet's eyes one final time before lowering her head between Bet's thighs. That look told Alex how much Bet was enjoying herself and how hungry she was for more. Alex used the tip of her tongue to brush lightly across Bet's soaked lips, savoring the aroma and taste of her salty wetness. Alex dipped her tongue into Bet's center, entering her deeply and with one stroke of her tongue felt Bet's body convulse with pleasure, her hips thrashed wildly onto Alex's face as her tongue plunged deeper and deeper inside.

Bet was panting wildly as Alex lifted her head and covered Bet's clit with her hot mouth. Bet cried out as she sucked her deeply into her mouth, her tongue wrapping around her clit as she kissed it frantically. Alex coated her fingers in Bet's soaking wetness and then slowly slid two fingers past her puckering lips. She pushed deeper inside and could feel Bet's muscles as they squeezed around her fingers.

Alex glanced up at Bet who was biting her lip to fight off the urge to scream. Alex began sucking Bet's clit in and out of her mouth as her fingers located and caressed Bet's G-spot. Bet reached over and grabbed a pillow, pressing it to her face as her moans grew louder and she feared waking Kylie. Bet's hips surged upward and she screamed into the pillow as her orgasm exploded. When her body could take no more, Bet reached down to find Alex's hand and pulled it toward her face.

Alex, taking the cue, slowly withdrew her fingers and placed a final soft kiss on Bet's throbbing clit. She moved back on top of Bet who took her face in her hands and kissed her with a blinding passion. Alex could still feel the trembling of Bet's body as she returned the kiss.

Bet moaned deeply into Alex's mouth, tasting herself on the lips of her lover for the first time. She wanted that kiss to go on forever but also wanted to give Alex the kind of pleasure she had just received. Still breathing hard, she pushed Alex onto her back.

"Are you okay?" Alex asked sweetly.

"I have never felt this good in my entire life." Bet laid her head on Alex's shoulder.

After her heartbeat slowed a bit, Bet reached out to touch Alex's breast, wanting so badly to make love to her. Alex watched Bet tentatively touch her hard nipples then gently pinch them, causing them to grow even harder.

Bet licked her lips and moved down to take Alex's breast in her mouth. Alex moaned with pleasure as Bet suckled her deeply, trapping her nipple against the roof of her mouth.

"Oh yes, baby," Alex whispered to encourage her new lover. "Don't be afraid to suck it hard." Bet immediately took Alex's breast into her mouth.

Bet's hand trembled with excitement as it moved between Alex's legs, touching another woman's wetness for the first time. Her fingers swam in the wetness and she enjoyed the velvety feel of it on her fingers. Bet brought her wet fingers up to Alex's breast and rubbed the wetness over the nipple, then replaced her fingers with her mouth to taste Alex for the first time.

The taste of Alex bombarded her tongue, leaving Bet hungry for more of the sweet nectar. Alex reached for Bet's shoulders and guided her down her body, her tongue burning rivers of fire on Alex's skin as she moved lower.

Alex spread her thighs to allow Bet to crawl between them. Bet parted her lips and lapped hungrily of her wetness. Bet's thumb brushed across Alex's clit and her body jolted from the sensation. Learning quickly, Bet slowly stroked Alex's clit with her thumb as she buried her face in Alex's wetness. Bet's tongue probed deeply as her face ground into Alex's wetness.

"Bet," Alex called out softly.

Bet lifted her face and looked into Alex's face. "I want to come with you," Alex said. "Turn around and straddle my face so I can taste you again."

Bet moved up to straddle Alex's head and then bent down to continue her oral assault on Alex's body. Alex took Bet's hips in her hands and lowered her onto her face. As Bet's tongue dipped deeply inside her, Alex's tongue parted Bet's lips and she entered her. Bet moaned as she experienced receiving pleasure while giving it to another. Her body went wild when Alex began stroking her clit with her thumb, and a gush of her warm juices covered Alex's face as Bet came quickly.

Bet covered Alex's clit with her mouth and entered her with two fingers, plunging deeply into her wetness. Alex bent her knees so her feet were flat on the bed and began thrusting her hips up to meet each plunge of Bet's fingers. Alex's right hand circled Bet's waist and she dragged her nails lightly down Bet's back and across her buttocks driving Bet wild with excitement. Alex felt her orgasm begin and she covered Bet's clit with her mouth sucking it roughly as her body gushed onto Bet's eager face. Bet's body also reached its peak and together they drank deeply of each other's passion.

Bet's hands spread Alex's legs wider and she continued to lap the juices flowing from Alex.

Alex slipped two fingers into Bet as her teeth nibbled her clit. Bet erupted in an intense climax, rocking her body over Alex's face as the violent contractions took over her body, leaving her breathless and exhausted as she lay on top of Alex.

Bet turned around and climbed into Alex's embrace, laying her head on Alex's chest as she listened to the pounding of her heart. "That was fantastic," Bet whispered.

"Amen," Alex said, letting out a big sigh.

Bet reached down and cupped Alex's wetness as they lay quietly together, both still reeling from the intense lovemaking they had shared.

"How much longer will Kylie sleep?" Alex asked.

"Probably for at least another hour, why do you ask?"

"I think we could both use a shower before she wakes up," Alex said with a grin.

"In a minute," Bet said as she snuggled into Alex.

They napped briefly before showering together. They took turns bathing one another and then Alex pinned Bet against the back wall of the shower as her tongue ravaged her body one final time, their moans echoing in the shower.

After drying off and dressing, they climbed down from the loft to find Kylie already up and playing quietly with Max. "I guess we are going to have to take quiet lessons from Kylie," Alex whispered before she turned Bet around for a short kiss. They walked down the stairs together.

Kylie looked up. "Hi Mommy, and Alex."

"Hi, sweetie," Bet said as she walked over to hug Kylie.

"You look pretty, Mommy," Kylie said.

Alex looked at Bet. She did look much more relaxed and there was still a faint glow on her face from their lovemaking.

"Why thank you, my sweet daughter," Bet said as she hugged her tightly.

"Do you feel better?" Kylie asked Alex.

"Yes, I do, Kylie, your mom has some really good hands indeed," Alex replied. The sexual innuendo was lost on the young Kylie, but Bet blushed profusely as Alex grinned.

"You think you could help me make a salad?" Alex asked Kylie.

"I sure can. Mommy says I make a good lettuce ripper."

Alex chuckled and headed into the kitchen to gather supplies to accompany the chicken breasts they would grill shortly. Sitting Kylie down at the table with a bowl and a head of washed lettuce, Alex watched as Kylie went to work on her assignment.

Alex moved to the sink where she washed vegetables and then sliced them to join Kylie's lettuce. "How do you feel about some cheese?" Bet asked as she gazed into the fridge.

"Sounds yummy to me," Alex said. "How about you, Kylie?"

"Yummy," she said as she continued tearing the lettuce apart.

"Grated or chunks," Alex asked Bet.

"Why don't I grate up some of this cheddar and jack," Bet replied as she joined Alex who was chopping veggies at the counter.

Together they created a large salad and placed it in the fridge for chilling. "What else would you like to go with the chicken?" Alex asked Kylie.

Without hesitation, Kylie said, "Macaroni and cheese, please."

Kylie was the first to finish the meal they created and she waited patiently for Alex and her mom to finish their meals. As soon as Bet swallowed her last bite, Kylie asked, "Can we have cake now?"

"Phew, I'm glad she asked," Alex stated. "I'm not sure I could have waited much longer."

Bet went into the kitchen and returned with three slices of yellow cake with chocolate icing. "You want some more milk?" Alex asked Kylie.

"Yes, please."

"How about you, Mom?"

"I think I will stick with tea. thanks." Bet watched Alex refill Kylie's glass, and pour one for her.

They all enjoyed the much-anticipated cake and Kylie and Alex ended up with matching milk mustaches. With a shared grin, they wiped their mouths and sighed with contentment. Watching the exchange between her daughter and her lover, Bet's heart swelled with love.

Alex picked up the kitchen while Kylie and Bet settled in on the front porch. The sun had set during dinner and the night air was cool so Bet sent Kylie upstairs to put on a light jacket. When she returned, Alex still hadn't joined them on the porch. "Where's Alex?" Kylie asked.

"I'm not sure, honey. Hang on and I'll go check on her."

Bet walked back into the house and finally found Alex in the laundry room ironing a pair of pants. She walked up behind Alex, slipping her arms around her, hugging her close from behind.

"Kylie was missing you, so I told her I would come find you."

"I was just trying to iron an outfit for work tomorrow," Alex said as she turned around to face Bet. "Was Kylie the only one missing me?"

"Well, Max didn't say so, but I'm sure he is missing you too." Bet stretched up to place a soft kiss on Alex's lips.

Alex took Bet in her arms and planted a fevered kiss on her lips, taking Bet's breath away.

"Wow, I'll let you kiss me like that all night long," Bet said as her hands slipped under Alex's shirt.

Bet's touch sent shivers of anticipation up Alex's spine. "I'll be finished here in just a few minutes, but you definitely keep that thought in mind," Alex said with a wicked grin.

"Count on it, babe." Bet gave Alex's breasts a gentle squeeze and then spun around to go back out to the porch.

Alex watched Bet walk away before returning to her ironing board. Finishing off her project, she folded the ironing board and put the iron away. She walked onto the porch and found Kylie sitting in her rocker. She walked over, picked her up, placing her in her lap as she sat back in the rocker.

"Did you get enough to eat tonight, Kylie?" Alex asked.

"Yes, ma'am, I did."

"Hmmmm. I could have sworn I felt an empty spot, right here," Alex said as she poked the ticklish child in the side.

Kylie broke out in giggles as she squirmed in Alex's lap.

"What are you two going to do tomorrow?" Alex asked Bet.

"I thought I would give the Board of Nursing a call about getting a Georgia license for starters," Bet said. "If you will loan us your car tomorrow, we can drive into town and change over my driver's license and I could stop by the hospital to see what kind of openings they have. I guess I should also check into getting Kylie registered for school."

"School? Really, Mom?" Kylie asked excitedly.

"Well, you have a birthday next week and you will be old enough to start pre-kindergarten," Bet replied.

"A birthday?" Alex inquired. "What day?"

"Wednesday," Bet replied. "A whole five years old."

"Sounds like you will have a busy day then. Pre-K is only half a day here so if you want, you can arrange for the bus to drop Kylie off at my office after school and she can keep Sandy, my office manager, company until I leave work," Alex suggested.

"How does that sound to you, munchkin?" Bet asked Kylie.

"Okay with me, Mom."

"I don't think school starts for another week or so, but Kylie can hang with me during the day if you get hired at the hospital right away," Alex said.

Kylie's eyes lit up at that prospect. "Can I really Alex?"

"Really," Alex assured her. "It may get pretty boring for you, though."

Bet had the feeling that Kylie would willingly suffer through absolute misery to spend time with Alex. Some mothers, she thought, would be jealous, but Bet was glad Alex made the effort to spend time with Kylie.

"Well, I imagine Tom will be here around seven thirty to tow your car, so you should have most of the day to run your errands," Alex said.

"Do you have any idea what you might want for dinner tomorrow night?"

"Why don't I treat us to the diner tomorrow night?" Alex said. "If you accomplish half of what you have planned, you are going to be worn out."

Kylie had gotten quiet while Bet and Alex chatted and when she looked down, Alex saw that Kylie had fallen asleep in her lap.

"You really wore her out today," Bet said.

"It's all the fresh air she's getting," Alex replied.

"Whatever it is, she sure is one happy little girl because of you."

"She is a real sweetheart." Alex smoothed Kylie's hair. "You want me to take her up to bed?"

"I think she would like that," Bet said as she worked the jacket off her sleeping daughter.

"I'll be back shortly then." Alex stood and carried Kylie up the stairs. She tossed the covers back and laid Kylie gently on the bed.

Kylie's eyes fluttered open as Alex pulled the covers over her. "I love you, Alex."

"I love you too, Kylie." Alex bent down to kiss her forehead. "Sweet dreams."

"Tell Mom I love her too, please."

"Will do," Alex said before she turned the lamp out and walked down the stairs with a smile so wide she felt like her face would crack. Not since her dad had died had anyone told her I love you, as genuinely as Kylie just did. Alex stepped out the door and lit two cigarettes, handing one to Bet.

"Kylie said to tell you she loves you," Alex said as she rocked back in her chair. "She even told me she loved me tonight."

"Well, you have to admit you are pretty lovable," Bet said as she placed her hand over hers.

"You are going to make me blush if you keep that up."

"Oh I hope to make you more than blush." Bet moved over to sit in Alex's lap.

"That sounds very intriguing, ma'am, just what did you have in mind?" Alex asked.

"I thought we might head upstairs and roll around naked in your bed for a while," Bet said as her fingers played in Alex's hair.

"Hmm, that does sound like it could be a lot of fun." Alex leaned down and tenderly kissed Bet.

"A few more of those and I will be putty in your hands."

Alex continued kissing Bet, her hand moving under her shirt to caress Bet's breasts, as their kisses grew more passionate.

Bet could feel her wetness soak through her sweats as her moans urged Alex to continue. "Oh, yes, baby," Bet managed to say as Alex's hand slid under the waistband of her sweats and her palm rubbed across Bet's throbbing clit.

Alex toyed with Bet's wetness, dipping her fingers inside her saturated lips and drawing her wetness over her swollen clit. Each stroke sent wave after wave of excitement through Bet. Alex played her body like a fiddle.

Bet's kisses grew hungry as Alex slipped two fingers deep inside her and began to rock in the chair. Alex's thumb stroked across Bet's clit as her fingers pressed deeper inside. Bet's muscles contracted around Alex's fingers as the first current of orgasm streamed into Alex's hand.

Breathless, Bet looked up to Alex. "I need to be naked with you right now."

Alex removed her fingers slowly and helped Bet to her feet and up the stairs to the loft. Alex sat Bet on the bed and removed her clothing before slipping out of her own. She then knelt on the floor between Bet's legs and placed her knees over her shoulders. Spreading her thighs wide apart, Alex used her fingertips to open Bet's lips and she began to slowly lap at the wetness flowing from Bet.

Alex teased Bet for several minutes, lightly kissing her wetness and stroking her tongue along the outside edges of Bet's clit. Bet needed release. She took Alex's head in her hands and guided her to the exact spot and Alex buried her tongue inside her. Alex's fingers rolled Bet's nipples as her tongue sank deeper and deeper into her wetness. Alex's face was soaked when Bet exploded. She moved her farther onto the bed and lay on top of Bet, slowly grinding her hips into Bet's and extending her orgasm for several minutes.

Bet wrapped her legs around Alex's hips, pulling Alex tightly into her body. Alex could feel her hard clit rubbing across Bet's and her body broke out in sweat as she struggled to hold back the flood of excitement running its course through her body. Bet shuddered; her body trembling with need as another orgasm approached. Alex covered Bet's mouth with hers and moaned deeply as her body released its passion into Bet.

Bet was panting, soaked with the exertion of their lovemaking as Alex moved to lie beside her. Each stroke of Alex's hand down her body sent renewed currents of arousal through Bet and her body ached for more of Alex's touch.

Alex read Bet's need as if they had been lovers for years. Her fingers teased and then parted Bet's lips, pressing deep into her wetness with three fingers.

Bet moaned loudly from the sensation of fullness as Alex worked her fingers inside Bet, stretching her walls and caressing her sensitive spots until Bet's body gushed, her juices filling Alex's hand with hot liquid.

"Another one of those and I won't be able to walk tomorrow," Bet said a few minutes later and she stretched and looked deeply into Alex's eyes.

Alex knew then that Bet had been satisfied for the night. She climbed higher onto the bed and took Bet into her arms. "Enough for tonight then," Alex asked as she pulled the covers over them.

"I could never get enough of you. You're a fantastic lover, and have taken me places I have never been, but we both do have big days ahead of us tomorrow," she said as she snuggled into Alex's warmth.

"I feel like I could stay up all night with you," Alex said as she caressed Bet's cheek.

"I have no doubt you could, baby," Bet said as she lifted her face to deliver a hungry kiss to Alex.

Alex felt her insides quiver as she responded to the kiss and wished the night would last forever. Their kisses slowed and Bet softly whispered, "Goodnight, lover." Alex drifted off to sleep with those words still ringing in her ears.

†

It was late on Sunday morning when Brian's thumping head finally woke him and he cursed himself for sleeping so late. It would be dark by the time he made it to the podunk little town in Georgia where Bet had last used her credit card and he would not be able to search for them until daylight came the next day. He managed to find a liquor store on his drive and then stumbled upon a dingy motel on the edge of town just as darkness fell.

Brian drank himself to sleep that night, his rest broken by dreams of chasing a wild animal through the forest.

58

Chapter Five

When Alex's alarm clock rang the next morning, she stretched and snuggled closer to Bet's warm body. "Good morning, sweetheart," she whispered into Bet's ear.

"Morning," a sleepy Bet managed to reply as she scooted closer to Alex.

"Don't get too comfortable," she said. "I have to hit the shower and get moving this morning."

"I know, but I just need one minute more with you," Bet pleaded.

Unable to resist, Alex curled her body around Bet's and held her for several more minutes. Then with a huge audible sigh, Alex crept out from under the covers and headed for the shower. Turning on the water Alex stepped into the steamy shower with hopes that it would help to bring her body awake. She had barely lathered her hair when she felt a slight draft as the shower curtain opened and Bet stepped into the shower with her.

"I turned the coffeepot on," Bet said as she soaped a washcloth and started at Alex's shoulders and worked her way down her lover's body. "What a tempting morsel you would make for breakfast." Bet's hands circled Alex's waist and she caressed Alex's chest with the soapy cloth.

"Would you settle for a midnight snack," Alex teased Bet, who had poked her bottom lip out in a pout.

"Tell me you really aren't going to make me wait until midnight," Bet asked as Alex turned in her arms.

"No way, darling." Alex kissed the pout from Bet's face.

Bet moved Alex under the flow of the water to rinse the soap from her body and then positioned her with a foot on the top edge of the tub, leaving her feet spread apart. Bet kissed Alex as her hand followed the trail of water down the front of her body until her fingers touched soft, damp curls. Alex sucked Bet's tongue deep into her mouth as Bet's fingers entered her wetness and began rocking in and out of her body. Bet knelt in front of Alex and took her clit inside her warm mouth. She began sucking on it with the same rhythm of her fingers moving inside Alex. She continued to lick and kiss Alex's clit until her body released a feral orgasm.

Bet knew Alex wanted and needed more of her sensual attention, but she wanted Alex to hunger today in anticipation of a night filled with their lovemaking. "Will that hold you to midnight?" Bet purred as her teeth grazed across sensitive skin.

"It will definitely give me something to look forward to today." Alex lifted Bet from her kneeling position to kiss her sweetly.

Alex rinsed off and left Bet in the shower to bathe. She dried off and dressed before going downstairs to get them each a cup of coffee. Alex stopped by her home office, and plucked a business card from her desk drawer and jotted down her home address for Bet. Tucking the card in her pocket, she climbed the stairs to find Bet dressing in the bedroom. Alex set the coffee on the nightstand and watched as Bet slipped a sweatshirt over tight-fitting jeans.

Bet walked over to where Alex was sitting on the bed. Alex lifted her hands to Bet's waist, and let them move down to cup Bet's buttocks with a gentle squeeze and then massaged down to Bet's thighs. "Come by the office when you get done later today and see if I am back in from the field," Alex said. "I would like to introduce you and Kylie to Sandy today if possible."

"I think we should be done no later than four, so we'll stop in around then, if that is okay."

"I'll make it a point to be done as close to four as I can then. If you give me your keys, I'll drop them off to Tom so he can go ahead and tow your car. I have also written down our address on my business card so you will have the information you need today," Alex said as she slipped the card into Bet's pocket. "It has my cell number and office address on it in case you need anything today." Alex sipped her coffee.

"May I fix you some breakfast before you go?" Bet asked.

"No, thanks, I want to get a jump on some things this morning so I'll pass on breakfast." Alex stood to leave the room.

"Good luck with everything today and call me when you get done. I left the car keys on the counter for you, and by the way, you look very sexy this morning."

"Thanks, sweetie," Bet said as she walked Alex to the front door. "Have a great day." She kissed her goodbye.

"You too," Alex said as she stepped outside the door and spoke to Max briefly before climbing into her truck and, wearing a broad smile, began the commute into town.

Bet turned to climb the stairs to wake her sleeping daughter. She was excited to start the day, which felt like a brand-new life, and one she sorely needed. Things were turning out wonderfully, all because Alex had given them the opportunity and encouragement needed to get a fresh start.

Kylie was still asleep when Bet walked into the room. She sat quietly on the bed watching the sleeping child. Bet caressed Kylie's face and slowly she began to stir. When her eyes finally fluttered opened, she smiled. "Good morning, Mommy," she said sweetly.

"Good morning, sweetie, how did you sleep?"

"Great," Kylie said as she stretched in the bed. "Where is Alex?"

"She has already left for work, but left instructions for us to meet her at the office later today."

"Okay, Mommy."

"Are you hungry?"

"May I have some Captain Crunch?"

"I think I can handle that," Bet said. "Why don't you get dressed while I fix you some toast and cereal?"

"I love you, Mommy," Kylie said, stopping Bet in her tracks.

"I love you too, Kylie," Bet said with tears in her eyes.

✝

Alex drove to town and pulled into the parking lot at the office. She had called Glen and told him she would meet him at the site later. She had stopped by Tom's to explain the situation regarding Bet's car to him and to drop the keys off. Tom promised he would call as soon as he could assess the damages, hopefully no later than Tuesday morning.

Alex climbed from her truck and locked the door as she walked toward her office, her feet barely touching the ground. Sandy, her office manager, was an early riser and always beat Alex into the office, starting the coffee and getting the mail ready to go out for the day. Sandy had seen her pull up and met her in the front office with a mug of steaming coffee. "Good morning, boss," she said. "You look like the cat that ate the canary," Sandy added as she noted the wide smile and glow that Alex wore this morning.

"Life is good," Alex said as she took the cup of coffee from Sandy. "I hired an assistant for you this weekend."

Sandy, truly startled by Alex's comment, stammered, "Is there something I don't know here, boss? I didn't think I had slowed down so much that you felt I needed an assistant," Sandy said with a worried tone.

Alex dearly loved Sandy and would never dream of replacing her, however, she couldn't resist a bit of teasing. Sandy had been a valued employee and friend ever since Alex had started her own business. "Well," Alex said with a straight face, "I felt we needed to have someone younger come in to help us out, so I asked her to stop by today for you to meet."

"Someone younger," Sandy said with her hands perched angrily on her hips.

"Yes, ma'am," Alex said, her lips twitching as she tried to hold in her smile. "She is four, soon to be five."

As expected, Sandy was confused and to Alex's delight had no idea what Alex was planning. Alex ushered Sandy into her office and sat her down in a comfortable chair as she explained the plight of Kylie and Bet.

"Well, that certainly explains the big smile on your face," Sandy said as she relaxed after hearing that Alex had no plans to replace her.

"They must be something special to have captured your heart this quickly," Sandy said with a grin. Sandy knew that Alex was lonely and in dire need of someone in her life that could make her happy. If her friend's attitude this morning was any indication, Kylie and Bet seemed the right combination to do just that. She hadn't seen Alex this excited about anything since she built her first home, and the look was good for Alex.

"You just don't know how special they are to me, Sandy," Alex exclaimed. "Kylie is such a great kid, and Bet has made me realize how badly I needed a human companion."

"My sister works in the Human Resources department at the hospital, so if Bet needs any help getting her foot in the door just let me know," Sandy said.

"Thanks, Sandy."

"I really look forward to meeting my new assistant too," Sandy said with a grin. "We need some fresh blood around here and you know you just can't start them off too soon these days."

"Just wait until you meet Kylie. She's almost five going on sixteen and if you don't watch her she will be taking over," Alex teased her friend. "She is such a smart cookie. I thought I might go out and get another computer and some games for her to play while she spends some time with you."

"Just leave me your credit card today and I will take care of it for you this morning," Sandy offered. "Being a grandma five times over now I have learned a great deal about educational software in the past few years. Besides I am pretty well caught up and could use a task to make my morning pass quicker."

"You've got a deal." Alex reached into her pocket and pulled out a Visa card. "I really appreciate your help."

"My pleasure, boss." Sandy picked up Alex's coffee mug and headed to the kitchen for a refill.

"Make mine to-go please," Alex requested as she looked over a set of plans. "I need to get out to the site and check on Glen and the crew."

Sandy met Alex in the front office moments later with a travel mug filled with steamy coffee. "One hot one to go," Sandy said as she handed Alex the mug.

After Alex left the office, Sandy picked up the phone and dialed the hospital to speak to her sister. After several minutes of conversation, Sandy had filled her sister Ann in on the situation of Bet's flight from Alabama and her need for a job until she could obtain her Georgia nursing license. Ann assured Sandy there were several positions and Bet could work until her license transferred.

She hung up with a promise from her sister that she would be on the lookout for Bet.

†

When Brian was able to pull himself awake Monday morning he decided to find something to eat and then begin his hunt for Bet. He couldn't remember the last meal he had eaten and the burning in his stomach was relentless.

Brian did not hold out any hope that Bet was still in this small town, but he wasn't going to move forward until he had searched every possibility or received confirmation that she had used her card in another location. Still reeking of last night's alcohol, he crawled up into his truck and found a small diner not far from the motel. He ordered coffee, a stack of pancakes, fried eggs, and bacon and ate like a starving man. The food did little to quell the fire in his stomach, but the coffee provided the boost of caffeine he needed to jumpstart his brain. He paid his bill and started toward his truck to check out the other local motel for Bet's car when he saw a tow truck coming toward him. He couldn't believe his blurry eyes when the truck passed him and the car in tow looked like her Honda. He ran the short distance to his truck and peeled out of the parking lot in pursuit of the tow truck.

He followed the driver for several miles until he reached a small garage and gas station. Brian cleverly pulled up to the pumps and began slowly filling his truck as he watched the driver release the small foreign car, and guide it into the garage. Brian got a glimpse of the license plate and sure enough, it was Bet's car. A slow, evil grin crossed over Brian's face as he watched the man toil with the car. *She is here. Now all I have to do is find her. Clever bitch thought she could outsmart me, but I have already tracked her down and it will be merely a matter of time before she is on her way home again,* Brian mumbled to himself as he pumped the gas.

He replaced the gas cap and walked inside to pay for his purchase. "Looks like someone has some big trouble," Brian said, pointing to the Honda.

"At the least a blown head gasket, but could be a burned up motor," the mechanic said as he took the offered bills from Brian and handed him his change. "It's a hard and costly lesson for people to learn about putting oil in their vehicles, but I guess it keeps me busy and off the streets."

Brian laughed with the man and then returned to his truck. Tracking Bet down couldn't be too difficult, since she was without a car. He drove to the other motel in town and sat in the parking lot, waiting to see if Bet or Kylie would exit any of the rooms. He sat for hours, his head pounding, under a small oak that provided the only shade in the scorching parking lot. He watched the motel's few customers come and go. Most looked like travelers who had stopped off for a night's sleep and then were eagerly on their way.

†

Bet buckled Kylie into the Outback and they took off for town. Their first stop was the Department of Motor Vehicles where Bet transferred her driver's license from Alabama to Georgia. The young clerk smiled when she read on Bet's application that she was living at Alex's address. "Welcome to Georgia," she said as she snapped the photo for Bet's new license.

"Thanks." Bet pulled out a twenty to pay for the new license.

"Tell Alex that Susan said hello for me, please," the young clerk said as she handed her the new license.

"Sure thing." Bet took the license and tucked it into her wallet. *I guess everyone knows everyone in a small town like this.* Bet retrieved Kylie from the waiting area and they walked backed to the car.

"Next stop, the elementary school," Bet announced as she tucked Kylie into the seat. Kylie was very excited about starting school and listened intently as the principal discussed the registration procedures and explained the orientation, which was set up for the following week for new students to become familiar with their teachers and with the school environment. Bet scheduled orientation for Kylie on Monday and took the list of school supplies Kylie would need with her.

"Welcome to Valley Elementary, Kylie," the principal said as she walked them out the front door.

"Thank you," Kylie said very politely, which produced a warm smile from the principal. "See you next week." Kylie waved goodbye.

"That went pretty well," Bet said as she cranked the car.

"Looks like a fun place. And the principal seemed really nice."

"Now, let's see if I can find a job," Bet said with an edge of anxiety in her voice. When she paid for the license, Bet realized her savings were dwindling fast. She was determined not to ask Alex for any assistance. She knew Alex would provide anything they needed without complaint, but Bet still had her pride and wanted to be able to provide for her daughter as they started their new life.

Kylie sensed her mom's anxiety and placed her hand on Bet's. "It will be okay, Mommy." She gave Bet one of her biggest smiles.

"Thanks, sweetie," Bet said as she pulled out of the school parking lot and headed toward the hospital.

When they had found a parking place, Bet and Kylie walked into the front entrance of the hospital and stopped off at the information desk to find out where the Human Resource office was located. The attendant gave her the directions and they walked down the hall to check out the vacancy board. Bet was relieved to find there were several RN positions available on the day and evening shifts. As they stood reading the announcements, a woman approached them. "May I help you?"

Bet introduced herself and told the woman, who had introduced herself as Ann White, that she was looking for employment while waiting for her license to transfer from Alabama to Georgia. Ann ushered both Kylie and Bet into her office and sat them around her comfortable desk.

"Do you have anything in particular in mind," Ann asked.

"Once I am licensed I would like to apply for the day shift in the ER or Intensive Care unit. Those are the two areas I enjoy the most, and it would allow me to spend time with Kylie after school."

"Have you applied for reciprocity yet," Ann asked.

"I was planning to call this afternoon when we finish here."

"I can help you with that, and if we let the board know we are waiting on your license to put you into a position it usually prompts them to move a little faster." She handed her a brief application to fill out with current information and took her Alabama license to make a copy. "Fill this out for me and I can send your application online while you start on a ton of paperwork," Ann said with a smile.

Bet quickly filled out the information Ann needed and handed her back the form. "I really appreciate all your help."

"I have a feeling you are going to be an excellent employee, so I will do everything I can to get you on board with us as quickly as possible. Besides, my part is easy, you have to complete all this." Ann handed her a thick packet of information. "You better get comfortable, Kylie," Ann said, "Mom's going to be here a while."

"Yes, ma'am." Kylie went to the coffee table, and picked out a children's magazine and then climbed up on a comfortable-looking couch.

Ann spun around in her office chair and began tapping on her computer keyboard as Bet started filling out the seemingly endless stack of papers Ann had handed her. As promised, Ann finished her task in no time and printed out a response that Bet's application would be reviewed and if approved she would be receiving her new license in a week to ten days.

"When did you want to start?" Ann asked.

"As soon as possible, if you have something I can do until my license comes in."

"We have an orientation class that will start on Wednesday and run for a week. By that time we should have an idea when your license will be here and if nothing else we can have you do case management reviews for a few days."

"That would be perfect," Bet replied, tears welling in her eyes. She busied herself with the paperwork and concentrated on holding back her tears. Everything was working out almost too perfectly and she said a silent prayer in thanks of her good fortune.

It took the majority of an hour for Bet to finish off the paperwork and writer's cramp was just beginning when she signed off on the last form. "Phew, all done," Bet said as she handed the packet back to Ann.

"Since we have openings in both areas of preference for you, would you like a tour of both units while you are here?" Ann asked.

"That would be fantastic!"

"Let's start with ICU then," Ann said. "Kylie, would you like to join us or would you prefer to finish your magazine?"

"Okay if I stay here, Mom?" she asked Bet.

"That would be fine, sweetie." Bet looked at Ann.

"Brenda, our receptionist, will keep an eye on her while we are gone."

Ann took Bet on the grand tour of the hospital. Bet was truly impressed with the well-equipped Intensive Care Unit and knew even before seeing the ER that she would choose ICU. They finished the tour and Ann asked, "See anything you liked?"

"All of it, but I was very impressed with the ICU and feel like that matches up with my experience."

"Fantastic! That is one of my hardest positions to fill." Ann admitted. "Susan, the unit supervisor, is off today, but I will make it a point to introduce you two on Wednesday during orientation."

"I will look forward to it," Bet said as they walked back into Ann's office to find Kylie dozing on the couch.

"We will see you on Wednesday then," Ann said as she reached out her hand.

Bet took the offered hand. "Thanks again for all your help."

"My pleasure," Ann said. "Welcome aboard."

✝

Bet and Kylie walked hand in hand out to the car, both wearing broad smiles on their faces. "Why don't we head back to the house and grab some lunch," Bet said. "You can take a quick nap afterward while I do some chores."

"Okay, Mommy."

Bet noticed her car up on the rack as they passed Tom's small garage and felt a little more relief now that she knew she had a job and could afford to fix her car. *Life was going to be okay.*

By one o'clock, Kylie was down for a nap and Bet had taken their dirty clothes as well as Alex's to the laundry room to catch up on the laundry. She noticed several pairs of pants and work shirts hanging in the small closet, and decided to go ahead and iron them for Alex while she waited for the laundry to finish. With loving care, Bet ironed in sharp creases with steam and starch. She had finished four outfits when the first load came out of the dryer. She folded the clothing and placed it in a basket for carrying upstairs. When the second load finished, Bet had a full basket and carried it upstairs to put away.

Bet quietly placed Kylie's shorts and underwear in the dresser and stood to watch her sleeping child for a few minutes. As she watched Kylie, tucked under warm covers in a deep sleep, Bet realized just how perfectly things were turning out. She fought off a small wave of fear, which threatened to creep into the back of her mind. Almost too perfectly, Bet thought again as the self-doubt inched its way into her thoughts. Fortunately, the buzzer on the dryer sounded, notifying her that it was on the last five minutes of the cycle, and that jolted her back to reality. Picking up her clothesbasket, she moved on to the next room, deposited her clean clothes into the dresser, and pulled out a few outfits of her own to iron for her upcoming orientation.

Bet climbed the stairs to the loft, and picked up a half dozen pairs of Alex's panties and walked to the dresser to put them away. She opened the first drawer, finding it filled with shirts and shorts, and moved down a drawer to find her underwear, sports bras, and panties. Bet placed the neatly folded stack in the drawer and began to carefully fold and stack the remainder of the drawer's contents. As she reached in the back for a stray sports bra, Bet's hand came to rest on a long cylindrical object. Her curiosity got the better of her. She pulled the item from under the bra and was surprised to find that it was a dildo with black elastic thigh straps. Her fingers caressed its length as her mind imagined what it would be like to have Alex use the toy on her. Bet felt a surge of wetness dampen her panties as her thoughts fed her arousal, reaching down between her thighs and sending a river of hot blood to her swollen clit. Cupping herself, Bet knew Alex would be in grave danger tonight as soon as Kylie was safely asleep and began to form her wicked plan.

Replacing the toy, Bet returned to the laundry room to iron several outfits of her own and to finish the laundry before slipping into a long, warm shower. She took great care in dressing in freshly starched jeans and a low-cut sweater, capping the outfit off with her favorite perfume. She hoped to end a perfect day with a night of lovemaking with Alex.

Chapter Six

The morning passed quickly for Alex as she inspected the reset beam and the morning's work by the crew. The extra time off over the weekend seemed to be very beneficial for the men, who were energetic and busily at work when Alex showed up at the site. Another few weeks and this project would be done and ready for final inspections. She would have to put in some extra time to finish off the plans for the next project. Alex always tried to give her crew a week or two off between projects to allow them to spend some time with their families, and she always rewarded her crew with handsome bonuses when projects finished on schedule. Maybe this week she would stay at home a few days to work on the plans and let Glen take over the daily inspections.

She called Glen outside to make the suggestion. Excited that she placed that much faith in his work, he eagerly agreed to the assignment. With that taken care of, Alex took off for the office to meet Kylie and Bet, anxious to see how Kylie and Sandy would hit it off. Sandy seemed truly excited about it. She had already called to say she had bought the computer and a small workstation for Kylie and would have them set up by this afternoon. *Life is good.*

†

Bet and Kylie had not yet arrived so Sandy excitedly showed Alex what she had done. She had set up a small desk beside Alex's that had Kylie's computer set up on it just like hers. She had even gotten a small desk plate with her name engraved on it, which gave the tiny workspace a miniature executive look. Alex was very proud of the job Sandy had done and was engrossed in the demonstration of the software Sandy had installed when Bet and Kylie pulled up.

Alex and Sandy met them in the front office and Alex made the introductions. "Sandy, why don't you take your new assistant and show her the workspace you set up for her," Alex suggested. Sandy took Kylie by the hand and led her to Alex's office. "You have got to see this," Alex said as she guided Bet to the office.

Kylie's squeals rang in their ears before they made it into the office. "Miss Sandy, this is great!" Kylie hugged the older woman's neck. "Thank you so much." She sat down in her small rolling chair in front of the computer and Sandy showed her how to boot up the computer. Alex pointed to the small nameplate and Bet smiled as she watched Sandy and Kylie interact. If Bet had any doubts about leaving Kylie with Sandy, they quickly vanished as she watched the two of them together.

"Let's get some coffee." Alex led Bet from the office and down to a small kitchen, where she spun Bet in her arms and kissed her passionately before Bet could say a word.

"Wow," Bet said when they finally broke their kiss. "I expect you have had a wonderful day too."

"It's been great, so how about yours?"

"We got a new driver's license for me and, by the way, a blushing Susan said to tell you hello. Kylie is all set for school and will go to orientation Monday, and I start this Wednesday in orientation at the hospital. Ann in Human Resources pulled a few strings and I should have my nursing license in seven to ten days. So after a week's orientation I will be doing chart audits until I can officially start nursing," Bet said, excitement raising the pitch of her voice.

"That sounds fantastic!" Alex was genuinely excited for both Kylie and Bet. "By the way, you look terrific, and you smell good enough to eat."

"We will have to test out that theory after dinner," Bet said with a wicked grin.

Alex poured a cup of coffee, but Bet declined the offer. The last thing she needed right now was more stimulant. The excitement of the day and the images of Alex that kept popping up in her head were more than enough to keep her hyped up for the next few hours.

Alex and Bet walked back to the office and watched Kylie and Sandy going to town on the new computer programs. Kylie was a quick learner, and had mastered the entry levels of the games so Sandy showed her how to increase the difficulty of each new game until she found a level that would challenge her skills.

Time passed quickly and Sandy suggested she give Kylie a tour of the rest of the office before it was time to head home for the day. With minimal instruction, Kylie shut down the computer and followed Sandy into the kitchen. Sandy opened the refrigerator to reveal small containers of juice, fresh fruits, and several after-school-type snacks she had bought for Kylie. After the tour, they once again joined Bet and Alex in the office.

"Well, boss, I think she is all set," Sandy said with a grin. "I know you are planning to work from the house some this week, but maybe you and Kylie can stop in a few times to check on me."

"I think we can handle that. As a matter of fact, I need to head over to the next worksite and take some pictures so maybe afterward we could stop by and I can print the pictures while you and Kylie pay some bills or something." Alex grinned.

"All right then. Well, I am going to head out for the day unless you need something."

"Go ahead, Sandy. I'll lock up. Thanks for everything today," she said as Sandy picked up her purse and headed to the door.

"Is anyone hungry?" Alex asked after Sandy left.

"Starved," Bet admitted and Kylie agreed.

"Well, let me lock up and I'll meet you at the last diner we passed yesterday," Alex suggested as she walked Kylie and Bet to the front door.

Bet opened the door and stopped. She turned around, kissed Alex on the lips, and smiled. "See you in a few minutes then." Bet took Kylie's hand and they walked out to the car.

Alex walked back into her office and shut down her computer, then flipped through a small stack of phone messages Sandy had left for her. Nothing that couldn't wait until tomorrow she decided and headed to the bathroom to freshen up a bit. She ran her fingers through her dark curls and sprayed a light misting of cologne on her forearms then brushed her teeth. A quick glance in the mirror brought a smile to her face. "It's been way too long since you primped for a woman, Alex Graves," she said to her image. Satisfied, she flipped off the light and locked the door behind her.

If Alex had looked to her far right as she left the building, she might have seen the black Dodge Ram parked in the back of the parking lot. She might have noticed the blurry-eyed, blond man behind the wheel who reached across his seat to take a long drink from a whiskey bottle. Her mind, though, was focusing elsewhere, so she walked to her truck without a glance.

✝

Brian was about to give up the search for the day and return to his motel when he saw an Outback heading down the road. There had been very little traffic on the roads, so Brian got a good look at the few cars he had encountered. As the black vehicle approached, he sat up in his seat when he saw a woman and small child as passengers in the vehicle. He was further astounded to see Bet behind the wheel as she passed by his location. "How on earth…" Brian muttered as he turned the key in the ignition and his truck came to life.

He followed the vehicle from a distance that would allow him to observe any turns, but would prevent Bet from recognizing him if she were to spot him in her rearview mirror. Brian saw her turn into a small office complex. He pulled into a stand of trees to watch as Bet and Kylie exited the vehicle and walked into the building. His patience rewarded several minutes later, when Bet and Kylie exited the building followed by a tall, dark-haired woman. He followed them as they drove to the same diner where he had breakfast this morning.

✝

"Hey, Alex," the server said as she approached the table.

"Hiya, Donna. How are you doing?"

"Doing great and you?"

"I am wonderful, thanks," Alex said and introduced Kylie and Bet.

"What's it going to be tonight, ladies?"

"Hmm, chicken and dumplings for me with corn and green beans," Alex said.

Bet laughed. "I'll have the country fried steak, mashed potatoes, corn, and another round of chicken and dumplings with corn and beans for the munchkin."

"We'll have it up in just a few minutes," Donna said as she walked toward the kitchen.

"I swear, I am beginning to really think Kylie is your kid instead of mine. You two are like peas in a pod all the way down to your food choices."

Alex winked at Kylie and said, "We can't help it if you don't know what to eat."

Kylie chuckled. "That's right, Mom, we know what's good to eat."

"Well, fine then. I will just eat my country fried steak and don't even dare to ask me for a bite."

"We won't, Mom." Kylie grinned toward Alex who winked at her.

"Hey, save some room, Kylie, they make great homemade pies here too," Alex told the young girl.

"Do they have coconut cream?"

"That's what I am having," Alex said with a laugh.

"Oh brother." Bet rolled her eyes.

As they chatted while waiting for their dinners to arrive, Bet's hand came to rest on Alex's thigh. She slowly massaged the strong muscles under her hand, while Kylie excitedly told Alex about school and the supplies she would need.

"I thought we might come into town in the morning and do some school supply shopping while you go take your pictures. Then you could come home for lunch before going into the office to print your pictures," Bet said.

"Sounds like a workable plan to me." Alex tried to keep her voice steady as Bet's fingers moved between her thighs.

Bet could feel the heat rising underneath her fingers as she caressed the crotch seam of Alex's workpants. Alex covered Bet's hand with her own and squeezed so she could feel the dampness growing between her thighs. She looked at Bet and smiled. Bet's plan to arouse her was working quite well and in a few hours, Bet would reap the benefits of her effort.

"I need to use the bathroom," Kylie said. Alex pointed to the restrooms.

"Need some help, baby?" Bet asked.

"No, Mom, I'm a big girl now remember."

"Hurry back then, big girl," Bet said to her laughing daughter.

As Kylie disappeared into the restroom, Bet leaned over and purred into Alex's ear. "I found something very interesting today while I was putting away your underwear. You think I might talk you into a demonstration later?"

Alex's cheeks flushed when she realized that Bet had come across the strap-on she had tucked away in the back of her drawer, forgotten for years. "I think that might be arranged," Alex said with a wicked grin.

Donna carried glasses of tea and milk over to the table. "Your food should be up in just a minute, and there is a fresh baked pie just waiting on you, Alex."

"How about boxing up a coconut cream to go, Donna, and we will take it home for dessert."

"Will do, Alex." Donna disappeared into the kitchen to check on their orders.

"Are you in a hurry, Alex?" Bet asked coyly.

"Are you kidding? If we take a whole pie home then Kylie and I can eat all we want," Alex said with a chuckle. She was anxious to get home, but she didn't want to let her know just how excited.

Donna followed Kylie's return to the table with plates of steaming food. "This looks wonderful." Bet cut a piece of the steak and dipped it into creamy gravy. "Oh my, Donna, this stuff is sinful." Bet took another bite.

"Glad you like it, honey. Is there anything else you need?"

"I think we're set for a little while, Donna," Alex replied.

"Just give me a holler if you need anything," Donna said as she went back to the kitchen with a tray full of dirty dishes.

It was Alex's turn to tease. She slid her hand between Bet's thighs moaning, "These dumplings are to die for." On cue, Kylie mimicked Alex, moaning loudly. Bet spread her thighs wider and

Alex cupped the wet spot that was growing hotter by the second. "So hot," she said as she gave Bet a gentle squeeze, and it was her turn to moan.

"When I can get my hands on some money I want you three to come back and do all that moaning for a commercial," Donna said with a laugh as she sat down next to Kylie. "Y'all make it sound so good, you are making me hungry."

"Donna this is incredible," Alex said.

"Well, I am glad to see you enjoying it so much," she said. "It's been a while since I have had that kind of compliments."

"You can count on us stopping in more often then," Bet said.

"I'll look forward to it. After the colors fade out, business gets pretty slow, so I have to depend on the locals for survival."

"Well, you've definitely got yourself two new customers," Bet said.

"You still want me to box that pie up for later, Alex?"

Alex looked at Kylie who just grinned. "Oh yeah Donna, we do, without a doubt."

"I'll be right back with it then," Donna said as she laid down their check.

Alex had finished her meal and was busily caressing Bet while she and Kylie finished their meals. "A cup of coffee and a slice of pie and I'll be set for the night."

"I'll brew a pot while you and Kylie change into something more comfortable," Bet volunteered.

"You've got a deal, ma'am."

†

Darkness had crept in as they ate, so Alex decided she would lead the way home. Bet followed her closely. Alex noted another pair of headlights trailing them as they turned off the road and into the drive. *That's curious. Why would anyone be out in this direction after dark?* She twatched as the truck slowed and turned around in her drive before heading back toward town. Alex couldn't help but shiver, as if an icy finger had drawn a trail down her back. *Probably just someone lost.* She pulled up in front of the house and watched as Bet pulled the Outback into the garage.

Moments later Bet and Kylie emerged and closed the doors. Max had met Alex at the truck and then ran to meet Kylie.

"Hiya, Max." Kylie hugged the big dog around his neck.

Alex walked onto the porch and held the door open as Max, Kylie, and Bet entered the softly lit house. "I'll let you take care of this, and Kylie and I will head upstairs," Alex said, handing the pie to her.

"I'll get the coffee going and slice up the pie. What do you want to drink Kylie?" Bet asked.

"Just some milk, please, Mom," she said as she raced to the stairs to catch up with Alex.

Kylie went to her room to put on her pajamas and Alex climbed up to the loft. Fresh linens were on the bed, and Alex opened her drawers to find everything neatly folded and stacked. She pulled open her underwear drawer and reached into the back. Her hand located the strap-on, which she took and placed in the bedside table—a much more convenient location. It had been several years ago, with her ex, that Alex had last used the toy. She strolled down memory lane, recalling the screams of pleasure her ex used to make whenever Alex strapped it on.

Alex sat on the bed and pulled off her work boots and clothes, dropping them into a now empty laundry basket. She noticed Bet had done some ironing too as she opened up her closet and pulled out some sweats and a soft T-shirt. Slipping these on, Alex located her moccasins and headed back down the stairs.

Kylie was already seated at the table and waiting for Bet to serve the pie. A large glass of milk and mugs of coffee were sitting on the table. Alex sat beside Kylie and watched Bet as she made her way to the table carrying two plates loaded with pie. "You aren't going to join us?"

"Not tonight," Bet said. "I am still stuffed from dinner."

"Maybe there will be some left for tomorrow," Alex teased as she cut a large bite. "Mmm, you don't know what you are missing."

"Probably about five hundred calories," Bet declared. "It will take days for me to work off that dinner."

"Maybe just a couple of hours," Alex said with a devilish grin.

"I certainly hope you are right, Alex."

"It's really good, Mom, you sure you don't want a bite?" Kylie asked, holding up a forkful of the delicious dessert.

"Okay, maybe just a little one." Bet took the bite offered by her daughter. "That is good," she said as the sugar swarmed her taste buds.

They finished off their dessert and placed their plates in the sink. Pouring fresh cups of coffee, Bet decided they should sit out on the porch for a little while. Kylie was already looking sleepy and certainly had a full stomach. Bet knew that a few minutes of rocking and Kylie would be down for the count. Sipping their coffee, they watched the fireflies as they danced across the night and rocked quietly until Kylie was asleep in her mother's arms. "Would you like a smoke before we take her up?" Alex asked.

"Yes, please." Alex walked over to light two cigarettes. "What a great day," Bet said as she took the smoke from Alex. "If you didn't notice, Kylie was in heaven at your office and I think she and Sandy will hit it off just fine."

"Sandy was so excited about setting up a workspace for Kylie that I thought she might pop," Alex said with a chuckle.

"That was really fantastic for you to do that for her."

"I'll be honest. I can't stand seeing kids parked in front of a TV. Sandy convinced me that there is plenty of computer software available to keep Kylie learning for years to come," Alex admitted. "I wouldn't be surprised if Sandy turned the books over to Kylie after a few years."

"You better be careful or Kylie might take over completely."

"That doesn't sound like a bad idea at all. We can sit in our rockers while she supports our bad habits," Alex teased as she crushed her cigarette out. "Are you ready to take her up?"

"Why don't you close up the house while I tuck her in for the night?" Bet stood and walked toward the door.

Alex whistled for Max and held the door for Bet while she waited on her canine companion. She watched as Bet climbed the stairs and disappeared into Kylie's room and then walked into the kitchen to reset the coffeepot. Alex made the rounds to lock all the doors and windows. A chill passed down her spine as she remembered the truck following them. She shook the feeling off and turned the lights down before heading up the stairs.

†

Brian had watched with a seething rage as they dined together, the laughter and the smiles on his wife's and child's faces burned straight to his soul. *How could they be so happy when they left him feeling so miserable?* It just wasn't right, and he would be sure to point this out to them when they were rightfully home again he promised.

As the sun went down, they left the diner and headed onto the road out of town with absolutely no clue that Brian was tracking them. He drove a half-mile behind the old truck and stopped at the edge of the drive to note the address as he watched the taillights disappear into the dense woods.

Very pleased with the results of his hunt, Brian turned around in Alex's driveway and headed back to town. "This calls for a celebration, Brian my boy," he said to himself as he drove back to his motel. "I know everything I need to know about their whereabouts. Now I just need to plan how I am going to get Bet and Kylie away from the tall, dark-haired bitch."

†

Alex lit the bedside candles before she went to the bathroom to brush her teeth. When she returned to the bedroom, Bet was sitting on the bed wearing only an oversized sleep shirt. Stepping out of her moccasins, Alex walked over to where Bet was sitting and knelt down in front of her, taking Bet's face in her hands for a long, slow kiss. Bet's hands slowly worked Alex's shirt above her shoulders and she broke the kiss long enough to slide it over Alex's head. Her hands were cool as they caressed the warm skin of Alex's chest, circling her nipples with soft fingertips, making them tingle with every stroke.

Alex's body shivered with excitement as Bet's hands cupped and caressed her breasts. She moved to stand before her. Bet licked her way up to Alex's nipple and covered her breast with a warm,

80

wet mouth as her hands slid beneath Alex's baggy sweats to massage her hips and buttocks. Alex's hands played in Bet's hair as Bet suckled each breast, driving Alex crazy with passion. Alex felt a trickle of moisture begin to flow down her thigh. She raised her right foot and placed it on the bed as she guided one of Bet's hands between her legs.

Bet moaned when her fingers touched the soft curls coated with hot, velvety droplets of Alex's excitement. Bet dipped her fingers into the wetness, coating them as her teeth grazed lightly over Alex's nipples. Bet's mouth feasted as she entered Alex with two long fingers, pressing deeply into her body. Alex rocked her hips onto Bet's fingers as they slid in and out of her heated body. Her breath quickened into short gasps for air. Bet felt Alex's body begin to tremble with the first sign of an impending orgasm and she began to nibble Alex's sensitive nipples. Alex's body gushed with pleasure. Bet slowly removed her fingers and slid Alex's pants down over her hips. Alex kicked them off and, after pulling the nightshirt over Bet's head, pressed her backward onto the bed.

Alex straddled Bet's hips and began to grind her way up her body, her hard clit caressing Bet's soft skin and leaving a trail of wetness in her wake. Alex's body was on fire as she moved up Bet's body. She took Bet's hands from her breasts and circled her hips with them as she moved to straddle Bet's face. Lowering her body onto Bet's waiting mouth, Alex watched as Bet's eyes closed and her tongue began lapping at the sweet juices flowing from her body

Alex leaned backward, reaching between Bet's spread thighs to find her soaked with excitement. Her fingers traced the outer lips of Bet's wetness causing Bet to begin thrusting her hips toward Alex's fingers as they teased her aching clit. Bet's hands pulled Alex's hips downward as she buried her face in Alex's wetness, her tongue working feverishly inside Alex, kissing her deeply. Alex rode Bet's face as wave after wave of pleasure ran through her body, covering Bet's face with her thick, sweet juice. Alex's fingers toyed with Bet's wetness. Bet's mouth covered her throbbing clit, sucking her deep into her mouth causing her body to explode again.

Fully sated, Alex moved to lie beside Bet. She licked her creamy juice from Bet's face as her fingers pinched and twisted Bet's erect nipples. "Are you ready for some loving?" Alex asked a fully aroused Bet.

"Yes, baby," Bet pleaded.

Alex moved from the bed and reached into the bedside table for the strap on, sliding the elastic bands around her thighs. Bet watched her closely, her eyes dark with desire and panting slightly with her arousal. The large toy dangled between Alex's thighs as she reached back into the drawer to pull out a condom that she opened and slid over the tip of the toy, rolling it down to tightly cover the rigid latex before laying back beside Bet. Alex draped a leg over Bet's thigh allowing the toy to rest on Bet's trembling thigh.

Alex's fingers teased Bet's nipples as she leaned down for another slow kiss. Bet's tongue danced wildly in Alex's mouth as she hungered for pleasure. Alex broke the kiss and looked into Bet's eyes. "You sure you are ready for this?"

"I am going to die if you aren't deep inside me soon," Bet groaned.

Alex reached behind her, and grabbed a pillow placing it under Bet's hips to raise her slightly off the bed and then settled between Bet's widely spread thighs. Bet had already soaked the bed with her juice and Alex could see her lips pulse with anticipation. Alex lowered her body onto Bet's, allowing the toy to slide across her wetness, coating it with her juices. Bet moaned as Alex's movements pressed the tip across her aching clit and her fingers moved down to spread her lips for Alex.

Alex placed the tip in the center of Bet's soaked lips and eased the head inside. Bet gasped as Alex dipped her hips and an inch of the toy entered her body. Alex froze until Bet's body slowly relaxed around the stiff toy. "You okay?" Alex asked with a note of genuine concern for her lover.

"Yes, baby, it's just bigger than I am used to. Please don't stop, though," she said as her eyes locked on Alex.

Alex began to rock her hips, penetrating Bet deeper with each stroke as she slowly buried the length of the long toy inside her. Bet's wetness flowed freely allowing Alex to move smoothly and deeply inside her. Alex noted Bet had begun to bite her lip and asked, "Too much?" Bet shook her head and wrapped her legs around Alex's waist.

Alex leaned forward on her hands, allowing the weight of her hips to press completely into Bet on each downward stroke. Alex could feel and hear the wetness as she thrust her hips into Bet, her strokes coming longer and faster as Bet's body began to writhe underneath her. Alex slowed her pace, working with the rhythm of Bet's body to drive deep with each stroke. She reached between them to rub her thumb across Bet's swollen clit and Bet's body erupted. She grabbed a pillow, pressing it across her face to muffle the scream as the orgasm made her body shake violently. Alex pressed deep into her and ground her hips into Bet as she gasped for air and thrust her quivering hips into Alex.

As Bet's body began to relax, Alex slowly withdrew the soaked toy and rolled off Bet, sweat running down her body. Still breathing hard, Alex reached up and removed the pillow from Bet's face. Tears were running down Bet's cheeks and Alex feared she had hurt her.

Bet saw the confused look on Alex's face and reached for her lover. "I love how you make me feel, Alex." Bet pulled Alex close. "That was the most intense orgasm I have ever had," Bet told Alex as she soothed her anxious lover. Alex relaxed and laid her head on Bet's chest to listen to the wild beating of her heart. Her hands slowly caressed Bet's body as she relaxed and buried her face in Bet's neck.

"The way you moved your hips, I now understand why you have such a nice ass," Bet said as she lifted Alex's face.

"Thanks." Alex grinned, her face still flushed from the exertion. "You think you have one more of those inside you?"

"There's only one way to find out."

"Roll over then and get up on your knees."

Bet rolled over, facing the bed and rose up to her knees. She allowed Alex to spread her knees wide to lower her body and give Alex full access from behind. Her position allowed her to look into the mirror at the head of the bed and watch Alex's face as she moved in close behind her. Alex slipped two fingers inside Bet to make sure she was still lubricated, and smiled as her fingers were surrounded by pulsing muscles and coated with Bet's velvety liquid. She withdrew her fingers and used them to guide the toy into Bet's waiting wetness, sliding in deep on the first stroke. Bet's moans grew louder as she watched Alex thrust deeper into her body, her hands on Bet's hips rocking her backward as her hips slapped into Bet's ass.

Bet reached down between her legs. She could feel the latex toy as Alex stroked deeper inside her. The feel of the toy inside her and the look of total bliss on Alex's face as she thrust into her was an incredible turn-on for Bet who moaned, "Yes, yes, yes," with each new stroke.

The verbal encouragement was all Alex needed to spur her on and she felt her orgasm begin to boil inside her. She reached underneath Bet and took her nipples in her fingers, allowing the movement of their bodies to stretch and twist her nipples as they rocked the bed and came together in a blinding burst of passion that left them both spent for the night.

Chapter Seven

Alex awoke Tuesday morning to soft lips on her neck and insistent fingers probing the wetness between her thighs. "Good morning, babe," Alex said to Bet.

"Morning, darling," Bet said as her fingers entered Alex's wetness.

"Mmm, do you always wake up like this?"

"Only with you," Bet replied as she took Alex's earlobe into her mouth. "Do you mind?"

"Heavens no." Alex placed her hand on top of Bet's and pressed her fingers deeper inside.

Bet moved sideways on the bed to take Alex's nipple in her mouth as her fingers plunged in and out of her wetness. Alex brushed the hair back from Bet's face so she could watch as Bet's mouth sucked eagerly on her sensitive breast. Alex's left hand stroked down Bet's back and then underneath to find her wetness, sliding two fingers inside her. "Come with me," she whispered as her fingers plunged deep inside. Alex's thumb rubbed across Bet's clit as she began lightly biting Alex's nipple.

Bet knew after last night's lovemaking that an orgasm this morning would be easy for her and she felt one quickly approaching. She desperately wanted to come with Alex so she kissed down Alex's body to take her clit into her mouth. Alex's moans as her tongue swirled around her clit rose in intensity and she began thrusting her hips into Bet's fingers and mouth. After several intense minutes, they came together in a rush of hormones.

"What a way to wake up," Alex said as she cradled Bet in her arms minutes later.

"Uh-hmm," Bet agreed as she snuggled back into Alex's warmth.

"How about a shower and then I will fix us some French toast for breakfast," Alex said.

"That sounds good to me. I'm starved."

In the bathroom, Alex bent down to start the water as Bet got out clean towels and set them on the sink. She spied the strap-on lying in the sink and picked it up, carrying it to the shower. Alex had already gotten under the water and had wet her hair when Bet joined her under the water. She placed the latex penis in Alex's hand as she covered her mouth with a searing kiss.

Alex backed Bet up against the shower wall and lifted her foot onto the edge of the tub, pinning her to the wall with her mouth. She parted Bet's soaked lips with her fingers and eased the tip of the toy into her wetness, sliding it slowly into Bet. Alex wrapped her fingers around the base and started pumping in and out until the toy was buried deep inside. Bet's hands were squeezing her breasts and her moans vibrated through Alex's body as Alex plunged the toy deeper and faster into Bet's trembling body. Alex bent down to take Bet's breast into her mouth, sucking it roughly as her fist slammed into her wetness with each stroke. Bet fought for control over her body but lost the battle as she came crying out loudly. Bet pulled Alex's mouth onto hers for a passionate kiss as Alex's hand slowed and then withdrew from Bet's body. She dropped the toy onto the floor of the shower, her arms circling Bet's quivering body.

Once Bet's body quieted, Alex soaped a washcloth and bathed her lover's body, and then washed her own hair as a tired, but content Bet looked on. Alex quickly finished her shower and then toweled them both dry. "Do you want to lie back down while I cook?"

"Not unless you join me in bed," Bet said with a sexy grin.

"There is nothing I would love more, but we have a little one that will be awake soon, if we haven't woke her up already."

"My whole body feels like melted butter," Bet said as she wrapped the towel around her body.

"Is that a bad thing?"

"Oh my God, no, it's absolutely heavenly." She pulled Alex close for a soft kiss.

Alex put on a soft terry robe and held one open for Bet before they headed down the stairs. Kylie was still sleeping so Bet whipped up the eggs as Alex prepared the griddle and pulled out a loaf of bread. Alex dunked the bread into the egg mixture and then placed several pieces on the griddle. Bet stood behind her with her arms wrapped around Alex's waist and watched her cook. Alex enjoyed the embrace and laid her head back against Bet nearly burning the first batch. "You better go get Kylie up before I ruin breakfast."

"Be right back then." Bet kissed Alex's neck and then spun away to go wake Kylie.

Alex leaned onto the counter for support. Her hips and legs were sore from last night's workout, but she couldn't help but smile to herself when she remembered the pleasure she gave Bet. The woman certainly had a healthy sexual appetite and Alex vowed she would do everything she could to satisfy that appetite, even if it meant not walking straight for days. She took the first batch of French toast off the griddle just as Kylie and Max came bouncing down the steps with Bet bringing up the rear.

"How about letting Max out for me please, Kylie," Alex said.

"Yes, ma'am." Kylie walked over to open the door and Max flew out the door in hot pursuit of a large gray squirrel that was frantically searching for nuts to stash away in his winter supply. Kylie watched as Max chased the harried squirrel up the tree and then walked into the kitchen to stand beside Alex. She reached up to tug on Alex's robe and Alex reached down to pick her up and put her on the counter so she could watch her cook.

Alex placed a second stack of French toast on the platter and looked over at Kylie. "Do you think this will be enough to get us started?" she asked Kylie with a wink.

"Me and you," Kylie said. "But what's Mom going to eat?"

Alex roared with laughter as Bet took the steaming platter over to the table. "Guess I had better grab a serving while I can then," Bet teased her young daughter. Bet took two slices off the platter, and poured melted butter and then warmed syrup over the top of the stack. "Do you want me to cut it up for you?" Bet asked Kylie.

"I think I can do it, Mom," Kylie said as she climbed up into her chair and picked up her fork.

Alex stood by the coffeepot watching the exchange between mother and daughter and smiled as she watched Kylie slowly cut off a bite with her fork and grin triumphantly as she placed the bite in her mouth. "Hey, save some for me," Alex said as she walked over to the table and sat down.

"This is really good," Kylie said as she cut another bite.

"It really is good," Bet said with a grin.

"Thank you, ladies. Just let me know if I need to cook some more to fill those ravenous appetites you two have," Alex said before taking a large bite.

Bet watched as Alex and Kylie both ate three slices. She couldn't believe Kylie was able to finish three pieces and sat in disbelief as she downed her last bite.

"More?" Alex simply asked.

"I am stuffed, Alex," Kylie said with a very satisfied grin.

"How about you, Mom, want more?"

"Stuffed here too," Bet said as she pushed back from the table to refill their coffee cups.

"I think Kylie and I will do some shopping this morning," Bet announced as she set a fresh cup down in front of Alex. "We got a list of school supplies from the teacher and Kylie is going to need some new clothes. I thought we would go to town while you go take your pictures."

"Well, why don't you drop Kylie off at the office after you are done and she can ride home with me later," Alex suggested.

"Sounds great by me," Bet looked at Kylie who nodded her head in agreement.

"Fantastic," Alex said as she stood to clear the table.

"Let me take care of this and you go get dressed," Bet said as she took the plates from Alex. "Why don't you head upstairs and take your bath, Kylie, so we can all head into town together."

Kylie raced ahead of Alex and quickly flew up the stairs. Alex stopped at the head of the stairs to turn and look at Bet, who was busy loading the dishwasher. Bet felt Alex's eyes on her and she straightened up and turned toward the stairs, a slight flush on her cheeks. Alex smiled and continued up to the loft where she brushed her teeth and dressed in the clothing Bet had laid out for her.

Bet came into the room as Alex was lacing up her boots and walked over to where Alex was sitting. She stood in front of her, placing her hands in Alex's hair.

"You sure do look nice, Ms. Graves," Bet said with a sultry tone to her voice. As her hands played in Alex's hair the front of her robe fell open, revealing the smooth, soft mound of Bet's breast.

Alex lifted her hand and cupped the warm flesh, leaning forward and softly licking the sleeping nipple. It hardened immediately. Alex chuckled and kissed the erect nipple before once again covering it with the soft robe. Her hands caressed up the back of Bet's legs to her ass as Bet stood before her looking deep into her eyes. Alex said, "I'll be back for more of this later."

Bet's knees felt weak and her heart beat wildly in her chest. "I feel like such a teenager," Bet said. "Every time you touch me or look at me like that, I just want to explode."

"This is a very good thing," Alex said as she stood. Her hand moved around Bet's body, her fingers dipping into the hot wetness between Bet's thighs. Alex removed her fingers and raised them to her lips, using the tip of her tongue to lick Bet's juices from her fingers. "Mmm, you're so delicious." Alex took Bet's chin in her hand and raised her face up for a soft kiss.

Bet could taste her juices on Alex's tongue as she parted her lips and her moans vibrated deep into Alex's mouth. Bet broke the heated kiss with a warning. "Unless your plans are to take me back to bed, I suggest you stop kissing me like that, Ms. Graves."

"Yes, ma'am," Alex said with a wicked grin. She stood and kissed Bet softly on the lips. "Call me when you and Kylie get back home from shopping, please?"

"Will you have time for lunch?" Bet asked.

"Will there be dessert?" Alex asked with a mischievous grin.

"There is still half a pie left," Bet teased, knowing that coconut cream wasn't exactly what Alex had in mind.

Alex laughed. "I guess that will have to do then." With a final squeeze to Bet's ass, Alex was off down the steps and, with a hug to Kylie, and a pat on the head to Max, out the door. "See you at lunchtime."

"Are you ready to go?" Bet asked Kylie as she slipped a shirt over her head.

"Yes, ma'am," Kylie replied.

"I'll be right down if you want to go ahead and let Max out, sweetie."

"Okay, Mom." Kylie opened the door for Max, and stood on the porch watching as Alex's truck turned onto the hard road and headed into town. As she watched Alex drive away, she saw a black truck pull out from the adjoining woods and onto the road heading to town. Kylie observed curiously as the truck stopped briefly at the mailbox and then pulled slowly away.

†

The door behind her opened and Bet walked out onto the porch. "All ready, baby?"

"Just waiting on you," Kylie said with a grin. "Stay, Max."

Their first stop was to the local department store to pick up the list of school supplies Kylie would need. With the basket half-full of paper, pencils, notebooks, and other supplies, Bet said, "I think we need to find you some new clothes too, honey."

Together they wandered through the children's clothing section and picked out several outfits. As Kylie and Bet carried them into the dressing room Bet caught a glimpse of Kylie's well-worn tennis shoes. Pleased with five of the outfits they had chosen, Bet steered Kylie over to the shoe department. "I think it is time for some new shoes too. Why don't you look around and see if there are any that you like." Bet sat on a small bench at the end of an aisle and watched Kylie inspect the rows of shoes. Out of the corner of her eye, Bet glimpsed a small rack of children's boots. Bet thought a pair of boots would be a good idea, since Kylie was going to be trekking around construction sites with Alex.

Kylie brought two pairs of tennis shoes over to her. "Do you like either of these, Mom?"

"I like them both." Bet told her daughter. "What about you?"

"I think I like these." Kylie pointed to the pair of plain white tennis shoes. "But I also like these." Kylie struggled to decide.

"Well then, why don't we do both?"

"Can we really, Mom?"

"Really, darling," Bet said with a smile. "As a matter of fact, I thought we might add a pair of boots too, since you are going to be working with Alex after school."

Bet wasn't a bit surprised when Kylie went directly to a pair of suede work boots that were identical to those Alex wore. "Do you like these?" Kylie asked.

Bet chuckled. "Those look fine, so come over here and let's get your foot measured for size."

Kylie sat and placed her foot in the sizing device. "My, my, someone has grown this summer," Bet said as she noted Kylie had gone up a full shoe size since the last pair. "Are those shoes hurting your feet?"

"They are a little tight," Kylie admitted.

"Well, let's see if they have your size," Bet said as they walked down the aisle together. They were fortunate to find both pairs of tennis shoes in the correct size. The boots, however, were out of her size so they selected a half size larger. Kylie tried on all three pairs and decided with thick socks, the boots would be just fine.

"As fast as you seem to be growing, you will probably outgrow these in no time," Bet said as she ruffled her daughter's hair.

"It's your good cooking, Mom," Kylie responded sincerely.

Bet hugged her daughter. "What a charmer you have become. Can you think of anything else we need to get?" Bet asked Kylie.

"May I get a book bag?"

"Ah, that's a great idea, honey."

Kylie picked out a black bag with a bright yellow piping on it. "This is the one."

"Okay, all done?"

"I think that's it," Kylie answered.

As Bet and Kylie paid for their purchases, Alex was wandering through the quiet woods at the site that she would be developing plans for a new mountain home. She had purchased the plot not only for the prime view, but also for the rippling cold-water creek that traversed the property and fed into a small pond that would be easy to stock with fish. The ten-acre plot also sheltered a small cave that Alex wandered across after she had purchased the property. There were several potential building sites on the property so Alex took shots from each one to help her decide which site to use.

As she walked the property, Alex finally decided that she would have the property surveyed and split into two five-acre plots. With the location of the creek and the available building sites, there would be ample room for two homes. Both owners would have enough space for privacy without detracting from the beautiful surroundings.

Alex sat on a boulder at the top edge of the property as she formulated a plan for the home that would rest at the top of the mountain. A home on stilts would provide the additional height, which would allow the owner a nearly three-hundred-and-sixty-degree view of the valley and surrounding mountain. Alex jotted notes on a notepad as she formed the house in her head. She sat so quietly that she did not even realize that she was under surveillance from a raccoon, which was watching her curiously. It took the chattering from the animal to make its presence known to Alex.

"Well, hello there," Alex said to the curious animal. The raccoon sat up on its haunches and stared at Alex as she quietly moved off the boulder, removed her camera from her pack and snapped a shot of the brave little critter. Kylie would get a kick out of that picture for sure and Alex made a note to bring some marshmallows up on her next visit.

Content with her shots, Alex packed up her bag and headed slowly down the mountain. It would take a four-wheel drive vehicle to make it to the top of the incline and Alex was determined to make the effort of the drive worthwhile by designing a home that was truly spectacular. Halfway down the mountain, her cell phone vibrated on her waist.

"Hello," she said.

"Hi, honey, we are all finished and will be headed back to the house in a minute," Bet replied. "How is your morning going?"

"It has been great. I've gotten some great shots and some fabulous ideas for the new homes."

"Well, Kylie and I have worked up an appetite and wanted to know when you will be home for lunch?"

"I am starved too. I should be there within an hour," Alex promised. "What do you have in mind for lunch?"

"How do some burgers and fries sound?" Bet asked.

"Sign me up. I'll make it there in forty-five minutes."

"Drive careful and we will see you soon," Bet said before hanging up.

Alex replaced the phone in her holster and picked up her pace as she hustled down the mountain. Arriving at her truck, the hairs on the back of her neck stood on end. Alex sensed that eyes were on her as she opened her door. She looked around, but didn't see anyone in this remote area. Shaking off the eerie feeling, Alex turned the key and steered the truck toward home. The disconcerting feeling of someone watching her movements eased as she drove down the undeveloped track back to the paved road.

✝

Deeper in the woods, Brian Stewart knelt next to a tree wearing the camouflage jumpsuit he normally wore while hunting. He watched Alex through the detachable scope, taken from his rifle, as she warily opened her door, looked around, and slipped in behind the wheel.

✝

Pulling onto the pavement, Alex planned the rest of her afternoon. After lunch, she and Kylie would drop by the office to print out the pictures she had taken this morning and then she would return home to begin drafting the design of the next home she would be building. She would work at home the rest of the week while Bet started orientation and then return to the office on Monday when Kylie started school.

Having Bet and Kylie really made life complete for Alex and the smile on her face grew wider and wider as she realized this fact. Her cheeks felt as if they would break when she pulled onto the drive up to their home and saw Max and Kylie playing in the yard. They both rushed to meet her when she turned the engine off, Kylie reaching up to hug Alex. Bending down to pick her up, Alex walked toward the house with Kylie chattering away in her arms.

"Wash up you two," Bet said as they walked in the door. "Lunch will be waiting when you get done."

Kylie and Alex disappeared into the bathroom to wash their hands and Max took up his spot beside the table. "I didn't forget you, Max," Bet said to the patient companion. "Your burger is cooling off as we speak." Max licked his chops in anticipation.

"Smells yummy," Alex said as she and Kylie sat down at the table. Bet brought over a plate piled high with french fries and sat it on the table.

"Dig in," she said as she returned to chop up Max's burger and place it in his bowl.

Alex dished out fries for Kylie as she created her burger and then placed fries on her plate, and passed them to Bet as she sat down at the table. "Looks like I'm not the only one starving here," Alex said as Kylie took a large bite of her burger.

"Well, shopping is hard work," Bet said with a chuckle. "After dinner tonight Kylie is going to do a fashion show to show off her new clothes."

"That sounds like fun," Alex said as she took a bite.

"Kylie and I thought we would cook an early dinner while you work for a bit and then we could relax and watch her show. How about I cook some spaghetti tonight?"

"Is that good for you, Kylie?" Alex asked.

"Oh yeah."

"Spaghetti it is then," Alex said.

"How long do you think you two will be at the office?" Bet asked.

"Maybe two hours tops, why?" Alex asked.

"I thought I might sneak in a bubble bath and nap while you are gone," Bet admitted.

"There is a nice bottle of French vanilla bubble bath under the sink in my bathroom," Alex said. "Help yourself and we will try to be as quiet as possible when we get home."

"Are you ready for some dessert, Kylie?" Alex asked.

"More pie," Kylie said. "Yes, ma'am, I am."

Alex laughed and walked to the refrigerator to retrieve the remainder of last night's pie. She cut the remaining pie into three sections, and placed them on small plates and carried them to the table. "Here we go." Alex said as she took a bite of the sugary pie.

They ate the slices of pie and cleaned the table together then Kylie disappeared upstairs to brush her teeth as Alex and Bet talked in the kitchen. "She is so excited about going with you today," Bet said as she wrapped her arms around Alex.

"I took a special picture for her today," Alex said as Bet snuggled into her chest. "I hope she likes it."

"If it is from you, I am sure she will like it. That kid really loves you, if you hadn't noticed."

"I love her too," Alex said. She was going to add she loved Bet as well, but Kylie came bouncing down the stairs at that moment, declaring she was ready to go. "Enjoy your afternoon," Alex said as she gave her a quick squeeze.

"You too," Bet said as she walked them to the door.

Kylie and Alex drove into town and met Sandy at the office, just returning from a late lunch at the diner. "Good afternoon, ladies," she said as they walked through the door together.

"Hi, Ms. Sandy," Kylie said. "Alex has some pictures to print, so I decided I would come in with her. Is there anything I can do for you?"

"I have some shredding I was saving for this afternoon if you want to do that," Sandy replied.

"Sure thing," Kylie said and went with Sandy as Alex booted up her computer.

"After that, you can play on your computer until Alex gets done," Sandy said as she showed Kylie how to use the shredder.

Kylie caught on quickly, and within minutes she was shredding away at the small stack of papers Sandy had saved for her. Sandy walked into Alex's office and said, "So, how is it going, boss?"

"Things are going very well, Sandy," Alex replied. "I was out at the new site this morning and have decided to subdivide it and make two parcels out of it. How about calling the surveyor and asking him when he could be available to survey it for me."

"Sure thing, boss," Sandy said with a chuckle.

"What?" Alex asked.

"Nothing, it's just good to see you happy for a change."

Alex grinned.

Sandy left the office and Alex started printing the photos she had taken that morning, separating the upper site from the lower and leaving the photo of the raccoon for last. When she had all her prints, she called Kylie into the office. Kylie climbed up into her lap and Alex said, "I want you to see who I met today." She clicked the mouse. The picture of the raccoon popped up on Alex's screen and Kylie burst out in laughter.

"He is so funny looking, Alex," Kylie said through her giggles.

"I thought so too," Alex said. "I thought maybe later in the week we could go back for a visit with a bag of marshmallows and see if we can get to know him a little better."

"You think he will like marshmallows?"

"I know for a fact that he will. I have never met a raccoon who could resist the temptation of marshmallows," Alex said with a chuckle. "Do you want to print a copy of him to take home and show your mom?"

"Yes, please."

"You see that button right there?" Kylie nodded. "Just push it and it will print."

Kylie leaned forward and pressed the key and watched as the furry raccoon came to life on the paper as it appeared from inside the printer. When it had finished, Alex picked it up and handed it to Kylie. "Why don't you go show Sandy and ask her for two file folders." She helped Kylie down from her lap and moments later heard Sandy's laughter from the front office.

Kylie returned with the file folders and handed them to Alex. "Let's put your picture in one and we can put my stack in the other," Alex said as she handed a folder to Kylie.

Alex shut down the computer and asked Kylie, "You ready to head home?"

"Yes, ma'am, ready when you are," she quickly replied.

"I'll be working at the house the rest of the week if anything comes up, Sandy," Alex said as she and Kylie walked toward the door.

"Okay, boss, have a good one," Sandy said with a smile.

"You too, Sandy, call me if you need to," Alex said with a wave.

"Bye, Ms. Sandy," Kylie said sweetly.

"See you later, Kylie."

✝

Brian seethed with anger as he watched his daughter walk hand in hand with the dark-haired woman. The smile on her face as they walked to the beat-up, old truck made his heart pound in his ears, intensifying the mind-bending headache he was already experiencing. He continued to watch as Kylie crawled up into the seat and buckled herself in just like a small adult and Alex walked back around the truck.

He watched as Alex pulled away from the office and headed in the direction of her home. His head was splitting, so he decided to return to the motel, certain that Alex was heading home for the evening. Brian drove the short distance to the motel, and popped a handful of aspirin into his mouth and then collapsed onto the bed. He tossed and turned in the sweat-soaked sheets, his feverish dreams filled with the plans he had for the dark-haired woman who was destroying his life.

Chapter Eight

Bet soaked in the luxury of the soft bubbles until the water started to cool. Toweling off, she slipped between the sheets and buried her face in the pillow, which still held Alex's scent. Filling her nostrils with the heady scent, Bet drifted off to sleep as Alex's body curled around her in her dreams.

Alex crept into the house quietly while Kylie and Max played together in the front yard. A note hanging from the staircase asked her to wake Bet up no later than five o'clock. Alex took the note and walked into her small home office, flipping the lights on inside. Placing the note on her desk, she booted up her computer. Removing the photos from the folder Alex arranged the shots of the upper plat onto an easel sitting next to her desk. After a few keystrokes on her keyboard, a drafting program appeared on her screen. Alex pulled the notepad from her bag and began to enter the dimensions of the building site she had chosen for the house.

She started by plotting the large beams that would serve to elevate the house then built in an oversized two-car garage that would rest under half of the first floor of the home. The other half of the space would be comprised of a large laundry room and a game/entertainment room, with a large picture window. Local river rock would encase the lower levels, and the upper floors would be finished in thick logs of fragrant cedar. Alex glimpsed at the clock on the computer to find that an hour had passed and it was a few minutes before five. Saving her work, she stepped to the front door and looked out to find Max and Kylie sitting quietly in the yard, as Kylie seemed to be telling Max a story. Alex smiled at the pair and walked up the stairs.

Bet's bare leg was resting on top of the covers and Alex let her fingers lightly trail up the delicate skin until she reached her hip. Sitting down on the edge of the bed, Alex gently removed the covers from Bet's naked body exposing the bare, tanned skin and soft mounds of smooth flesh. Bet rolled onto her back searching for the covers, further revealing the fullness of her body to Alex.

Alex bent forward, her warm breath caressing Bet's skin as the tip of her tongue circled a sleeping nipple, and her fingers brushed down Bet's body into the soft curls nestled between her spread thighs. Alex could smell the fragrance of the bubbles on Bet's skin as she licked the sensitive skin surrounding Bet's nipple. Her fingers met a warm, dampness as they stroked through the soft curls and Bet's body became alive with arousal. Alex's fingers coasted through the wetness between Bet's legs and her lips slowly brushed across Bet's swollen clit. Bet's eyes flittered open and she realized she was not dreaming.

She spread her legs wider as her hands reached for Alex's head, placing her mouth directly onto her throbbing clit. Alex's fingers dipped eagerly into Bet's wetness as her tongue swirled around the sensitive flesh. Bet's moans grew louder. Alex watched her lover's eyes glaze over. She bit her lip to hold back a scream of ecstasy as her body convulsed with pleasure.

Licking the tasty dew from her lips, Alex asked, "Will that hold you over until tonight?" Still breathing hard, Bet smiled and nodded her head, unable to speak for a few seconds more.

"That felt totally fantastic," she finally breathed as her hands reached to touch Alex's cheek, caressing her with soft fingertips. "If I didn't know better I'd think I had died and gone to heaven." Bet stroked Alex's face with a loving hand.

"Well, I hate to bring you back to earth, but your note said to wake you at five."

"You can wake me like that anytime," Bet said as she pulled Alex onto her and kissed her deeply, tasting the desire on her lips. When she broke the kiss she added, "I hope you are ready for tonight."

"Just what do you have in mind, ma'am," Alex inquired as she rolled over onto the bed.

"I guess you will just have to wait and find out," Bet said as she stood and dressed in shorts and a pullover. "I would suggest you eat a healthy meal tonight, though, because you are going to need all your energy." With a final kiss, she was gone down the stairs.

Alex was left sitting on the bed grinning wildly at the prospects the night held for her. She had planned to work a little longer while Bet cooked dinner and then they would relax and watch Kylie's fashion show. Kylie was walking in the door with Max as Alex walked back down the stairs. "Hey, you two," she said.

"Hi, Alex, hi, Mom," Kylie said as she walked into the kitchen.

"You want to make the salad for me, honey?" Bet asked.

"Sure, Mom." Kylie went to the bathroom to wash her hands.

"I will be in the office if you need anything," Alex said.

From her office, Alex listened to Bet and Kylie as they toiled together in the kitchen. She pulled up her file and began to detail the plumbing for the bottom floor, her mind already skipping ahead to the second and third floors. This house would be a masterpiece of her work and she was eager to put her ideas down on paper. She couldn't remember the last time her mind burned with such creative force, and she wanted to ensure she harnessed the energy to capture a magnificent plan. This home would be the largest built yet, and Alex was certain there would be buyers eager to purchase it before the project was complete.

Alex completed the plumbing sketches and added a large hot tub to the entertainment room, which would be dressed with accent lighting and in-wall speakers for a stereo and theater system. She grew more and more excited with each keystroke, the faint noises from the kitchen dwarfed by the pounding of her heart. She pushed aside the mouse and picked up a sketchpad and pencil. She quickly drew the outline for the second and third floors and, as an afterthought, added a fourth, containing a widow's walk with a full, 360-degree view of the entire mountaintop. The widow's walk would be a gem. A ten by ten, square room, fully enclosed with glass and accompanied by a bench that wrapped the entire room to allow for hours of comfortable viewing.

The third floor would house two large open loft bedrooms with separate baths and a staircase up to the widow's walk. Both rooms would open up to full-length decks that would allow for excellent views of the valley. Alex flipped the page of her sketchbook and began to pencil in the second floor with two slightly smaller bedrooms sharing a full bath. A full island kitchen would be equipped with brilliant stainless steel appliances, and the dining room would open onto a large deck perfect for grilling out on a star-filled night. In her vision, the living room, accented with a large stone fireplace, would have a built-in entertainment system, complete with a large flat-screen television, and all the high-tech equipment necessary to bring a show to life.

Alex was so busy sketching she had not realized that Kylie had come into the office and was sitting next to her, watching intently as her pencil created the house of her vision. Kylie waited patiently until Alex paused in her drawing to whisper, "Mom says dinner is ready."

Alex jumped when the young child spoke. She turned to see Kylie sitting next to her. Kylie chuckled and said, "I didn't mean to scare you, Alex, but you know how Mom gets when it's time to eat."

"That's okay, I just didn't realize you were sitting next to me," Alex said. She turned the sketch toward Kylie. "So what do you think?"

"It's going to be big isn't it?"

"Huge," Alex said as she ruffled Kylie's hair and set the sketchbook down. "We better get a move on." Alex stepped into the bathroom to wash her hands before walking into the kitchen.

"Smells great," she said.

"How are the plans coming?"

"The rough draft is moving right along," Alex said as she took her seat at the table and reached for their hands for Kylie's nightly prayer. Afterward, Alex picked up the garlic bread and took a slice before passing it on to Bet. Alex swirled a large forkful of the spaghetti and popped it into her mouth as Bet cut Kylie's into smaller bites.

"Fantastic," Alex exclaimed as she wiped a drop of spaghetti sauce from her chin.

"Mom, makes great spaghetti doesn't she, Alex?" Kylie piped in.

"She certainly does, Kylie. She's a great cook," Alex said with a smile to Bet.

"Are you all set for your fashion show?" Bet asked.

"Yes, ma'am, I am," Kylie said excitedly.

"When we finish dinner you can go get dressed in your first outfit while I clean the kitchen," Bet instructed.

"Did you show your mom the picture you printed today?" Alex asked.

"Yes, I did, and she thought he looked funny too," Kylie said with a giggle.

"Well, they can be pretty funny creatures," Alex said. "Especially when they know they have an audience to perform to. Toss in a couple of marshmallows and they get real goofy trying to eat the squishy treat."

"I can't wait to see that." Kylie took another bite of her spaghetti, the sauce spreading wider across her face as she grinned.

"Maybe we can go up this weekend," Alex suggested with a look toward Bet.

"Sounds good to me, maybe we can pack a picnic lunch for the hike," Bet replied.

Kylie asked to leave the table as soon as she finished her dinner. "Be sure to wash your face good before you put on your new clothes," Bet reminded her young daughter. "Yell down to let us know when you are ready for your show."

"Yes, ma'am." Kylie bounded up the stairs and disappeared into her room.

Bet carried plates to the kitchen and rinsed them while Alex finished her meal. "She is so excited to show off her new look for you."

"I can't wait to see her," Alex said with genuine excitement.

"Give me that plate and go get comfy on the couch. I will be there in a just a minute," Bet said as she took the plate from Alex.

Alex went to the living room and sat down, propping her feet up on the large wooden coffee table. Moments later Bet joined her on the couch sitting next to her with a warm hand resting on Alex's thigh. "How is it coming, Kylie?" Bet yelled up the stairs.

"Almost ready," Kylie answered.

Bet snuggled into Alex and let her hand run down the length of Alex's strong thigh, feeling the muscles twitch under her touch. The door to Kylie's room opened and she slowly came down the stairs, wearing the first of the new outfits she and Bet had picked out that morning. Beaming with pride, she walked to the fireplace and turned in a full circle to give her audience the full view of her outfit.

"Very nice, Kylie," Alex said. Kylie grinned and headed back up the stairs.

Kylie repeated the sequence for each of the outfits until she came to the very last one. "The next one is just for you," Bet whispered as they waited for Kylie to return. When the door opened again and Kylie walked down the stairs, she was wearing light tan work pants, a safari print shirt, and her suede work boots. "Kylie calls this one her going to work with Alex outfit," Bet narrated as Kylie made her turn and then raised her foot up to the coffee table so Alex could see the work boots that matched her own.

"I love it," Alex said as she hugged Kylie tightly. "I know Sandy and the boys will love it too. As a matter of fact, Sandy may have to order us all some of those shirts to wear when we meet with customers and inspectors."

Kylie's eyes twinkled with delight from the praise she received from Alex. She crawled up onto the couch to squeeze between Alex and her mother. "You are going to be the envy of the preschool," Alex said to Kylie.

"She even picked out a black and gold book bag," Bet said.

"Really," Alex remarked. "Maybe we will have another Tech fan in the house after all. Those are Tech's colors and that was the school I graduated from, Kylie."

"I know. I saw the picture in your office and I liked the colors," Kylie admitted.

Alex chuckled. "Well, I guess when it starts to cool off we will have to get you a Tech sweatshirt."

Kylie's eyes lit up. "Can Mom get one too?"

"I think we can manage that," Alex said with a grin as she lost herself in thought for a moment.

Attending Tech for her degree was never in doubt for Alex, fulfilling her father's dream. He was in his second year at Tech when his father passed away and he gave up his college dreams to return home to support his mother and two younger siblings. Shattered, but proud to step into the role, her father built his business and kept his dream alive with the knowledge that one day, his child or children would have the opportunity to get a college education.

Maybe that Bet and Kylie were now a part of her life, she would dream of Kylie following in her footsteps at Tech and taking over the business from her one day.

"Time for you to hit the bath and get ready for bed, young lady," Bet said. "I'll hang your clothes up while you get clean and then you can come back down to say goodnight to Alex."

"I'll be in the office for a bit," Alex said as Bet and Kylie headed up the stairs. "Thanks for the fashion show, Kylie."

"You're welcome, Alex," Kylie said as she followed her mother upstairs.

Alex settled back into her office. She tore the page with the widow's walk off the sketchpad and taped it onto the easel along with the pictures. Alex picked up her pencil and started sketching more detail into the second floor. Immersed in the drawing, she looked up when Kylie returned. She walked over to Alex and reached up for a hug, kissing Alex on the cheek. "Goodnight, Alex."

"Sleep tight, Kylie." Alex watched as Kylie climbed the stairs, ready for bed.

Alex went back to work, focusing on the sketch when she felt a pair of hands slide down the top of her chair to the buttons on her shirt. She put the pencil down as the fingers slowly worked the top three buttons of her shirt loose and the soft hands slid beneath the fabric, teasing her erect nipples. "Mmm, feels good," she said as Bet's touch became firmer. Alex could feel a rush of dampness growing between her thighs. Bet removed her hands and spun the chair around to face her. She reached down and pulled the hem of Alex's shirt from the waistband of her pants, and loosened the remaining buttons, opening her shirt wide.

Bet had also changed clothes while she was upstairs and was wearing a long T-shirt and nothing more. She straddled Alex's body and sat down in her lap, the warmth of her body enveloping Alex. Her mouth found Alex's as her hands worked to push the shirt off Alex's shoulders and off her body. Her fingers worked under the sports bra and she broke the kiss long enough to pull it over Alex's head, leaving her naked from the waist up. Bet's hands cupped and massaged Alex's breasts as her tongue probed deeply into Alex's mouth, muffling her moans as she ground her crotch into Alex. The seam of Alex's pants rubbed roughly across Bet's clit and her kisses became more fevered with every thrust of her hips.

Alex could feel the tremors as they grew in Bet's body. She severed the kiss to remove Bet's shirt. Bet leaned backward, her body resting on the desk. Alex leaned forward to take a breast into her mouth and sucked it deeply into her mouth, chewing lightly on the blood-gorged nipple. Her thumb reached down to stroke Bet's clit as she continued to thrust onto Alex's body. Bet was soaked and Alex could feel her own wetness growing as she continued to lick and nibble Bet's breasts.

Alex cleared a spot on the desktop with one swipe, settling Bet on the top of the desk then knelt before her. Placing her hands under Bet's knees, Alex spread her legs wide as her tongue drove deep into Bet's wetness, her face coated with the sticky sweetness. Bet managed to lock her heels around Alex's neck, pulling her deeper as she came all over Alex's face, grinding into her with each new wave of orgasm.

Bet lifted Alex's face from her lap and sat up on the desk. She slowly licked the juices from Alex's face as her hands loosened the belt and worked the fastener of Alex's pants open. Alex lifted her hips to allow Bet to pull the pants and underwear down to her knees then Bet used her feet to slide them the rest of the way to the floor. She knelt in front of Alex, removing her boots and pushing the pants away from her body, tilting the chair slightly backward as she raised Alex's thighs and rested them on top of her shoulders. Bet's fingers teased Alex's wetness until she felt as though she would explode and when Bet looked into Alex's eyes they begged her for release.

Bet stood and pulled Alex to her feet and led her quietly up the stairs to the loft, pressing her backward onto the bed. Bet opened the nightstand beside the bed and lifted out a large ribbed vibrator that she had carefully tucked away in her belongings during her escape from Alabama. She crawled onto the bed next to Alex, placing the toy between them. Bet's mouth covered Alex's breast as her hand stroked down her tense body and came to rest between her soaked thighs. Bet pressed two fingers deep inside Alex as her teeth grazed lightly over her sensitive nipples. Alex's hips thrust upward, urging Bet deeper inside as her body screamed for relief. Bet slowly withdrew her fingers and picked up the toy, twisting the top to turn the vibrator on low. Bet could hear the soft buzz as she laid the toy across Alex's quivering lips. She felt Alex's body vibrate with her moans. Bet rolled the toy atop Alex coating it with her ample juices before placing the tip of the toy against the opening of her womanhood. Alex reached down to cover Bet's hand with hers as they slowly eased the large toy inside Alex.

Alex spread her legs wider and pressed Bet's hand sending the toy deeper inside. The pressure of Alex's hand on hers was a real turn-on for Bet. She slowed her movement, allowing Alex to control the depth and speed of this experience. With her thumb, Bet turned the top of the vibrator turning up the speed of the vibration and Alex groaned as her back arched, and her body began to convulse from the increased sensation.

Bet was totally engrossed with the sensual way Alex's body responded. She moved down between Alex's legs releasing her grasp on the toy, replacing her hand with Alex's. Alex's need had grown so imminent it didn't matter that Bet's hand was no longer giving her pleasure as she drove the toy deeper inside. Bet lay between her thighs and reached up with her fingertips to spread Alex's lips and watch as Alex stroked her body faster. Bet watched as the toy was buried deep inside Alex on each downward stroke and then withdrawn almost the full length only to disappear once again deep inside her. Alex's body began to quake with pleasure and Bet reached up to increase the vibrator to full speed, the powerful vibrations echoing inside Alex's body as she buried the toy deep inside her and left it buried there as her hips bucked wildly.

Bet's hand covered Alex's wetness to ensure the toy remained in place as Alex writhed in pleasure then leaned forward and covered Alex's clit with her hot mouth, sucking her deep. Alex gripped the sheets, her body arching off the bed as her body surged with a flow of juice escaping around the vibrator, running down Bet's chin and between her trembling thighs. Bet moved her mouth down between Alex's legs to capture the flow with an eager tongue as she slowly withdrew the toy from Alex, turning it off and laying it on the bed.

Bet climbed on top of Alex's sweat-soaked body and listened as the wildly beating heart of her lover pounded in her chest. Alex wrapped her arms around Bet and held on tightly to the woman whose passion both inspired and intoxicated her. Tears of joy slipped quietly down Alex's cheeks. Bet looked up into her face and softly brushed away the tears with a gentle hand.

Bet moved further up Alex's body, taking the covers with her as she snuggled deep into the hollow of Alex's neck and, with her body draped over Alex, drifted into a deep, peaceful sleep.

Chapter Nine

The alarm clock woke Bet at six the next morning and she struggled with the temptation to snuggle back into Alex's warm body. Today was her first day of orientation at the hospital and while she was eager to return to work, her body longed for the physical comfort of sleeping next to Alex. As quietly as she could she slipped from the bed and closed the bathroom door behind her as she ran a nice hot shower. As she bathed, the memory of last night's lovemaking was renewed and Bet could barely restrain herself from waking Alex with some early-morning loving. Instead, Bet dressed and crept downstairs to retrieve the scattered clothing from the office and pour the coffee.

When she returned to the bedroom carrying steaming coffee, Bet found Alex awake and propped up on pillows at the head of the bed. "Good morning," Alex whispered as Bet set the coffee down on the table and crawled onto the bed.

"Good morning, lover." Bet picked up a mug and handed Alex her first cup of coffee.

"Are you excited about today?"

"I am, but it sure is tempting just to crawl back into bed with you and love the morning away," Bet replied with a wicked grin.

"I'll be ready and waiting when you get home today and you won't miss a thing," Alex promised as she caressed Bet's cheek.

"That will definitely give me the energy to make it through the day," Bet said as she stood and kissed Alex on the lips. "Right now, I better get moving or I am going to be late." "Have a great day," Alex said as Bet started for the stairs.

"You too, sweetie." Bet whispered and then she was down the stairs and out the front door, followed closely by Max.

Alex stretched once more in the bed and headed for the shower to wake her stiff body, the warm water soothing the still exhausted muscles. The intensity of her orgasms last night surprised Alex and the tenderness in her body served as a pleasant reminder of just how much she enjoyed it. She remained under the flow for several minutes as her body slowly relaxed.

✝

Brian awoke at the motel to the clanging sound of the town's lone garbage truck as it noisily emptied the motel's ancient Dumpster. He sat up on the still made bed and his head began to throb. The pounding headache had become a constant part of his life. He struggled to his feet and stumbled over the empty whiskey bottle he had dropped beside the bed the night before. He walked to the single window in the dingy room and pulled back the faded curtain. "Just fucking great," he said aloud as fog swirled around the building. There was no sign of the sun yet, but the glare from the fog seemed to burn a hole right into his brain.

Brian cursed again loudly as he searched for the bottle of aspirin and poured four tablets into his palm. Walking toward the bathroom, Brian popped the pills into his mouth and bit down on the bitter-tasting medicine. He turned the water on in the sink and bent down, cupping water in his hands to wash away the taste.

When he raised his head from the sink, he looked into the mirror at his face. His dark eyes, laced with red streaks surrounded by dark circles. His unshaven face added to the manic look in his eyes. He looked directly into the eyes of a man possessed.

✝

Kylie had finished her breakfast and was outside playing with Max as Alex continued to draft the house plans. She was very pleased with her progress so far and only mildly disturbed by the vibration of her cell phone.

"Hi Alex, this is Glen. I hate to bother you, but old man Johnson will be out to certify the final electrical panel today and he called to say that he expects you to be there."

"That old fart just never passes up an opportunity to flirt," Alex said with a chuckle. "What time will he be there?"

109

"Straight up eleven he said before he hung up on me this morning."

"Okay. I'll drop Kylie by the office and then meet you out at the site."

"Thanks, Alex," he said. "I really did hate to call you, but you know how he can get and I don't want him holding up the project."

"I needed a stretch break anyhow, Glen, so I'll see you in a bit."

She walked to the door and stepped outside onto the porch. "There's been a change of plans, Kylie. I need to meet an inspector out at the site for a little while, so would you mind spending some time with Sandy? Then we can head to the diner for a late lunch."

"Sounds good to me," Kylie said as she walked onto the porch with Max.

"Let me grab my keys and we will be on our way then." Alex disappeared into the house.

Kylie climbed up into the truck, buckled herself into the seat, and waited for Alex. "Be back in a little while Max," Kylie said as the big dog followed Alex to the truck.

Alex started the engine and down the drive, they went.

†

Brian had arrived early, hidden in the fog, and watched as Bet drove away without Kylie in the car. He waited to see what would develop. As Alex passed his location, he slowly pulled his truck from the woods and followed them to town. He watched Kylie jump down from the truck and walk into the office with a wave to the driver of the truck. The dark-haired woman was finally alone so Brian chose to continue to track his prey. This may be my best shot, Brian thought, as he watched Alex head out of town. Surely, she will be coming back this way soon to pick up his daughter and when she did, he would be waiting for her. He followed Alex for nearly three miles out of town before he spied a spot that would play perfectly into his plan. He turned into a small pig trail and waited for Alex to return. Hidden in the trees, he had an excellent view of the highway. Brian would be ready to set his plan in motion at the first glimpse of her return.

†

Alex arrived at the worksite where Glen greeted her, looking nervous. "Relax," Alex told him. "Mr. Johnson is just a grumpy old man who needs some attention. How is the project coming?"

"Still ahead of schedule," he replied, which took his mind off his nervousness for a moment.

Glen walked around with Alex who performed a last-minute check of the electrical system and then showed her the progress they had made during the week. "This looks really good," she praised Glen. "Maybe I should leave you boys alone more often."

"No way, Alex, these guys work much better when you are around."

"That's because we like how she cracks her whip better than you," one of the carpenters said, and the whole crew broke out in raucous laughter.

"Is this a worksite or a damn comedy club," a booming voice said from behind them.

"Hi, Mr. Johnson," Alex said as she walked over to the old man and hugged his neck.

"Always good to see you, Alex," Mr. Johnson said, his face itching to break into a smile. "Looks like you have another beauty on your hands here."

"Definitely one to be proud of," she answered as they walked the old man to the main electric panel.

Mr. Johnson completed his inspection of the panel and then crawled up into the attic access to inspect the wiring. "Damn, it gets hotter every year," he claimed as he made his way through the house checking outlets, switches and GFI plugs.

"Perfect as usual," Mr. Johnson told Alex as he signed off on the paperwork and sticker for the main panel and handed them to Alex. "Keep up the good work, young lady," he said with a wink to Alex. "Don't let these ole boys pull ya down to their level." He laughed and was gone.

"I don't know why that old man gets to me so bad," Glen admitted to Alex.

"Could it be that he is just as big a perfectionist as you are?" Alex questioned.

Glen smiled with relief as he laughed. "As usual, boss, you're right again."

"Of course I am," Alex, teased. "And now I am going to let you buy Kylie and I lunch at the diner since you disturbed my lunch plans."

"A price gladly paid for your assistance." Glen walked her out to her truck. "Be back shortly, guys, so why don't you knock off for lunch so nothing gets screwed up while I'm gone," he hollered as he walked to his truck.

Alex was already well down the drive when Glen made it to his truck. She hit the hard road a good half-mile ahead of him. Glen was happy they had finished that inspection with a perfect score and hoped Alex was as proud as he was of the work they had completed. He was reveling in these thoughts when he saw a fast-moving, black truck fly out from the woods and ram Alex's pickup, pushing the lighter truck off the side off a steep embankment. Glen watched in horror as Alex's truck rolled down the side of the mountain and the larger truck sailed through the air, bursting into a fireball as it landed nose first into the earth.

An eternity seemed to pass before Glen's truck slid to a halt at the spot where Alex's truck had left the road. Her truck had finally come to rest on a large oak, tires still spinning wildly. Glen fumbled with his cell phone to dial 911 as he searched for a way to get down to Alex. He finally remembered he had a long length of rope behind his seat. After tying off to the bumper, he slowly made his way down to Alex as sirens filled the air. Glen reached in and turned off the ignition, afraid that her gas would begin leaking and he sure didn't want anything to spark a fire. Blood rushed down the side of Alex's head, as she lay slumped in the seat. Glen called to her and heard only a faint moan, but that was enough to let him know that Alex was still alive.

Glen looked up to see paramedics rappelling down from the embankment, towing a basket and emergency supplies behind them. He grabbed the basket and guided it to earth as the two medics rushed to evaluate Alex. "Looks like the other driver is beyond help," one said to another, "so let's concentrate on this one. Why don't you climb back up to the road, mister," the lead paramedic said. "When we get her extricated and secured, it's going to take a lot of manpower to get her back up this mountain."

"You get her ready and I'll get her up," Glen promised. He took out his cell and called back to the worksite. "Bill, this is Glen, Alex has been in a wreck, and I need you and the boys to get the Bobcat and a block and tackle down to the Old Town Road as fast as you can."

Glen grabbed his rope and started to scramble back up the mountain. Once at the top, he looked down the mountain at the burning heap of metal.

A county deputy asked Glen, "Do you have any idea what happened here?"

Glen told the deputy about him and Alex heading into town for lunch and the black truck that appeared from the woods, hell-bent, and ramming Alex off the road. Glen had no idea who was driving the truck.

He excused himself promptly from the deputy when Bill and the crew rushed onto the scene with the Bobcat and supplies. A fire truck had also arrived and was blasting water down the mountain to extinguish the blazing truck. The scene was chaotic with men and equipment rushing around everywhere. Glen and Bill went to work rigging the block and tackle onto the Bobcat, which they would extend enough to clear the side of the mountain. Once securely in the basket, they could lower the rope down and using the block and tackle and muscle from Alex's crew, they would get their boss safely up the mountain and into a waiting ambulance.

From the top of the mountain Glen watched as the two paramedics worked to free Alex and place her onto a backboard, and finally into the awaiting basket. Glen could hear the crackling of the paramedic's voice over the radio as he called in Alex's condition. "Vital signs are stable but she has not regained consciousness, suspect broken left arm and leg and possible skull fracture," the paramedic reported to the hospital staff that would be waiting their arrival. He finally gave a thumbs-up to Glen and they began to lift Alex slowly into the air and up the side of the mountain. A second pair of paramedics took over at the top of the mountain. They quickly loaded Alex into the back of their ambulance and with sirens screaming were out of sight in a flash.

Glen had his crew to take the equipment back to the site and said he would call them as soon as he knew how Alex was doing. As he walked back to his truck and gathered the rope, he saw the two paramedics were still down the mountainside looking into the smoldering remains of the black truck. On his way to the hospital, he called Sandy at the office and explained what had happened, intentionally leaving out the seriousness of Alex's injuries until he knew more information. Sandy told him that Kylie was with her at the office and that she would keep her overnight if needed. Glen thanked her and promised to call as quickly as he could.

As soon as Sandy hung up, she picked up the phone and called her sister Ann. Bet needed to know what was going on. Ann said she would pull her from orientation and bring her up to speed. The next task Sandy dreaded. She called Kylie into the front office and sat her in the chair next to hers. Sandy knew how much Kylie loved Alex and as gently as she could, she explained to Kylie that Alex had been in an accident and that Alex needed her thoughts and prayers. Kylie's bottom lip trembled, but she never shed a tear. She walked back to her computer, and began creating a card for Alex as her little mind prayed to God to make Alex all right. Sandy called the diner for lunch which neither she or Kylie could eat. They sat waiting by the phone for news of their beloved friend.

†

Ann cracked open the door to the auditorium and luckily Bet was sitting at the end of an aisle. She crept quietly over to her and whispered, "Grab your stuff and come with me, please." Bet had a shocked look on her face, but she quickly assembled her belongings and followed Ann out into the hall.

Ann located a small waiting room and led Bet inside. "Sandy just called to tell me that Alex has been in a bad accident and is being transported here." She watched the color drain from Bet's face as she fumbled for a seat. Ann placed her arm around Bet's shoulders to steady her and they sat silently for a moment.

"Do you know what happened?" Bet asked.

"All Sandy knew was that a driver ran Alex off the road as she was coming back from a site visit."

"A site visit, oh my God, Kylie is with her today!"

"No, no, Kylie is fine. Alex dropped her by the office. Sandy has her safe and sound, and will keep her as long as needed, so don't worry about Kylie. Ann could feel Bet's body slump with the relief that her daughter was safe.

"How bad is Alex?"

"Sandy didn't know but I heard the ambulance pulling up as I came down after you," Ann said. "Let's go up to the ER and see what we can find out."

Bet stumbled as she stood up, and she felt faint. "Are you okay," Ann asked.

"I'm okay. Just a little too much overload there for a second." However, she still took advantage of the steadying arm Ann offered.

When they walked into the ER waiting room, Glen was already at the desk trying to get an update on Alex. The nurse was telling Glen that she had just arrived and was being evaluated, and stabilized. There was no initial report yet, but someone would talk with him as soon as possible. Ann and Bet walked over to Glen. Ann made the introductions and suggested they wait in the family waiting room while Ann snuck back to see what she could find out.

Glen paced the floor while Bet collapsed onto the armchair, a bit dazed yet from the news. "It's my damned fault," Glen said as he paced.

"Why on earth, would you say that, Glen?"

"Because, if I would have done my job, and handled that inspection by myself like she had planned there would have been no need for Alex to be on that road today."

"Glen, Alex thinks the world of you and would do anything in her power for you, so don't even think that way."

"I still can't help but believe that if I hadn't called her that black truck would have never have run her off the road," Glen said with tears in his eyes.

"What black truck?" Bet asked. Her heart started hammering even harder in her chest.

"There was a big black truck that came barreling out from the woods and ran Alex off the road and down the mountain," Glen said. "The damned fool driving it crashed at the bottom of the mountain and is probably nothing more than a pile of ash right now."

"Oh shit! My husband Brian has a black truck." Bet said as the realization of what could have happened hit her full in the face.

"It was possibly a Ram with lots of chrome," Glen said.

"Oh my God! It sounds just like his truck." Tears rushed down her face. "How could Brian have found us so quickly? Why would he want to harm Alex?"

Glen moved beside Bet and placed a comforting arm around her shoulders. "Look, Alex told me about how your husband treated you and how you ended up here. I am so sorry all of this has happened," he spoke sincerely to her. "Alex is a strong woman. She will fight with all her might to make it through this battle." Bet's sobs racked her body. Glen could not think of any other comforting words, so he just held Bet while her tears soaked his shirt.

Several minutes later the door to the waiting room opened and Ann walked through. "Dr. Lee said that Alex's vital signs remain stable. They have sent her up for x-rays and an MRI to determine the extent of injuries caused by the crash."

"Has she been awake at all?" Bet asked.

"Not that I am aware of," Ann answered. "I asked Dr. Lee to come in and give us a status report as soon as he could, but I am afraid it's going to be a long night. Glen, Sheriff Jones is waiting out in the lobby. He asked if it would be okay if he came in to speak with you for a few minutes."

Glen looked at Bet, who nodded her head. "Go ahead and tell him to come in, and thanks for all your help, Ann."

"I just wish there was more that I could do."

Sheriff Jones stepped into the room and introduced himself. "Glen, I have just a few questions for you and then I hope we can put our heads together and answer some other questions. First, tell me what you know about the incident from the time you left the site this morning."

"Alex and I were on our way back to town to pick up Kylie, Bet's daughter, and we were going to have lunch at the diner. Alex left the site a few minutes ahead of me in her truck, and as I came onto the paved road, I saw her just ahead of me. Then I saw a large, black truck appear from out of the woods and the driver steered right into the side of Alex's truck. Everything seemed to be moving in slow motion as I watched Alex's truck flip on its side and begin to roll down the side of the mountain. The black truck went out of control and took flight over the edge of the mountain." Glen scowled as he remembered the facts. "I can still hear the roaring of the motor as it soared down the mountain and burst into flames when it made impact at the base of the mountain."

"Were you able to recognize the driver of the vehicle or the vehicle itself," the sheriff asked.

"It wasn't a vehicle I had seen before and I didn't see the driver at all. My eyes were glued to Alex's truck as it continued to roll down the side of the mountain," Glen said with a hollow sound to his voice.

"Well, there was very little evidence left in the wreckage to give us any clue to the identity of the driver, but I have my office calling around to the various motels in the area to see if there were any guests registered that may have been driving a truck of that description," the sheriff continued. "We were able to salvage part of a license plate number and to verify it was an Alabama plate, so we at least know where to start."

Bet had remained silent during the interview. "What was the license number you found," she asked.

"BDK are the first three letters but the remainder was too damaged to determine."

"The rest of the license will probably be 36I," Bet said as she hung her head. "The driver was likely Brian Stewart, my husband for almost five years," she said as she started her story. "The relationship was an abusive one and last Thursday night, my daughter and I fled Alabama in hopes of finding refuge from the physical and emotional torment Brian put us through. We made it as far as Alex's drive before my car became disabled. Out of the kindness of her heart Alex welcomed us into her home." Bet burst into tears. "I had no idea Brian would track us down and place Alex in jeopardy or I would have never accepted her kindness."

The sheriff and Glen sat and listened to Bet's plight, and the sheriff chuckled at Bet's last statement. Bet looked at him a bit confused, and he immediately blushed with embarrassment.

"I am sorry," he said, "but you will quickly learn that once Alex Graves makes up her mind to do something that there is no force in this world strong enough to prevent her from accomplishing her goals." He smiled warmly at her. "I know Alex well enough to know she sees something in you and your daughter that touched her heart, and there was no way she could allow you to continue in that sort of life.

"Thank you for sharing that information with me. It will certainly make a lot of the investigation go more quickly. I feel obliged to say I am sorry for your loss, but in an unofficial capacity, I feel like you and your daughter are much better off." The sheriff blushed as he stood, and exited the room.

Glen followed the sheriff out and went to get fresh coffee for the two of them. When he returned, he handed a cup to Bet and said, "I am sorry your life included the abuse you and Kylie endured, but I am very pleased that your path has led you into Alex's heart. I have known and worked with her for years and I have never seen Alex as happy or inspired as she has been this last week. You and Kylie are the cause of that."

Bet covered Glen's hand with hers. "Kylie and I are truly the fortunate ones here, but I sincerely appreciate your support."

Ann poked her head back in. "Are you ready for some company?" Bet nodded her head, and the door opened and Kylie flew into her arms.

"I couldn't keep her away any longer," Sandy said. "So we thought we would stop by to see how things are going."

"Mommy, is Alex going to be okay?" Kylie asked with huge tears in her eyes.

"I sure hope so, honey. I know she is getting good care so we will have to just pray and see how things come out." Bet hugged her young child tightly.

"I brought her a card I made for her, and I have been praying for hours," Kylie innocently said as she handed Bet the card.

"Alex will love this I will make sure it is the first thing she sees when she wakes up."

"Would you mind spending the night with Ms. Sandy tonight so I can stay with Alex?" Bet asked.

"I can't stay with you?" Kylie asked.

"I'm afraid not, sweetie, at least not tonight." Tonight would be Alex's hardest fight and Bet did not want Kylie to see Alex hooked up to all kinds of equipment and wires. "I bet Ms. Sandy will bring you by in the morning, but it will probably be a day or so before Alex will be ready for visitors. I will make sure she knows you were here though."

"Okay, Mom." Kylie stood to leave with Ms. Sandy. "Be sure to tell Alex I love her, and I love you too Mommy," she added with a hug and a kiss.

"Love you too, munchkin," Bet said, struggling to show her daughter a bright smile. "Thanks Sandy."

"My pleasure, Bet, just call if there is anything I can do."

Another hour passed before the door opened again. This time a young doctor came in and introduced himself as Dr. Lee. "I know this seems like it is taking forever, but we want to make sure we have a thorough assessment of Ms. Graves's injuries. So far, we know that she has a broken left arm and leg and one nasty cut above her left eyebrow. It took eight staples to close it, but hopefully the scarring will be minimal. The biggest worry right now is the blow to the head that she took. We have run CAT scans, an MRI and have been able to rule out a skull fracture. However, there's a dangerous amount of swelling on her brain, that has me worried.

"I inserted a temporary shunt, which will help the fluid drain and hopefully relieve some of the swelling, but we will have to keep her heavily sedated for the next few days and hope that the residual effects will be minimal," he continued. "I understand you are an ICU nurse, Ms. Stewart, so I'm sure you are aware of the procedures, but if you have any questions, please don't hesitate to track me down. How she comes through tonight will tell a lot. I plan to be here all night in case there are complications, so just page me. After we receive the last CAT scan results, the staff will prepare her to move to ICU. Once she is settled in, you can begin to visit, but don't expect a response for a few days until the swelling subsides. There is a private nap room right outside of ICU and I would recommend you take advantage of it and get as much rest as you can." He smiled at Bet. "The nursing staff is very good and will wake you if anything changes," Dr. Lee promised. His pager vibrated, and he excused himself to go check the test results.

"Okay, now that he is gone, tell me what he just said in plain English," Glen requested.

"Well, the broken bones are simple breaks and not complicated fractures that would require surgery to repair," Bet explained. "The swelling on the brain is more difficult to treat and may have some long-term or even permanent damage associated with it. The shunt is a small tube that will assist the brain in flushing the excess fluids and relieve the pressure on her brain. To make sure that she doesn't have a convulsion or seizure that could cause more damage he will keep her heavily sedated in a coma state for the next few days." Bet sighed, knowing the procedures very well from experience. "There will be a ventilator to help her breathe if needed, since she will be so deeply sedated, and probably several IVs running to provide her fluids, nutrition, and medication while her body tries to heal itself."

"I want to stay until she gets taken to ICU if that's okay with you," Glen asked. "I need to see her before I leave."

"Just be prepared that she will look very different right now and there will be a great deal of swelling in her body," Bet warned, knowing that nothing she could describe would prepare him for his first visit.

"I will call Sandy and the guys to give them an update when I leave," Glen promised. "Is there anything I can do for you?"

"Could you check on Max for me?"

"I can do better than that. I will drive out to the house and pick him up. He can play with my boys for a few days. So don't worry about Max, he will be well taken care of, I promise."

"Thanks, Glen," Bet said as the door opened once more.

Ann stepped into the room and told them they were preparing Alex for the move to ICU, and they could visit in about thirty minutes. Ann said she would meet them upstairs shortly and left the room.

Bet and Glen walked outside and found the sun had already sunk below the horizon and the temperature was dropping quickly. An older man was standing outside smoking a cigarette and Bet asked him for one. The first drag rushed straight to her head, but the taste had a way of calming her nerves so she continued to smoke the strong tobacco.

Finishing her smoke, Bet dropped the butt into the ashtray and took Glen's offered arm as they walked to the elevator to travel up to the ICU floor. As promised, Ann met them at the nurses' station and introduced them to Cindy, the charge nurse who would be working with Alex. "This isn't exactly the kind of orientation we wanted you to have at the unit, but rest assured you can visit all you need," Cindy said. "I do have orders though that you are to at least lay down for a couple of hours in the nap room." Cindy grinned.

"Alex looks pretty rough right now, but if you are ready, you can go in for a short visit," Cindy told Bet and Glen.

"We're ready," Bet said, and Glen nodded his agreement.

Cindy led them to room with the lights turned down low. "I will be at the station if you need anything."

Bet and Glen stepped quietly into the room. Bet glanced at Glen to find that the color had drained from his face as he looked at Alex, tears running freely down his cheeks. Bet placed an arm around his waist for comfort as much as support as they stood beside the bed.

The staff had shaved the left side of Alex's head and Bet could see the faint line of the shunt as it disappeared behind her ear. Her face was swollen and deeply bruised. They had placed air splints on her arm and leg until the swelling subsided and they could set her up with plaster casts. There were monitors and IV bags surrounding the bed. Bet checked the readings to find everything was working fine. As promised to Kylie, Bet taped up her card on the closest monitor where Alex could see it when she again opened her eyes. Her nursing instincts kicked in temporarily masking the personal devastation she was feeling at the sight of her lover lying motionless on the bed.

Glen had had all he could bear and he leaned down to whisper to her, "Call me if anything changes or you need anything at all." He silently left the room.

Bet collapsed into the chair beside the bed overwhelmed with the ocean of emotions coursing through her. She placed her hand on top of Alex's and laid her chin on the edge of the bed. "I am so sorry to put you in the middle of this, baby," she whispered as her fingers stroked the cool, dry skin. Bet could no longer hold back the flood of tears that finally came when she was alone with Alex.

Chapter Ten

The rhythmic pulse of the ventilator droned in the darkened room and Bet found her head nodding as she searched Alex's face for any sign of response. Around midnight, Dr. Lee stepped into the room. He opened Alex's chart as he sat next to Bet. "She is responding well to the medications and the pressure on her brain is slowly dropping," he said without raising his head. "We still need to keep her under for a while yet, but I feel encouraged by her initial response."

"Are there any signs of permanent damage?"

"I can't be one hundred percent sure, but I haven't seen any indicators yet that would lead me to believe that any of her major systems will be affected." Dr. Lee placed a reassuring hand on Bet's shoulder. "It's going to be a long night, so why don't you lie down and get some rest. I will have the nurses wake you if anything changes, but I feel safe that for now she's as good as she can be."

Emotionally drained, Bet doubted sleep would come, but allowed Dr. Lee to escort her to the "nap room," which she found surprisingly comfortable. On the wall next to a coffeepot, Bet noticed a bronze plaque. She walked over to it and read the inscription under the picture of an elderly man with the same strong, dark eyes she saw when she looked into Alex's eyes. The inscription read, *Dedicated to the families of seriously ill patients in the memory of Ben Graves, loving father, friend, and mentor, who fought a gallant fight within these very walls. His battle done, he now rests with his Maker.*

Bet took comfort from the fact that Alex had spent time in this very room as her father battled the cancer that slowly took him from her. With that thought on her mind, Bet lay down on the plush bed and let thoughts of Alex surround her as she drifted off to sleep.

Cindy woke Bet three hours later to inform her that Alex had spiked a fever briefly, but she was back down to a slightly raised temperature. When Bet returned to her side, she checked monitors and found that Alex's vitals were stable and her eyes were roving side to side, indicating she was dreaming. Bet covered Alex's hand and whispered, "I hope those dreams are pleasant, darling." She felt a slight twitch in the muscles in Alex's hand. "There is so much we have yet to do and we need you in our life really badly, so don't go getting any ideas of checking out early on us. Kylie has made you a beautiful card and everyone in town is praying for you to have a fast and full recovery." She knew from her many years of experience in the ICU that even though a person may be deeply sedated they can still hear, and comprehend conversations and can remember them after the crisis is over, so she kept talking to Alex throughout the night.

At one point during the early morning, Bet noticed tears running down Alex's cheek and worried that Alex was in pain. With a soft tissue, Bet slowly dried the tears even as her own began again. "I love you, Alex Graves," Bet vowed as she caressed the right side of Alex's face.

"I do believe you got a response on that one," Cindy said as she slipped into the room. "Did you see that sly little grin?"

Bet looked back into Alex's face and sure enough, there seemed to be a grin on Alex's face. Bet squeezed Alex's hand to let her know that she had seen it and she was still at her side.

"I have to take her down to the lab for another CAT scan, so why don't you head down to the cafeteria and grab some breakfast and fresh coffee while we are gone. You need to stay strong for Alex, and you can't do that if you don't rest and eat."

"Yes, Mom," Bet teased knowing that she had uttered those same words to distraught family members on several occasions.

"Be gone then. We should be back in about an hour."

Bet was surprised how hungry she was. She loaded up a full breakfast on her tray in the cafeteria and found a quiet spot to eat and watch the sun come up. She was just about finished with her coffee when a husky voice spoke from behind her. "May I join you?"

Bet turned in her seat and found Glen standing beside her. "Of course you can, Glen."

Glen sat down across from her and reached in his pocket to pull out a pack of cigarettes. He slid them across the table to her along with a lighter. "My wife thought you might need these," he said rather shyly.

"You must be married to an angel."

"Ninety-five percent of the time she is," Glen said, leaving the remaining five percent dangling for Bet's assumptions. "How is Alex this morning?"

"She is very strong and had a good night. I got the boot when they took her down for another CAT scan."

"Were you able to get any rest?"

"I slept for a couple of hours in the nap room. Did you know that room was a memorial to Alex's dad?"

"The room, and the new section of the ICU, was purchased by Alex in appreciation of the staff's care of her dad during his battle with cancer. During the last few weeks of his life, she only left his side for a shower and a few hours of sleep each day. When Ben passed, I thought we would have to commit Alex somewhere. Her dad had been her entire world for most of her life and Alex struggled for months after his death. It's only been this last week that Alex has had the light in her eyes that she had when her dad was alive."

Bet blushed. "How about going outside with me so I can smoke one of these and then we will head back upstairs."

"Sandy called and said that Kylie didn't eat much, but she was sleeping well," Glen relayed. "Don't be surprised if they stop by sometime this morning to visit you. Sheriff Jones will also be stopping by to see you this morning. He called me last night too, and said he had discovered some things he felt he needed to share with you."

"I sure hope it's not more bad news."

"I don't think it is, Bet, I think he uncovered some answers for you and wants to give you some peace of mind is all."

Glen held the door open for Bet as they entered the hospital and walked to the elevator. As the elevator doors opened, they found Ann standing there, waiting. "Ah, just the woman I was looking for."

"Good morning," Bet and Glen said in unison.

"I just wanted to make sure you know that you have been excused from orientation for the rest of this week or until you feel you can resume."

"Thanks, Ann, that means a lot to me right now. I appreciate everything you have done," Bet said with tears in her eyes.

"Cindy said it was like having a free nurse with her patient last night and regrets you chose the day shift," Ann relayed. "She was very impressed with your knowledge and would love to have you on overnights."

"Maybe when Kylie gets a little older, or if you get in a bind and need me on a temporary basis, I could do that," Bet responded, thankful of the opportunities Ann had given her.

"Lord, don't let Cindy hear that or she may fire someone just to get you on. By the way, I passed them downstairs in X-ray and she said to tell you they would be back in about twenty minutes. Alex looks stronger already." Ann stepped past Bet to press the button to call the elevator. "I've got to run for now, but I wanted to make sure you are taking care of the important things right now." Ann placed her hand on Bet's arm.

"I had a full breakfast and a few hours of sleep last night, so I'm good to go for a while."

"That's a good start. Let me know if there is anything I can do," she said as she stepped onto the elevator.

"Will do." Bet watched Ann disappear behind the closing doors. "Is everyone up here always this nice?"

"Generally yes, it's just a good old small southern town, but when I say there is gossip to be had, this place will buzz." Glen chuckled.

Bet and Glen stepped back into the "nap room" to pour fresh coffee and to wait for Alex to return. Sheriff Jones knocked on the door and popped his head inside. "May I have a few minutes with you, Ms. Stewart?"

"Of course, Sheriff, come on in. May I get you some coffee?"

"No, ma'am, I have already downed two pots this morning."

They sat together in the small room and the sheriff shuffled his feet as he thought of a way to begin. "First off, we have a definite confirmation that the driver of the truck was indeed your husband, Ms. Stewart. He has apparently been in town searching for you since Sunday. We discovered he was staying at the small motel just on the edge of town. We entered the room he had rented and found a variety of papers, notes mostly. Apparently, your husband tracked you through your use of a gas card and a tracking program we found on his phone. We located an old bill that had notes written on it from where you gassed up just south of Montgomery and then again right after you crossed over into Georgia. I would say that it was just short of miraculous that he stumbled upon you here and was able to track your movements for several days, without any of the locals getting suspicious. From the looks of his room I would also say that he had been drinking pretty heavily since his arrival."

Bet sat in stunned silence as she listened to the sheriff describe how Brian had so easily tracked her down, knew where her damaged car was, where she was living and what vehicles she and Alex drove.

"I know you have your hands full here but I was wondering if you had the number of a family member that I could contact to make arrangements to ship his remains back home?" The sheriff immediately blanched at the word remains.

The term didn't even phase Bet. She gave him the number of Brian's parents in Alabama.

"Unless you instruct me otherwise, I will keep your whereabouts confidential and explain to them that he was involved in an automobile crash involving alcohol. No need to further muddy the man's name."

"I would greatly appreciate that, Sheriff. Brian was an abusive man at times, but he did have some redeeming qualities, and he was their only child."

"I will give them a call and our office will handle all the arrangements then," the sheriff said as he stood to leave. "I hope Alex gets well quickly."

"Thank you, Sheriff." Bet closed the door behind him.

"I thought I had been so careful. I never dreamed Brian would go to that length to track us down." Bet sat down heavily in the oversized chair.

"I think his actions say a lot," Glen said. "He was obviously obsessed with you, and would go to any length to possess you again. Had his plan not been flawed, leading to his death, who knows what may have happened to you and Kylie."

Glen's last statement sent a chill through Bet and she realized just how true his words were. Brian would not have stopped pursuing them had he survived the crash and both she and Kylie would have been in great jeopardy. Bet silently pondered Glen's words until a knock on the door startled her.

Cindy stuck her head in the door. "We're back if you are ready to visit. Hi, Glen," she said when she saw him sitting beside Bet.

"Morning, Cindy."

"Are you ready?" Bet asked him.

Glen nodded and they walked with Cindy into Alex's room. "The results from the CAT scan were amazing. Dr. Lee said he might move her into step down unit today if her progress continues," Cindy stated.

"That is excellent news." Bet watched Glen closely. Glen, stunned by Alex's condition last night, appeared relieved to see her in a better light this morning. "Would you like a few private minutes with her?" Bet asked.

"Thanks, but no. No offense, Cindy, but this place gives me the creeps." Glen was obviously uncomfortable.

"I am so hurt, Glen." Cindy punched him in the arm. "You would think the big, bad high school quarterback could handle a little ole hospital room."

"Quarterback huh?" Bet joined in the teasing.

Glen blushed. "Enough already, Cindy," he said with a grin that lit up the room.

"Oh yeah, he had a fantastic arm, but he broke the heart of all five women in our class when he chose to date a girl from another school, and then ended up marrying her. I swear the woman must be a saint to have put up with you this long."

"I'll be sure to give Dee your regards when I get home tonight." Glen smiled. "Now I guess I better get to work before Alex wakes up and sees me loafing. Call me if you need anything, Bet."

"That man is a true sweetheart, and has made a fantastic dad," Cindy said after Glen was out of earshot.

"I can tell."

"I am off in five minutes, but I will be back tonight and will find you if Alex gets moved today. Susan, your supervisor, will have Alex today and will see you get anything you need. Just let me know if you change your mind about moving to overnights." Cindy winked and was gone.

Finally alone with Alex Bet walked over to kiss her forehead and sat beside her to hold her hand. Her hand felt warm and Bet instinctively looked at the monitor to check her temperature. She was relieved to find that she was sitting right at normal. She checked the readings on the ventilator and noted they had begun to wean her off the machine, allowing her normal respirations to take over. "You are looking good, babe. Looks like you are going to move out of here today." She gently squeezed Alex's hand. "I bet you will get plastered today so you will be sporting a cast on your arm and leg for a while." Bet opened a drawer and pulled out a tube of moisturizing lotion. "I am going to lotion you down so hopefully the itching under the casts will be minimal." Bet spoke to Alex as she poured lotion into her hand and rubbed it as far under the air splints as she could without disturbing them. She carefully massaged the lotion into the rest of Alex's body, stimulating blood flow to help prevent any breakdown in her skin. "Hopefully in a day or so, I can give you a nice bed bath. That and getting your hair washed will make you feel much better." Bet massaged lotion on Alex's shoulders.

"Good morning," Susan said as she entered the room. "How is she doing this morning?"

"Very well, so it seems."

"How are you holding up?"

"I am doing fine."

"Sandy and Kylie are waiting for you in the nap room. I'll have to take Alex downstairs to get plastered soon, so why don't you take a break, go home, shower, and get some fresh clothes. It looks like Alex will be moving into step down today, so a nice pair of pajamas would probably be a welcomed relief from these hospital gowns. It's probably going to be a few hours downstairs so if you want to grab a nap too, there should be plenty of time."

"I'll make a run out to the house, but am too wired for sleep right now. Do you think Kylie can sneak in for a quick visit once Alex is in step down?"

"How old is she?"

"Oh, my goodness, she will be five tomorrow." With everything going on, she had nearly forgotten about Kylie's birthday.

"The vent will be removed and a lot of the monitors and maybe one of the IVs will be gone. Will Kylie be upset if Alex isn't awake to talk to her?"

"I don't think so if I explain things to her in advance. She is pretty mature for an almost five-year-old."

"I think we can bring her in for a short visit then. Just don't leave her too long if she seems to be upset." She caught a glimpse of the card Kylie had made for Alex. "Is that from her?"

"Yes, so please make sure it makes the move with Alex."

"Why don't you pick up some colored markers then and let Kylie put some artwork on Alex's casts. It may help to distract Kylie from the fact Alex isn't awake and will give Alex big smiles when she does wake up."

"That is a fantastic idea. I know Kylie will love it." Bet hugged Susan's neck and left to find her daughter and Sandy waiting for her.

"Hey, Mom," Kylie said when she walked in. "How's Alex doing?"

"Good morning, you two. Alex is getting much better, sweetie. So good, in fact, they are going to put the casts on her arm and leg and move her to a different room today. And you know what?"

"What Mom?"

"I have a very important project for you."

"I need you to bring your markers to the hospital and draw some art on Alex's casts so when she wakes up she will see your work and know that you were here with her."

"Can I really do that, Mom?"

"Yes, you can, sweetie. Would you mind giving us a ride out to the house so I can shower and get some clean clothes and pajamas for Alex," Bet asked Sandy.

"I'd love too."

"When we get back, Alex should be in her new room, and then we can all visit."

"Let's get to it then," Sandy said as she picked up her purse. Kylie jumped up and headed for the door, truly excited about her "project."

On the ride to the house, Bet talked to Kylie about Alex and let her know that Alex would still be asleep but could hear every word Kylie said. She also tried to prepare Kylie for the bruising on Alex's face and the swelling in her body. Kylie listened intently as Bet explained to her how important Alex's sleep was to her right now and how it would help her get well quicker. Kylie floored her with a question Bet had not been prepared to answer when she asked, "Mom, why would Daddy want to hurt Alex?"

"How did you know it was your daddy's truck?"

"I overheard someone talking about it at the hospital."

Sandy also looked at Kylie in shock that she would ask that question. "I don't know the answer to that question," Bet admitted. "I think your daddy was sick and wasn't thinking very well and Alex, unfortunately, got hurt because of it." It was the best thing she could think of to answer her young daughter.

"Is he dead?" Kylie asked.

"Yes, honey, I am afraid he is," Bet said, bracing for Kylie's response.

"So he can't hurt us anymore?"

"No, sweetie, he can't hurt anyone anymore."

Kylie was silent for the remainder of the trip until they pulled up into the yard. "Where's Max?" she asked.

"Glen came and got him last night," Bet said. "He is going to keep him for a while until Alex gets better."

"I am going to miss him," Kylie said sadly.

"Well, you know Glen lives really close to me and I bet he would love for you to come by to visit Max and meet his kids," Sandy said.

"All right," Kylie said as she opened the door and ran up on the porch, dancing with excitement.

Bet and Sandy remained seated in the car. "You handled that very well," Sandy said. "I would have never been able to answer those questions like you did."

"Thanks, Sandy, I swear that kid is much older than her five years sometimes."

"Without a doubt," she answered with a wide grin.

Chapter Eleven

When they returned to the hospital, they found Alex was now in a progressive care unit. Sandy and Kylie sat in the waiting room while Bet checked with the nurses' station to verify what room Alex was in and to check her progress. Martha introduced herself as the charge nurse and the nurse assigned to Alex's care. "Susan said you would be coming back and that I should turn my back on a little one visiting, even though it is against hospital rules," Martha told Bet. "Since you are one of us and Alex is so special, I think I can do that without a problem."

"Thanks. That would mean a lot to my daughter, Kylie, and me too."

"The vent is out and Dr. Lee dropped a couple of her monitors, but she will still be heavily medicated until sometime tomorrow when Dr. Lee begins to reduce her sedatives. Ann in Human Resources also had maintenance deliver a small rollaway that shouldn't be too uncomfortable for you. Ann said there would be no way we could convince you to go home tonight so we might as well make you comfortable." Martha grinned.

Bet laughed. "She knows me so well already. Thanks for all the information and for allowing Kylie to visit, I promise she won't be staying all day."

"From what I heard, she is so well mannered, I'm sure she wouldn't be a problem."

"She is a great kid." Bet turned to walk to Alex's room and immediately spotted Kylie's card still taped to an IV pole right next to Alex's bed. Bet bent down and kissed the top of Alex's forehead, and whispered, "Hey, sweetie, I love you. Are you ready for some company? There are a couple of folks waiting down the hall to see you so I will be right back."

Bet stepped into the waiting room and asked, "Are you gals ready?" Kylie bounced up and waited for Sandy to stand and together they walked into Alex's room. Kylie's eyes lit up when she saw her card next to Alex's bed. She asked her mom to hold her up so she could kiss Alex's cheek. "I love you, Alex," the soft, tiny voice said. "Can I could sit on the end of the bed, Mom?" Kylie reached into her school bag and pulled out her markers.

"I think so just remember to be gentle with Alex."

"I will, Mom." Kylie carefully crawled onto the bed and sat between Alex's legs.

Sandy sat beside the bed, and carefully stroked Alex's hand and spoke quietly to her as Bet wiped Alex's mouth with a damp washcloth and then coated her chapped lips with Vaseline. She sat down across the bed from Sandy and watched Kylie as she went to work on the cast covering Alex's left leg. Bet and Sandy watched as Kylie took great care in moving around on the bed as she drew a picture of a boat on a lake with a black dog and a little girl. The sun shone brightly down on the lake and the little girl was holding a fishing pole, the line dangling into the bright blue water.

Kylie moved slowly up to Alex's thigh and took great pains in drawing a raccoon that was sitting up on his back legs with a big marshmallow stuffed between his front paws. Bet couldn't help but chuckle when she saw what Kylie was drawing. "Alex is going to love that, Kylie."

"It looks just like the one in your picture," Sandy added, praising Kylie's artwork.

Kylie beamed with pride as she colored in the stripes on the raccoon's puffy tail, the tip of her tongue poking out of her mouth as she concentrated on her artwork. When she finished the raccoon, she sat back on her feet and looked at her artwork. She had covered up a good portion of the leg cast and was eyeing the cast on Alex's leg arm and a smile came across her face.

"I need your help now, Mom."

"What do you need, sweetie."

"Will you outline some letters for me on Alex's arm and prop me up on your lap so I can color them in."

"Sure I will. What did you have in mind sweetie?"

"I thought we could start down by Alex's hand about here—" Kylie pointed to her own wrist "—and you could draw the letter I for me and then a big open heart and then the word you and then Alex's name. But do it so it goes up Alex's arm so she can read it."

"Excellent idea," Sandy said to Kylie as she slowly climbed down from the bed.

"I thought Alex might like that."

"I am sure she will," Sandy agreed.

Kylie picked up her markers, and walked around to where Bet was sitting and then placed them on the bed as she climbed up into Bet's lap.

"What color do we use?" Bet asked.

"Green is her favorite color so let's use green for the words and red for a big red heart," Kylie said, certain of her plan.

Bet was astonished that Kylie knew what Alex's favorite color was and she silently wondered what other private conversations Alex and Kylie had been having. "Green it is then." Bet picked up the marker and drew a large capital I just below Alex's wrist. Then she picked up the red and outlined a large heart on Alex's forearm and then the green again to write the word you in big bold letters starting at Alex's elbow and up her arm. "How's that look?"

"That looks great, Mom. Can we do something else, Mom?"

"Sure baby, what is it?"

"Well, I know my birthday is tomorrow, but can we put it off until Alex gets better?"

Bet looked over at Sandy, who also had tears in her eyes. "I think that would make it an even more special birthday, Kylie."

"That's what I thought too, Mom." Kylie hugged her mother.

With that settled, Kylie went to work coloring in the large red heart and then the green letters of her message to Alex. Bet looked at Sandy again who shook her head with a smile. She too thought that was a very generous offer from a five-year-old. Most children her age would have been horribly disappointed to delay the receiving of gifts even one day. They watched in silence as Kylie finished coloring in the green letters and then they all sat back to admire Kylie's work.

"I couldn't have done better myself, honey," she told Kylie as she kissed her daughter on the cheek. "Alex is going to love it, when she wakes up."

"When do you think that will be?"

"It's hard to tell, Kylie, maybe tomorrow or it could be the day after. It depends on how well Alex's body heals, but I would say so far she is doing pretty well," Bet added to ease Kylie's worries.

"When she does can I stay up here at night with you?"

"Well, by then she should be moved to a regular room, so maybe we can arrange that. Alex will still need plenty of rest, but we'll see."

"That's okay, Mom. Ms. Sandy has been teaching me how to play Parcheesi, and she says I am getting really good at it."

"She has beaten me twice already," Sandy said from across the bed.

"She can be pretty ruthless at games," Bet said, tousling Kylie's hair.

"Are you ready to head into the office with Sandy?"

"I guess so, but can we come back later tonight?"

Sandy nodded her head and Bet said, "Why don't you two come back after work for a visit and we can grab some dinner downstairs afterward."

"I have a better idea," Sandy said. "Why don't Kylie and I stop by the diner and pick up some real food."

"I can't argue with that," Bet said.

"Me either, Mom," Kylie added.

"Let's plan on it then." Sandy stood to leave.

Kylie turned around in Bet's lap and hugged her. "I love you."

"I love you too, baby."

Kylie leaned over and kissed Alex's cheek. "I love you too, Alex."

Alone again with Alex, Bet said, "She loves you so much, honey. I can't wait for you to see your casts." Her voice held a note of laughter. "She took a great deal of care in getting everything just right for you." Bet moved around to the other side of the bed to take Alex's hand in her own and laid her head down on the edge of the bed.

Martha woke her twenty minutes later when she came to check Alex's vitals. "Why don't you nap for a bit this afternoon? You look like a couple of hours of sleep would do you good," Martha said. "The artwork is great, did Kylie do this?"

"Yes, she did." Bet stood and walked over to the small bed. "Would you mind waking me up later?"

"Not at all," Martha said as she lowered the lights in the room and left.

Bet laid her head on the pillow and within seconds her exhausted mind and body was asleep. Dreams broke the rhythm of her sleep, but she did manage to sleep for almost three hours before Martha woke her.

"Dr. Lee will be making his rounds soon, so I thought you might want a few minutes to wake up first," Martha said.

"Thanks, Martha." Bet walked to the sink to splash cold water on her face.

"Things are looking good for, Alex," Martha said. "Dr. Lee will probably order one more CAT scan and then if the results are good, he will begin reducing her medications."

"I sure hope so. I will rest easier once she is awake and talking again."

"I know you will, honey, but these things take time. Just remember that and don't expect too much too fast," Martha reminded her. "After all, Alex has been through quite a bit of trauma over the last twenty-four hours."

Dr. Lee knocked and entered the room. "Good afternoon, Ms. Stewart, how are you today?"

"Doing good and yourself?"

"Just fine, thanks." He seemed rather cheerful for someone who had gotten very little sleep last night.

"Looks like Alex is doing very well," he said, looking over her chart. "Let's get her down for a CAT scan, Martha, and call me when they have the results. And you, young lady," he said to Bet, "get some sleep while she's downstairs."

"Yes, sir," Bet answered and with a nod Dr. Lee was gone.

"You heard the man, hit the sack and I will wake you when we have the results."

Bet watched as Martha expertly wheeled Alex's bed out the door to take her down to the lab before she lay down. She slept soundly for almost two more hours before Martha woke her again with good news.

"Dr. Lee was pleased with the test results and has ordered to drop the medications by a third every twelve hours, so maybe you will get to see those sexy, dark eyes sooner than we think. Tomorrow, he said, you can also start some ice chips which should help to ease the horrific sore throat she is certain to have," Martha added.

Martha checked Alex's vitals and chuckled when she saw Kylie's artwork. "I sure hope I am on duty when she wakes up and sees this." Martha pointed to Kylie's raccoon. "She's going to love it."

"Things are sounding really good, Alex," Bet told her after Martha left. "Looks like you may be waking up some tomorrow. I love you so much honey." Bet's fingertips traced the top of Alex's hand.

Bet watched as tears rolled down Alex's cheek. "Are you hurting, baby?" Bet asked, knowing there would be no response as she softly wiped away the tears. "I know you can hear me, Alex, I just wish you could answer me." Alex's fingers twitched underneath Bet's and she wondered if that was Alex trying to respond to her or if the movements were involuntary contractions of the muscles that were slowly coming back to life.

The door opened quietly and Kylie crept in to stand beside her mother. "How's she doing, Mom?"

"She's much better today, honey. Hopefully by this time tomorrow she will be awake."

"That sounds very promising," Sandy said as she set a large bag of food down on the bedside table. "How are you doing?"

"I'm tired but good," Bet replied.

"I sure hope hungry is in there somewhere," Sandy said. "Kylie and I brought enough food for an army. Kylie picked out your dinner and dessert, and we picked up some sodas on the way up." Sandy set out a feast before them.

"I got you country fried steak, Mom," Kylie said. "I got chicken and dumplings so we can share if you want to."

The room was filled with the fragrance of the home-cooked meal and Bet hoped Alex could smell the aroma of the food she so loved to eat. Sandy opened a final small bag and placed three large slices of apple pie with melted cheese on their table.

"You two are angels," Bet said as she eyed the still steaming pie.

"Nope, we're just hungry." Sandy smiled. "We worked up an appetite today answering the phones with calls checking up on Alex. Kylie was busy on her computer today too," Sandy said, prompting Kylie.

Kylie pulled out two envelopes, and handed one to her mom and then set the other next to a vase of flowers delivered earlier in the day. Bet opened the envelope and pulled out a card that Kylie had made for her and tears filled her eyes. She had covered the front of the card with beautiful red roses, and when she opened it inside was a note written by Sandy and signed by Kylie. *I miss you both. Hurry home. Love, Kylie.* Kylie had drawn a big red heart under her name. As Bet read those words, Alex moaned. They watched as a crooked smile grew on her face and then Alex began to snore as she drifted back to sleep.

Together they ate the rest of their meals followed by the sumptuous dessert. Sandy noticed Bet was starting to nod off as they sat and listened to the purring of Alex's snores. She winked at Kylie and said, "I think it's time for us to head home so your mom can get some rest."

"I think you are right." Kylie giggled as she watched Bet's head snap back up when she realized she was drifting off to sleep. Kylie walked over to her mom and reached up for a hug and a kiss. "Sweet dreams, Mom. I love you," she added with an extra hug.

"We will stop by tomorrow, if that's all right," Sandy said.

"That would be great." Bet walked them to the door. "Thanks again for everything, Sandy."

"I have had a great time with Kylie. I hope even after Alex comes home that Kylie will still come to visit from time to time."

"I'd like that, Ms. Sandy," Kylie said as they walked out the door and down the hall.

Bet watched as they made it to the elevator. Kylie looked back toward the room and Bet waved and blew a kiss as she walked onto the elevator with a smile. Bet went back into the room and watched as they walked across the parking lot and disappeared into the darkness, gone for the evening. She pulled out a cigarette from the pack Glen had brought her and headed downstairs. She stopped at the gift shop to pick out a birthday card for Kylie along with a small stuffed bear before heading outside to smoke.

She was sitting on a bench outside of the emergency room, smoking, when Glen walked up. "You look really tired Bet, how are you holding up?"

"I am ready to go home and sleep in our bed, but I can't bear the thought of leaving Alex."

"I am sure she would want you to rest." Glen sat down beside Bet.

"I will get some sleep tonight."

"So how is she doing?"

"She is looking really good. Why don't you go see for yourself? Room 332," Bet said, offering Glen a few private moments with his beloved boss.

"See you in a few?"

"I think I will stretch my legs for a few minutes and maybe grab some coffee. Can I get you anything?"

"No, ma'am, I had a big dinner before I came to visit, but thanks." Glen stood and walked inside the hospital.

Bet sat outside in the cool air for a few minutes and watched an orange harvest moon rise and wished Alex were awake to share the beauty of it with her. She walked into the hospital, down to the coffee shop and poured a cup of hot dark coffee that would surely give her a boost. Taking her cup, she rode the elevator up to the small maternity ward and peeked into the nursery to see the three new babies sleeping soundly in their bassinets. It seemed like only yesterday that Kylie was that tiny, so fragile looking, but in a blink of an eye, it seemed she was growing up.

Bet walked back into the room and saw the relief on Glen's face as he held Alex's hand and spoke to her quietly. When he looked up into Bet's face, she could see the love Glen fostered for his boss. "Is she really going to be all right?" Tears were in his eyes.

"Tomorrow should reveal a lot to the doctors. The progress she has made already is a very positive sign."

"She's got us all so worried," Glen admitted. "They were finally able to get her truck up the mountain today and when the boys saw what was left of it, several of them got sick. It normally takes a lot to shake those guys, but after seeing Alex's truck I decided to let them go home for the day because they couldn't seem to concentrate." He smiled as he looked around the room. "I see several of them have sent flowers." He motioned toward the growing number of vases of fresh, cut flowers.

"A couple of them stopped by earlier in the day to check on Alex, but they didn't come in for a visit. I encouraged them to come back Saturday morning when Alex should be awake and strong enough for visitors."

"I don't think they wanted to see Alex in a vulnerable state. They look upon Alex as our rock. She has done so much for our crew when they have had personal tragedies of their own to deal with."

"She is an incredibly strong woman." Glen nodded his agreement.

"Tomorrow is going to be a short day for us. Would you mind if I stopped by after lunch?"

"Of course not, Glen," Bet said as she punched him in the arm. "You can stop in anytime you want."

"Is there anything you need?"

"I'm doing fine. Thanks for asking, though."

"Just call if there is anything."

"I promise." Glen smiled and ducked out the door.

A nurse came into the room to check Alex's vitals and to administer her medication, a dose that had reduced again. "I wouldn't be surprised if she is awake in the morning," the nurse said as she charted on Alex. "You better get a good night's rest tonight. I have a feeling tomorrow is going to be a long, emotional day."

"I don't think that will be a problem tonight."

"Rest well then and we will be quiet when we come in to do our rounds."

Bet walked over to the bed, and kissed Alex softly on the lips and whispered, "Goodnight, sweetheart, I love you." Utterly exhausted, Bet crawled between the sheets of the small rollaway and slept peacefully for hours.

Chapter Twelve

Bet woke around four to the sound of Alex moving in her bed during her slumber. She went to Alex's side and caressed her face until she quieted and drifted into a deeper sleep. Bet laid her head down on the edge of the bed and let sleep overtake her once again.

Two hours later, Bet woke up to the feel of fingers softly stroking her hair. When she raised her head, she saw Alex was awake and her eyes were smiling at her. Alex struggled to move her lips, but no words would come. Bet could see the frustration grow on Alex's face.

"Take it easy, babe. You were pretty far under and it will take some time for everything to return to normal. Your throat is going to feel like it is on fire for a while, so Dr. Lee said we could start with some ice chips this morning. Are you ready? Alex nodded her head and Bet bent down to kiss her lips. "I will be right back then," she promised as she slipped from the room to get ice chips and to let the nurses know Alex was awake.

Bet returned to the room and raised the head of the bed slowly to elevate Alex's body and prevent her from aspirating the liquid from the ice chips. Bet watched Alex for signs of discomfort as the bed lifted the upper part of Alex's body. There was no sign of pain in the huge grin Alex had on her face when her eyes came to rest on Kylie's artwork. "I guess you can see Kylie has been pretty busy." Bet lifted a spoonful of ice to Alex's lips. "Just let it melt on your tongue. Bet could read the relief on Alex's face as the ice melted and the coolness coated her raw throat and offered another bite. "Kylie has made you a private card, but I am going to wait and let her give it to you later today, if that's okay with you."

Alex nodded her head weakly and laid it back against the pillow. "Sandy has been fantastic about keeping Kylie. They have visited you several times a day along with Glen and several others."

Dr. Lee walked into the room. "I heard you were awake," he said. "I imagine you still feel like you were run over by a freight train, so take it easy today. Another day of rest and we will start getting you out of the bed some." He looked at her chart. "Has she tried to speak yet?" he asked Bet.

"Yes, but it's still too early."

"That's right, Alex," Dr. Lee said. "We had to keep you heavily sedated to prevent further injury, and the vocal cords usually are the last to come back to life. You were also ventilated, which severely irritates your throat so you will probably experience a lot of pain when you speak for the next few days. Try to take as much of the ice as you can and later today, we can start on some pudding and maybe ice cream if you can tolerate those well. I will stop back in later today, so get some rest." With a nod to Bet, he was gone.

"He's a great doctor and you have had some really fantastic nurses working with you." Bet spooned more ice into Alex's mouth. Bet continued to chat with Alex until she saw her lover slowly begin to fade. "I am going to let your bed back down so you can rest for a bit, sweetie, but I will be right here when you wake." Bet coated Alex's lips with some Vaseline and kissed her forehead. "Sweet dreams, baby," she whispered, but Alex was already out.

Bet walked downstairs and smoked a cigarette, enjoying the crispness of the early morning air on her cheeks. She grabbed a toasted bagel and a glass of fresh-squeezed orange juice before starting back upstairs, a broad smile covering her face. She silently ate her breakfast as she sat beside Alex's bed and watched her sleep, knowing that each time she woke up she would be a little stronger.

Ann stopped by to check on Alex and was pleased to hear that she had been awake earlier. She promised to stop back in later after Alex had rested. Bet watched the rise and fall of Alex's chest, and her rhythmic breathing had a hypnotic affect, making Bet's eyes grow heavy. She battled the urge to close her eyes, afraid that Alex would wake up while she was napping, but weariness overtook her and she dozed with sweet dreams for nearly an hour.

Bet had barely brushed the cobwebs from her sleepy mind when Alex began to stir again. Alex stretched slowly as her body started to wake. She watched quietly as Alex's eyes fluttered then opened, the gentle strength in those dark eyes warming Bet to the bone. "Hey, sweetie." Bet leaned over to kiss Alex on the lips then raised the head of the bed slowly, allowing Alex time to adjust to the new position. "Want some ice?" Alex nodded her head and Bet fed her ice chips to ease her burning throat. "Are these helping any?" Alex nodded and tried to clear her throat, the pain registering immediately on her face.

"I wish I could make it easier on you, baby," Bet said as she spooned more ice. Alex took the ice and crunched it between her teeth. "I bet you are hungry. Are you ready to try some pudding?" Alex's eyes sparkled at the mention of real food. Bet walked to the nurses' station to see what options there were. She returned with a small container of butterscotch pudding. She spooned out a small bite of pudding and slid it between Alex's lips.

Alex swallowed the tasty morsel painfully and then smacked her lips to cue Bet that she was ready for more. With each bite, the fire in her throat began to ease as the soft, cool pudding coated her parched throat and Alex felt her muscles start to move more freely. After she finished the container of pudding, Bet fed her several more spoons of ice to help her wash the sweetness of the pudding away. Alex moved her lips to get Bet's attention and then she hoarsely whispered, "I love you too."

Tears streamed down Bet's face as the first words Alex chose to speak rang in her ears. "Oh, Alex, I love you so much and I thought I had lost you forever." Bet's fingers stroked the side of Alex's face as her tears continued to flow. Alex reached up with her fingertips to trace Bet's tears down her cheek then outlined the delicate curves of her lips. Her fingers reached behind Bet's head, pulling her down onto her lips, kissing her slowly, her tongue tasting the sweetness of Bet's mouth for the first time in days.

Bet was breathless when the kiss ended and wanted nothing more than to crawl into bed with Alex and snuggle the day away, but she knew she needed to be honest with Alex and tell her what happened to cause her accident. Taking a deep breath, Bet sat back on her chair. "I need to talk to you about something. I don't know how much you remember about the accident, but I want you to know that you were almost killed because of me." Alex looked confused as she listened to her. "It was Brian who ran you off the road. I stupidly used a credit card and he was able to track me down with it. From what the sheriff has been able to determine, Brian stalked us for several days until he had the opportunity to attack you while you were alone. If I hadn't ended up in your driveway and gotten you involved then you wouldn't be lying here in this hospital and your life wouldn't be so disrupted," Bet said, tears dripping from her face.

Alex took Bet's hand and placed it over her heart. "It's not your fault," she hoarsely whispered. "I love you, and we are all okay and that's all that matters," Alex said as the fire returned to her throat. She opened her mouth to speak again, but her vocal cords had once again locked up. The frustration of not being able to talk, to soothe the guilt Bet was feeling took its toll on Alex, draining the energy from her tired body. Alex used her remaining strength to scoot her body over to one side and then patted the bed to invite Bet to lie down with her. Bet carefully climbed onto the bed and lay beside her, placing her head on Alex's chest as Alex circled her with a loving arm. Listening to the beat of Alex's heart, Bet cried herself to sleep.

Alex was awake and watching Bet sleep when Kylie and Sandy walked quietly through the door to her room. When Alex saw Kylie, her eyes sparkled with joy. She lifted her arm from around Bet and waved to Kylie as she walked around to take Alex's hand. "Hi, Alex," Kylie softly whispered.

Bet awoke at the sound of Kylie's voice. She sat up in the bed, disoriented for a moment until she remembered where she was. She turned to see Kylie sitting in the chair beside the bed with Sandy standing behind her. "Hey there, sweetie, how is my birthday girl today?"

"I'm doing great, Mom," Kylie said with a grin. "Ms. Sandy and I made cupcakes this morning and we brought one for you and Alex." She turned to take the small bag from Sandy.

Bet swung her legs over the side of the bed and Kylie crawled up beside her on the bed and then carefully leaned down to kiss

Alex on the cheek. "I am so glad you're awake, I have missed you," Kylie told Alex. "Max has too."

Alex swallowed hard and whispered softly, "Happy birthday, Kylie."

Kylie's eyes lit up when she heard Alex's voice, and she hugged Alex around the neck. "My wish came true," Kylie whispered as she snuggled into her neck.

Alex raised her arm and circled Kylie's tiny body, hugging her close. "Mine did too," Alex said with a wink and a grin.

Sandy sat down next to the bed and Bet asked, "Are you ready for some ice?"

Alex nodded her head. "Feels like I have been swallowing glass."

"I can only imagine. I'll be back in a few minutes then." She climbed off the bed and left the room.

"It is good to see you awake and talking some," Sandy said. "You had us all really scared for a while, boss."

"Sorry," Alex managed to say before she lost her voice again.

"Take it easy, boss, don't wear yourself out trying to talk. There will be plenty of time for catching up once you get out of here."

Alex pointed to the casts on her arm and leg and gave Kylie a big smile and thumbs-up. "Love it," she whispered painfully.

"I was hoping you would," Kylie said. "I wanted you to know I was thinking about you even though you weren't awake yet. I made you this card too." Kylie handed Alex the envelope on the bedside table.

Kylie carefully opened the card that had a picture of she and Max on the front of it and Alex opened it to read the note Kylie had so carefully dictated to Sandy and then signed herself. *We miss you and hope you can come home soon, Mom. Love, Kylie and Max.*

Alex's eyes watered when she read the word Mom. She never thought that a child would look to her as a mom and the fact that Kylie felt this way made her heart swell with love. Even though her battered body ached with every movement, Alex hugged Kylie close and kissed her on the forehead. She managed to squeak out the word "Thanks," as she held Kylie close.

Bet reentered the room carrying a pitcher full of ice chips and another carton of pudding. Kylie reached for a spoon and slowly fed Alex ice chips as she chatted about what she and Sandy had been doing all day. Alex grinned at her excited chatter.

When Alex looked over at Bet sitting at the end of the bed their eyes locked and the look of adoration in Bet's eyes made Alex's heart skip a beat. Some might think that Alex had hit a streak of bad luck with her accident, but she knew that her luck had never been better. She had a woman and child that loved her deeply and her life felt right for the first time in years. Maybe sometimes it takes a hard knock to the head for some to realize just how fortunate they really are Alex thought as she watched the twinkling in Bet's eyes.

"Do you want some pudding, Alex?" Kylie asked.

Alex shook her head and looked at the cupcake instead. "You want your cupcake?" Alex nodded her head.

Kylie looked at her mom who said, "Try a small piece and let's see how it goes down."

As instructed, Kylie pinched off a small bite and gently placed it in Alex's open mouth. Alex slowly chewed the fresh cake and moaned with pleasure at the sweetness that exploded in her mouth. "Now give her some ice. That will help her swallow," Bet told Alex's young nursemaid.

Kylie fed Alex several mouthfuls of ice and then offered her another bite of cupcake. Bet was uncertain which of them was enjoying the interaction more as half the cupcake and a large container of ice chips disappeared. She could see that Alex's energy was fading and knew she would need to rest soon. "Why don't we go downstairs and grab a bite to eat and let Alex rest for a while," Bet suggested.

Kylie kissed Alex. "I will see you tomorrow."

Alex smiled back at her and waved to Sandy as they left the room.

Bet lowered the head of the bed and Alex laid her head back on the pillow, grateful for a short period of rest. "I'll be back soon, babe," Bet said before she picked up a small bag and joined Kylie and Sandy in the hallway.

"Alex looks so much better today," Sandy said with a tone of relief in her voice.

"Yes, she does," Bet agreed as they walked toward the elevator. "I think it's safe to say she's out of the woods now." Bet added for her benefit as well as Sandy and Kylie's.

They each ordered cheeseburgers and fries in the snack bar and then slid into a booth to await their food. Bet slid the small bag across the table to Kylie and said, "I know this hasn't been a great birthday, but I wanted to give you this until we can do your birthday up right."

"Don't worry, Mom, it's been a good birthday," Kylie said as she opened the bag and pulled out the card and small stuffed bear. "Aw, he's so cute, Mom," she squealed with excitement. Kylie leaned over to kiss Bet. "What do you think we should call him?"

"I don't know, honey, do you have something in mind?"

"Gilbert." She giggled and held the bear to her chest.

"Gilbert it is then," she said to her beaming daughter.

Kylie opened the envelope and removed the card. Her eyes grew wide with excitement. "Is this me and Max?"

"Yes, it is. I thought you should have a special card with you and your new best friend."

"This is the bestest card ever," Kylie said as she showed Sandy the card. When she opened the card, she laughed. "No, he didn't sign my card."

"Yes, he did, and it barely left me room to write anything." Bet chuckled. "He's such a card hog," she exclaimed for Kylie's benefit.

Kylie burst into a fit of the giggles. "A card hog dog, that's funny, Mommy."

"Happy birthday, sweetie," Bet said as she returned Kylie's kiss.

"What do you think about going out to the house tomorrow and getting some clean clothes and then having a slumber party up here tomorrow night?" Bet asked Kylie.

Kylie broke into a big grin. "Can we, Mom? Really? What time?"

Bet looked at Sandy and asked, "Will nine be too early."

"Heaven's no. We can easily be here by nine."

"I need to make a few calls to Alabama to check on some arrangements, and take a nice long shower," Bet admitted. "Alex should be moved to a regular room tomorrow and then hopefully discharged Monday or Tuesday, if all goes well. Would you call Glen and ask if he and the crew could make a temporary ramp so I can get Alex into the house in a wheelchair?"

"I think they would love that. What do you think about having them move a bed downstairs for her also?"

"That would make more sense. It's going to be weeks before her casts come off. I'll bring you an extra key tomorrow if you can make arrangements with Glen."

"Kylie and I will give him a call tonight as soon as we get home. Can you think of anything else she may need once she comes home?"

"Not that I can think of, Sandy. I will need to ask another favor of you next week, though. I will need to go back to Alabama for about two days to take care of some business down there. Would it be possible for you to stay out at the house with Kylie and Alex, if she's discharged, one night while I am away?"

"That's no problem at all. I think Kylie and I can handle anything that might come up. You go take care of business and we will keep Alex out of trouble."

"I will let you know as soon as I can make arrangements."

The clerk called their number and Kylie helped Bet carry their food to the table. Bet asked, "Will you be okay staying up here without me for two days?"

"I'll miss you, but I go to school Monday so I will be busy." Kylie sounded too grown up for a five-year-old.

After finishing their meal, Bet walked Kylie and Sandy out to her car and saw them off. The cool night air felt good on her skin as she found a quiet spot to enjoy a smoke before heading back up to Alex's room.

Alex was awake and sitting up in the bed when Bet walked into the room. She was struggling with a cup of ice chips and a spoon. "Here let me help you with that." Bet took the cup from Alex's hand and sat on the side of the bed.

"Thanks," Alex whispered and opened her mouth. "Feels good," she said as the melted ice trickled down her fiery throat.

Even though Alex was in pain, the smile on her face warmed Bet's heart. "How would you like a bed bath tonight and a pair of pajamas?"

"Fantastic."

"Well, let's get some more ice and pudding into you and then I will give you a bath and wash your hair." Bet went down the hall and returned with a container of vanilla pudding and a small pitcher of ice water. "Vanilla tonight, darling, and Dr. Lee left orders for you to take some fluids if you can handle water." Bet poured a small cup of water.

Alex's eyes glittered at the sight of the cup of water and she eagerly reached for the cup. "Take it slow," Bet warned.

Heeding her warning, Alex took a small sip through a straw and winced as the pain in her throat erupted as she swallowed. Despite the pain, Alex took another sip, this time less painful and then asked Bet for some pudding.

The joy on Alex's face as she swallowed the pudding was like that of a child on Christmas morning. Bet spooned bite after bite into her mouth, grinning wildly at her. Alex drank more small sips of water and then asked, "I'm still hungry; may I have more pudding?"

"Of course you can, sweetie. What flavor would you prefer?"

"Butterscotch if they have it, please."

"Be right back then." She kissed Alex's lips. At the nurses' station, she plundered through the refrigerator until she found butterscotch pudding and then opened the freezer to find Popsicles. Choosing a banana flavored one she quickly walked back to Alex's room. "I hit the jackpot," Bet crowed as she stepped inside the door waving the Popsicle.

Bet removed the paper wrapping and handed the frozen treat to Alex, who eagerly stuck it into her mouth, biting off a chunk and allowing it to melt in her mouth. "Oh, my goodness, this tastes so great." Alex offered a bite to her. She took a small bite and watched as Alex slowly finished the treat and then she opened the pudding.

Alex ate heartily. Bet was relieved to see the strength returning to Alex as she finished off the pudding. As promised, Bet went into the bathroom, drew a pan of warm water, and returned with soap and a washcloth. Starting with her face, Bet slowly washed down Alex's body, careful of the bruises and scrapes as she tenderly bathed her lover. Bet lowered the head of the bed, removed the pillows, and helped Alex scoot up so her head hung slightly off the end of the bed. Bet changed the water in the pan and then began to wet Alex's hair, slowly lathering her dark curls. Bet noticed the area that the nurse shaved to allow the doctor to place the shunt had started to grow hair again, and the hair that was growing back was much lighter in color than her original dark curls. It would still be a few days, but Bet felt certain that the hair was growing back gray from the trauma to her head.

"It looks like you are going to have a light spot here," Bet said as she rinsed Alex's hair.

"What do you mean a light spot?"

"You're going to have a gray streak just over your ear, darling."

"Will you still tell me you love me every day?" Alex's question took Bet off guard.

"Of course I will, sweetie."

"Well, then it can all turn gray." Alex smiled.

Bet toweled Alex's hair dry and brushed it back on her head, the damp curls shining in the soft light. Bet poured lotion and rubbed it into Alex's feet and her right leg and hips before she slipped a pair of pajama bottoms over Alex's cast and up over her hips. She massaged lotion into Alex's shoulders and arm and then down her back and stomach with loving hands before placing her pajama top on, completing her promised bath.

"This feels so much better, Bet. Thanks for everything."

"I brought some socks too if you would like those."

"Toasty feet would be nice." Bet placed the thick, soft socks on her feet.

Bet sat beside Alex on the bed, her fingers playing in Alex's hair. "You know I like the look of a little gray in your hair. It gives you a very distinguished look."

"Distinguished, huh," Alex said with a chuckle.

"Very." Bet stroked the short gray hairs growing above her left ear. "By the way, Dr. Lee says you get real food tomorrow and are going to be moved to a private room. I hope you don't mind, but Kylie and I have scheduled a slumber party with you tomorrow night."

"That sounds like fun."

"I asked Sandy to give Glen a call to see if he and the crew could build a temporary ramp to get you into the house and she's also going to ask them to move your bed downstairs as well. I need to go out to the house in the morning to make some calls, get cleaned up and get us all some clean clothes. Sandy is going to visit with you while Kylie and I go out to the house. I need to call Brian's parents to see what arrangements have been made, and I thought I would close out the house and bring up some more of our stuff if that's okay with you."

"I just wish I could go with you. I know you have things you need to take care of that aren't going to be easy for you."

"Well, I don't plan on being gone for more than two days and Sandy has already agreed to stay out at the house with you and Kylie if you get discharged before I return. Would you mind if I took your Outback?"

"I don't think I will be doing any driving anytime soon. Of course it's all right for you to use the car. It's going to cost you, though."

"What's the price?"

"Lots of long, slow, kisses when you return." Alex pulled Bet onto the bed beside her and kissed her sweetly.

"I will gladly pay that price any day." Bet entwined her fingers with hers.

"I love you, Bet."

"I love you too, Alex."

Dr. Lee knocked on the door and walked in. "You two look cozy," he said with a smile.

"She was threatening to get out of bed earlier so I decided I better stick close just in case."

"You are looking really good, Alex. How are you feeling?"

"I still feel like I have been hit by a train, but at least my throat has eased up quite a bit." "I know that has to be a big relief. Are you keeping the pudding down okay?"

"I've had several containers today and I feel like I could eat a case of the stuff."

"Do you think you could handle a sandwich and maybe a cup of soup tonight?"

"Oh heck yeah!"

"Well, why don't we send your private nurse downstairs to pick up a grilled cheese and maybe some ice cream for you instead? It may still be too soon for hot soup on your throat."

"What flavor would you like, sweetie?"

"I'd love some chocolate, please."

"I'll try to hurry," Bet said as she climbed off the bed. "Better watch her close, Doc, she's a fast one."

"I'll keep her busy with an examination while you are gone." He grinned.

Bet walked out the door and Dr. Lee began a neurological exam on Alex, checking her reflexes and for signs of edema throughout her body. "Any problems with blurry vision, light-headedness, or nausea?" he asked as he instructed Alex to squeeze his hand.

"No, other than having a raw throat and a sore body, I feel surprisingly good."

"Any headache?"

"Off and on but it's usually just a dull throb that goes away after medication time."

"You were incredibly fortunate that your injuries were not more extensive. I am amazed by how quickly your body responded to the treatments. Frequently we have to keep patients with that type of head injury heavily sedated for up to a week while the body begins to heal itself. Try to take it easy and not push your body too hard for a few more days." He completed the exam and said, "We will move you into a private room tomorrow and maybe by Wednesday you can head home. After that, lots of rest and about six weeks more in the casts and you should be as good as new."

"That sounds great to me. Nothing personal, but I am ready to go home."

"I can imagine. We will get you home as soon as possible."

Bet returned with the sandwich and ice cream and handed half of the sandwich to Alex. "Go slow," she instructed.

"Yes, ma'am." Alex took a bite of the sandwich.

"Well, ladies, I think I will head home for the evening. I am off duty tomorrow, but will be available if anything changes. I left strict orders to call me for any changes. Both of you get some rest tonight," he said and was gone.

"This is heavenly," Alex said as she finished half the sandwich and took the remainder from Bet.

"Better get the ice cream ready," Alex said with a grin.

"Yes, ma'am," Bet said, smiling at her hungry lover. "Real food must taste really good to you right now."

"I can only think of one thing that would taste better." Alex grinned wickedly.

"My, my you must be feeling better."

"I am getting stronger with every bite."

"I am so glad to see that sparkle back in your eyes."

"That sparkle is all for you, darling," Alex said as she eyed the container of ice cream.

"Me or this ice cream," Bet teased as she offered a bite to Alex.

"All you, babe, the ice cream is a nice bonus."

"That was a very good answer."

"Do you think you could bring my sketchpad back with you tomorrow?" Alex asked.

"Of course I can."

"While you are gone maybe I can do some work on the new homes to keep my mind occupied. I am missing you already and you haven't even left yet. Will you take my cell phone with you too so you can call me and let me know how things are going?"

"Yes, and I'll get my own when I return."

"I don't see how you've survived this day and age without one," she teased.

"It was another of Brian's control issues."

Alex flinched at the reminder of the man who brought them all so much pain.

Bet leaned in and stroked her face. "I promise I will make it back as quickly as I can. I wish circumstances were different and I didn't need to go, but I really need to get closure on some issues."

"I know you do, honey, I just wish I could be there for you. Don't think I'm rushing you home either so take whatever time you need. There will be plenty of time for catching up once you get back."

Bet tossed the empty container into the trash and sat down in the chair next to Alex's bed. Covering Alex's hand with her own, Bet felt the familiar tingling she experienced every time she and Alex touched. She felt herself smiling and Alex asked, "What are you thinking about right now?"

"I was enjoying the feel of our bodies touching and thinking how important you have become in my life. I never realized how precious our time is together until the accident threatened to take you away from me." Tears filled Bet's eyes.

"Well, I have plans to grow old with you so you better get used to having me around a while yet." Alex lifted Bet's hand to her mouth and kissed it softly.

"I do love the sound of that, Ms. Graves. It's getting late, though, and you need to lie back and get some sleep." Bet stood and covered Alex's body with the sheets and blankets. "I will be right over there if you need anything." Bet pointed to the small rollaway beside Alex's bed.

"I do need one thing."

"What's that?"

Grinning, she said, "one of your long, slow, kisses to hold me until the morning."

Bet walked back to the bed and leaned, her lips pressing into Alex and then her tongue slipped inside Alex's mouth for a tender, burning kiss. When Bet broke the kiss, she could see the passion burning in Alex's eyes. "Goodnight, lover," Bet whispered softly to Alex.

"Goodnight, darling."

Chapter Thirteen

Bet awoke to the sound of breakfast trays being delivered and sat up to find Alex feasting on scrambled cheese eggs, bacon, and toast. "Morning, darling," she said as she took a bite of crispy bacon.

"Good morning, honey." Bet walked over to the side of the bed and opened Alex's juice container for her. "That looks really good. After you finish, I think I will head down to the snack bar and get some breakfast too."

"I am good here, honey, if you want to go ahead. Maybe you could sneak me up a bagel with cream cheese," Alex said rather sheepishly.

Bet chuckled and left to go to the snack bar. When she reentered the room, she found Kylie sitting up on the bed with Alex, and Sandy sitting beside the bed. Bet set her breakfast down and handed Alex the bagel. "Good morning, you two," she said to Sandy and Kylie.

"Morning, Bet," Sandy said.

"Hey, Mom," Kylie said sweetly.

"Have you two had breakfast already?"

"Yes, ma'am, we had pancakes and bacon."

"Mmm, that sounds good," Alex said.

"I promise I will fix you some next week when you get to go home," Sandy said.

"Sandy, you have yourself a deal." Alex grinned widely.

Bet opened the bagel and handed it to Alex. "You better cook a huge stack," Bet said. "All of a sudden Alex has become a bottomless pit."

"I think I can handle it. May have to buy a pig or two," she shot back with a chuckle.

"Hey, now!" Alex exclaimed. "I am not that bad yet."

"Yet," Kylie said with a laugh.

"Oh no, not you too, Kylie," Alex said with a smile.

"Yep, me too, Alex." Kylie said as she hugged Alex.

"Is there anything in particular you would like from the house, Alex?"

"My robe and a basket of food." She grinned.

"Woman, you are relentless. Kylie and I will see what we can scrounge up for you." Bet reached for her young daughter. "We will be back as soon as we can."

"Take your time, sweetie, and please remember to pick up my sketchpad so I can doodle some."

"Yes, ma'am, will do." Bet leaned in to kiss Alex on the lips. "Love you."

"I love you too," Alex replied as she watched as Bet and Kylie leave.

"You definitely have a keeper there," Sandy said as she saw the joy on Alex's face.

"No, Sandy, I have two."

"I stand corrected, boss." Sandy chuckled. "May I get you anything?"

"I could drink some more apple juice if you would get some from the nurses' station."

Sandy returned a few moments later with two cartons of juice and opened one for Alex. "Thanks, my throat is better, but the fire still returns when I talk sometimes."

"Just lay back and relax then," Sandy said. "I will be here if you need anything."

"Thanks, Sandy." Alex handed her the empty juice carton. "I think I will take a nap if you are sure you don't mind."

"No, not at all, you go ahead." Sandy pulled out a magazine. "I will just catch up on the soap opera scoop."

✝

Kylie and Bet walked out to the parking lot and it took Bet several minutes to remember where she had parked. The three days Alex had been in the hospital seemed an eternity to her. With a keen eye, Kylie spotted the Outback. "There it is, Mom." Kylie pointed toward the vehicle.

When Bet and Kylie arrived at the house, they found Glen and the crew already working on a ramp for Alex. The front yard buzzed with the sound of saws, hammers, and men as Bet and Kylie made their way over to Glen. "Wow, this looks fantastic already."

"Nothing but the best for the boss," Glen said as he smiled with pride.

"Alex will be very pleased, Glen. Will you also move her bed downstairs while you are here?"

"Sure thing. Do you want us to go ahead and do that now or wait a bit?"

"If you could do it now, I can go ahead and put fresh linens on it before I hit the shower."

"Not a problem," Glen said as he waved to one of the crew to follow him into the house. Under Bet's instruction, they moved the living room furniture back against the wall to make room for the bed. Bet stripped the linens off the bed and sent Kylie downstairs with the pillows. With the help of two more men, they were able to carry the large frame downstairs in one trip and the mattress and box springs quickly followed to complete the move. Kylie helped Bet make the bed with fresh linens then went outside to watch the construction project while Bet showered.

Sitting on the edge of the tub, Bet dialed the phone and spoke briefly with Brian's mother, who told her Monday was the memorial service. Bet was relieved that Brian's mother was cordial, fearing she would blame her for Brian's demise. Mrs. Stewart was quick to let Bet know they were aware of Brian's drinking problem and had worried for years that his life would end exactly as it did. She was glad to hear that Bet would be present for the memorial and sympathetic to the reason for Kylie's absence. Bet ended the conversation with a promise to call as soon as she got back to Mobile.

Donning faded jeans and a sweatshirt Bet began to pack for her trip to Alabama. She would leave Sunday and be back no later than Tuesday night. She hung her robe next to Alex's in the bathroom and couldn't help burying her face in the soft terry coated with Alex's scent. She breathed deeply, filling her lungs with the earthy scent of Alex's cologne.

Sighing deeply, Bet finished packing her bag, and began to pack an overnight bag for Alex with fresh pajamas, socks, and some hygiene products. She carried the two bags downstairs and placed them on the couch then returned upstairs to pack a small bag for Kylie. Placing the bag beside the two already packed, Bet checked the supplies in the kitchen and was content that there was plenty of food to hold Sandy, Kylie, and Alex until she returned. Bet went to Alex's office, located her sketchpad, and collected the drawings she had already placed on the easel, placing them in a small briefcase along with several mechanical pencils.

Bet walked out to the porch to find Kylie and Glen in deep conversation as the crew completed the ramp. "It looks good, huh, Mom?" Kylie asked.

"Fantastic! Can we fix you guys some sandwiches or drinks or something?"

"No, ma'am, we are good. Everyone is eager for Alex to come home."

"Well, I expect she will be moved into a private room today and may be discharged as early as Monday or Tuesday. I know she is anxious to get back to work, but it will be a few more weeks before she can get back onsite. She did ask me to bring her sketchpad back today so she can continue working on the new projects."

Glen laughed. "That sounds just like Alex, already working on the next project before the current one is done."

"She is really excited about these next two homes."

"She's like that. Alex gets an idea in her head and it burns inside her until she gets it down on paper."

The crew had finished packing up their equipment and waved their goodbyes, sending well wishes to Alex as they left the yard. Glen stood to leave also and Bet took his hand. "Thanks for everything, Glen," she said as she walked with him to his truck. "Nice truck." Bet looked over the new Chevy. "Guess we'll have to be doing some shopping soon to replace Alex's old truck."

"Let me handle that," Glen said. "My brother-in-law works at a nearby dealership and will cut us a good deal. Just pick out the color and I will do the rest."

"Green," Kylie said. "It's Alex's favorite color," she reminded them.

"Green it is then," Glen said. "Give me a few days and I should have something worked out." He climbed in behind the wheel.

"That sounds great to me." Bet took Kylie's hand and walked back to the house. They walked up the ramp and onto the porch. "You want to help me carry the bags out to the car, sweetie?"

"Yes, ma'am." Kylie ran ahead into the house.

Bet walked slowly into the house that had become her home. She longed for Alex and Max to be sitting quietly in front of the fireplace. The house seemed eerily quiet without them and she hoped that once she returned from Alabama, life would settle down and the house would fill again with Max's soft voice and Alex's warmth.

Kylie watched her mom look around the quiet house and said, "Too quiet, isn't it?" Kylie had a knack for reading her mother's thoughts, which at times scared Bet, but at that moment, it was comforting to know that Kylie missed them too.

"I'll be glad when everyone is home again," Bet said as she hugged her daughter.

"Me too, Mom," Kylie said and hugged Bet close.

"Run upstairs and get your backpack. Don't forget you will be starting school Monday," Bet said as Kylie raced upstairs.

Kylie bounced back down the stairs with the backpack securely draped across her shoulders. "All set," she said with a huge grin. Kylie grabbed a bag from the couch and headed toward the door. Laughing, Bet picked up the remainder of the bags and followed her daughter out the door.

When they returned to the hospital, they went to the desk and were informed that Alex had been moved into a private room. When they walked into the new room, they found Alex asleep and Sandy dozing over her soap opera magazine. Sandy's head snapped up when she heard the door close. She smiled at Bet and Kylie. "Guess I slipped off for a second."

"That's easy to do around here," Bet said with a smile. "The quiet creeps in around you and before you realize it your eyes are closed and an hour has slipped away."

"Yes it does." Sandy smiled as she watched Kylie crawl up onto the bed quietly.

Alex must have sensed their presence in the room and when her eyes fluttered open she saw the three of them watching her. "Have I grown three heads or something?"

"No, Alex," Kylie said, "we were just watching you sleep."

"Well, come here and give me a hug then, munchkin."

Kylie crawled up beside Alex and gave her a soft hug then remained snuggled into her body. "Mom says we can have a slumber party tonight," Kylie said with a giggle.

"Oh, that sounds like a lot of fun. Who's bringing the popcorn and snacks?"

"I think we can find whatever we need downstairs," Bet said with a wink to Kylie.

"I guess I will head on out to the office then unless there is anything else you need," Sandy said.

"You have been a tremendous help already. Just tell the boys I said hello, and make sure Glen cracks the whip now and then."

"You got it, boss," Sandy said with a warm smile. "Kylie, do you want to stay here or go to the office with me?"

Kylie looked at her mom who nodded. "Go ahead if you want, honey, we certainly aren't going anywhere." Bet saw the excitement in her daughter's eyes.

"Are you sure?" Kylie asked Alex.

"Absolutely, I see your mom has brought my sketchpad so I may try to do some drawing and then probably nap the afternoon away."

Kylie kissed Alex on the cheek. "I love you, Alex."

"I love you too, Kylie," Alex replied, a twinkle of delight burning in her eyes.

Bet bent down and hugged Kylie. "Love you, munchkin, see you later today."

"Okay, Mom, love you too," she answered as she and Sandy walked to the door.

Bet bent down and kissed Alex warmly on the lips, and sat next to her on the bed. "How are you feeling?"

"Much better, and good enough to do some work," she said as she looked at the sketchpad at the end of the bed.

"Fair enough. I'm going to go down to the gift shop and snack bar then and see what kind of snacks they have for our slumber party." She handed Alex the pad and placed a few of her drafting pencils on the bedside table.

"Is there anything in particular you want?"

"Something chocolate would be very nice."

"I think I can handle that request pretty easily. Is there anything else?"

"Nope, that and some popcorn will suit me just fine." Alex took up a pencil and turned to the page she had been working on earlier in the week.

"I will be right back," Bet said as she left the room.

Alex propped the pad on her lap and began to sketch out the images in her head, slowly bringing to life the first of the two homes she had planned for the next project. Glen and the crew should be getting close to finishing the current home. She thought she would give them a week off to rest while a contractor cleared a road up to each of the lots. She would work with Glen to order the materials and lay out the foundation and hopefully they would be well into the framing by the time Alex was able to visit the site to monitor their progress.

Downstairs, Bet picked out their slumber party supplies and then found a paperback that looked interesting. She would kick back and do some reading while Alex sketched for a bit and then maybe lay down with her for a short nap later in the afternoon. When she walked into the room, Alex was intent on the sketchpad and didn't hear her return until Bet sat down next to her.

"Welcome back, honey."

"Miss me?"

"Every moment you're away." Alex noticed the paperback in Bet's hand and asked, "You going to do some reading today?"

"I thought I would read for a while to give you time to sketch and then maybe after lunch we can take a nap together."

"That sounds like an excellent plan." Alex returned to the pad and began drawing again.

Bet watched her sketch for a few more minutes and then cracked open her book. She was several chapters deep into it when she heard the clanging of the lunch carts coming down the hallway. She looked up when the aide entered the room and placed the tray next to Alex.

"You are looking much better today, Alex," the young woman said with a grin.

"Thanks, Karen, I feel like I just might make it after all," Alex said with a grin. "So what did you bring me today?"

"You're lucky, today is fried chicken day. It's paired with mashed potatoes, gravy, green beans, and a slice of peach pie."

"That does sound good."

"They serve it down in the cafeteria too if you want to go down and get a lunch," she said to Bet. "This is one of the best meals you will get while you are in here."

Bet helped Alex put her drawing materials away and set her tray up for her. "Mmm, I think I will go downstairs for one of these."

"Go ahead, sweetie, I will wait on you."

"Oh, no you don't, Alex. You need to eat this while it's still hot. It won't take me but just a few minutes so you go ahead and get started."

"Yes, ma'am." Alex took the fork and began attacking the meal.

"Be right back, hon."

Bet stepped outside for a quick smoke before entering the cafeteria to order her meal. The day was quickly fading away. She glanced at the trees with their leaves starting to change into the brilliant colors of fall. With autumn on the way the daylight was beginning to get shorter and shorter each day. She pressed out her smoke, and in just a few minutes she was on her way to the room, lunch in hand and a large glass of sweet tea.

Once back in the room, she noticed Alex struggling one handed with the chicken breast. "Hang on, let me get that for you." Bet pulled the moist white meat off the bone for Alex. "I thought we might trade desserts too." She picked up her bag and pulled out a huge slice of coconut cream pie.

Alex's eyes lit up when she saw the slice of pie Bet dangled in front of her face. "Are you sure you want to trade that?" Alex said, her mouth watering already.

"Yes I am, darling." She placed the pie on the small table and began to eat her lunch.

They finished eating and Bet cleared the meal from the bedside table. "Do you want to sketch a while longer before we nap?"

"Another hour tops and then I think I will have done enough for one day," Alex said, taking the pad in hand.

"Very well then," Bet said and settled back into the chair with her book.

After nearly an hour had passed, Bet could feel her head begin to nod. She looked over at Alex in the bed and saw that she too was fading fast. Laying her book down, she stretched and walked over to the bed. "I think it's time we took that nap," she said and received no argument from Alex.

Bet placed the sketchpad and drawing supplies beside the bed and then carefully crawled in beside Alex. Alex wrapped her right arm around Bet's shoulders as she snuggled in close to her body. The warmth of Alex's body welcomed Bet, and within minutes, both women were sound asleep.

Alex was the first to stir when Kylie entered the room. She smiled brightly at Alex. Alex gently stroked Bet's arm and whispered, "Time to wake up, sleepyhead, our party has arrived."

Bet slowly stirred and sat up as Kylie joined them on the bed. "Hey, sweetie," Bet said as Kylie kissed both of them.

Kylie looked over to Sandy. "May I tell them the news, Miss Sandy?"

"Sure thing, Kylie, go right ahead." Alex and Bet sat in anticipation of her news.

"A man came by the office today and said he wanted to buy the house Glen and the boys are just about finished with," Kylie said with a huge grin, proud of delivering such good news.

"Really?" Alex asked. "That is good news indeed, Kylie."

"Mark from the real estate office dropped by to say a couple of professional ladies from Atlanta had inquired about the home and were prepared to make a substantial offering on the place," Sandy added to Kylie's message. "Mark said to name your price and give him a call when you are ready to deal."

"That's fantastic news! If you will run the final budget figures for me on Monday, I will give him a call, hopefully from home."

"Home, that sounds so good," Kylie said, once again amazing the three adults with her aged wisdom.

"Yes, it does, Kylie, and I can't wait to get there," Alex added.

"Is there any news on a discharge yet?" Sandy asked.

"Nothing official, but I am praying for early Monday," Alex said.

"Well, I will drop by the office tomorrow and run those figures for you and then be here bright and early to take you home and Kylie to school. If there is anything you need this weekend, just give me a call." Sandy stood to leave.

"Thank you for everything you have done for us, Sandy," Bet said with tears in her eyes. "I don't know what we would have done without you, Glen, and the boys."

"That's what family is for." Sandy hugged Alex and Bet and gave special kiss to Kylie.

"Are you hungry, munchkin?" Bet asked.

"I'm starving, Mom."

"Why don't you and I go down for some burgers and we will get this party started," she said with a grin. "Alex can check out the movie schedule while we are gone and we'll settle in for the night. Fries or onion rings?" she asked Alex.

"Onion rings," Alex said, her eyes alight with anticipation as Bet and Kylie headed down to the snack bar.

Chapter Fourteen

†

As the door closed behind Bet and Kylie, Alex felt a sharp pain stab behind her left ear, and her vision went blurry, the picture on the TV fading as a wave of nausea overtook Alex. Several minutes passed before the pain subsided and her stomach quit lurching, leaving Alex feeling a knot in her midsection. A thin layer of perspiration had broken out across her forehead, and Alex struggled to gain control over her body before Bet and Kylie returned to the room.

†

Kylie placed their orders and paid for their meals as Bet sat at a booth and waited for her daughter to return. "Good job, sweetie," Bet said as she took the change Kylie, who was wearing a huge smile, and slipped it into her pocket.

Kylie crawled up in Bet's lap for a hug. "I have really missed you and Alex," Kylie said with a look of concern on her face.

"We have missed you too, honey, and hopefully Alex will be home soon so we can all be together again." Bet tried to reassure her daughter that all was okay.

"I know, Mom. I'm glad Alex said it was okay for me to spend the weekend up here with you two, though. Ms. Sandy is great and I have so much fun with her, but she's just not you."

"That is so sweet of you to say, honey." Bet hugged her daughter tightly, tears threatening to run down her cheeks. She held Kylie close for several minutes until the woman behind the counter shouted out their number to notify them that their food was ready.

Entering Alex's room Bet immediately noticed how pale Alex had become. Then she saw the thin sheen of perspiration covering her face. "Are you feeling all right, Alex?" Bet asked with a look of concern on her face.

"Just feeling a little queasy is all. Nothing that a good meal won't fix I am sure," she said as Kylie climbed up on the bed with her and handed her a cup full of iced tea.

Bet placed the bags of food on the bedside table and reached over to feel Alex's forehead. "Well, you don't feel like you are running a temp." A growing uneasiness settled in the pit of Bet's stomach.

"I am fine, worrywart," Alex teased and a little color seemed to return to her face. "Just feed me already, will you. I am dying here smelling those onion rings and you want to make small talk."

"Better feed her quick, Mom, before she starts to get ornery," Kylie teased.

"Ornery," Alex said. "Where on earth did you pick up that word I wonder? Maybe hanging around a bunch of construction workers isn't such a good idea."

"Oh Alex, Mom used to get ornery all the time."

"Hey now, don't go telling all my bad traits," Bet said as she opened a bag of onion rings and placed them on the table in front of Alex. "Kylie, can you open some ketchup for your partner in crime there?"

"Sure thing, Mom." She grinned then began tearing open packets of ketchup and pouring them into a pile on top of the wax paper.

"Thanks, sweetie." Bet cut the hamburgers into smaller portions, making them easier for Kylie and Alex to eat.

"Sure smells good, and tastes good too." Alex dipped a ring into the ketchup and popped it into her mouth. Her stomach still felt nauseous, but she was determined not to worry Bet or Kylie, hoping it would pass soon.

Bet sat back in her chair and watched as Kylie and Alex ate. Something just didn't look right with Alex, but she couldn't put a finger on what it was. She took a bite of her burger and watched as the two she loved so deeply shared their meal. Smiling to herself, she sent up a silent prayer of thanks for having Kylie and Alex in her life.

After dinner, Kylie snuggled under Alex's right arm and Bet propped her feet up on the end of the bed as they watched the movie *Ice Age*. Bet disappeared near the end of the movie to sneak down to the nurses' lounge to pop popcorn and purchase sodas for them to share.

"Yummy, Mom," Kylie said when Bet returned and took a bowl of popcorn and placed it in Alex's lap and began to feed Alex.

"Very yummy, indeed," Alex said as she munched on the salty, buttered treat Kylie was busy feeding her.

Bet scrolled through the TV listings until she found another movie, portioned out another large bowl of popcorn, and opened a bag of M&M's before she settled back into the recliner by the bed. Kylie was having a blast feeding the candy and popcorn to Alex and they paid little attention to the movie. Bet watched with a growing discomfort as Kylie and Alex finished their snacks and finally settled down to watch the rest of the movie.

Within an hour, both had drifted off to sleep, Kylie tucked comfortably under Alex's arm, smiles playing on their faces. It was still early yet, so Bet decided to turn the TV off and do some reading before retiring for the evening. Within the next hour, she found her head nodding and she was rereading the same paragraph numerous times, so she gave up the fight. She quietly covered Kylie with a blanket and then slipped between the sheets of the visitor's bed.

Bet's sleep was restless as dreams invaded her sleep. Dreams that terrified her as they showed Alex relapsing into a coma, this time not drug induced, and she feared for her lover's life. Bet tossed and turned in the small bed as the horror of her dreams came to life.

Alex's arms flailed wildly, waking Kylie. At first, Kylie thought Alex was dreaming and tried to wake her. She patted Alex's cheeks imploring her to wake, but Alex failed to respond. Kylie's eyes filled with panic as she screamed for her mother's help. "Mommy, something's wrong with Alex," she cried. Tears were streaming down her cheeks as she looked at Alex's convulsing body.

Bet shot straight up out of the bed, recognizing Alex was having a grand mal seizure. She grabbed Kylie, swinging her off the bed in one swift motion as her nursing instincts kicked into high gear. "Run get the nurse," Bet said to Kylie, more to get her young daughter out of the room than anything. Bet pressed the call button and told the nurse on duty she needed her STAT as she tried to keep Alex's convulsing body safe from entanglement in the bed rails and causing further damage to her broken body.

A team of nurses entered the room while one of the younger nurses stayed outside with Kylie. Linda, the charge nurse, assessed the situation quickly, instructing one of the other nurses to page Dr. Lee, who would still be making rounds, then left the room, returning with a syringe. Linda quickly pushed the Ativan injection through Alex's IV, and within seconds the violent thrashing of her body began to subside.

Bet stepped outside the room to check on Kylie and found tears streaming down Kylie's face. Bet took the small child in her arms and held her close as she smoothed her daughter's soft hair. "She will be all right," Bet softly whispered as much for her own benefit as Kylie's.

Dr. Lee came rushing down the hall and within minutes had the nurses were rolling Alex's bed down to the CAT scan lab. When Dr. Lee came from the room he stopped to update Bet. "I think Alex's seizure was caused by a blockage in the shunt we installed, but we will not know for certain until we get the CAT scan results," he said. "Hopefully it will be a blockage that we can remove fairly easily."

Bet steeled herself for the worst and asked, "What if it isn't a blockage, Dr. Lee?"

"Well, there could have been more significant neurological damage done than what we realized, but I don't want you jumping to conclusions until we have more information. Why don't you and Kylie wait in her room and as soon as I know anything I will be back to talk with you."

Bet nodded her head and led Kylie back into the room. She sat back in the oversized recliner and held Kylie close as tears continued to fall. "Alex will be just fine, Kylie," Bet promised as she rocked them in the chair. Slowly, Kylie's tears began to fade and Bet looked down to find that she had cried herself to sleep. She stood and carefully placed Kylie on the small bed and pulled the covers over her emotionally drained body and then slipped from the room to pour a cup of strong coffee as she settled in for the painfully long wait.

Twenty minutes later, Linda stuck her head into the room and whispered, "They have Alex in the CAT scan now so it should only be an hour or so."

Bet whispered "Thank you" to Linda and sat back in the chair praying that Alex would indeed be all right. The seconds on the clock ticked away slowly and echoed in the stillness of the quiet room like the banging of a drum. Each minute seemed an eternity and Bet could feel the vise grip of anxiety tighten in her chest as her ears strained for the sound of Dr. Lee's approach.

Chapter Fifteen

Thirty minutes passed with no sound in the room other than the monotonous ticking of the clock and the slow, deep breathing of Kylie's slumber. Bet could feel her heart pounding in her chest, the blood coursing through her veins as her imagination ran wilder with each passing moment. She and Kylie had both found the love they had searched for and she feared they would be shattered beyond repair if anything were to happen to Alex. Pushing these thoughts to the back of her mind, Bet shifted her thoughts to the strength of her memories made with Alex in the short life of their relationship. She focused on Alex's laughter and the smile she wore when she played with Kylie and Max and the genuine love she shared with them. The tears that had welled up in her eyes spilled over and she covered her face with her hands to hide the sobs from the sleeping Kylie.

✝

Down in the CAT scan lab, Alex's body was rolled into the machine. She lay motionless, exhausted from the intense convulsions and suffering the sedating effects of the injection. The machine hummed to life as it began recording images of Alex's brain. Dr. Lee waited anxiously for the test to be completed. He had not seen any indicators of any further problems and the sudden seizure left him puzzled and worried. Alex's recuperation had progressed very smoothly and he felt blindsided by this recent development.

The technician nodded to Dr. Lee and several monitors lit up with the images of Alex's brain. His first instinct was correct. The shunt he had inserted to help reduce the swelling on her brain had indeed become blocked with a very small blood clot. Fortunately, the clot was near the draining end of the shunt and with a bit of luck Dr. Lee felt he could clear the blockage and prevent any further damage.

He wrote orders that Alex be prepped for the procedure then went upstairs to talk with Bet.

"It's just as I thought, Bet. The shunt is blocked with a small blood clot, and the combination of toxins placed pressure on Alex's neurological system and triggered the seizure. I feel that if we can quickly remove the blockage, the shunt will continue to drain the toxins and Alex will continue to progress. I will want to keep her in the hospital a while longer until we can be certain the pressure on her brain is completely removed and there is no further threat of clotting."

"So what is the next course of action?"

"Alex is being prepped as we speak. I will clamp off the shunt and remove the clot and hopefully be able to drain some more of the toxins off her brain. It should take about forty-five minutes to complete the procedure and I want to put her back in ICU for precautionary measures."

"I'll call Sandy then and ask her to come pick Kylie up for the night and will wait for you in ICU."

"I will let you know how the procedure went as soon as I finish up," Dr. Lee promised.

Bet took a deep breath and reached for the phone. She dialed Sandy's number with trembling fingers trembling.

Sandy answered the phone on the second ring. "Sandy, I apologize for calling so late, but there has been a problem," Bet said, her voice cracking with emotion.

"What's wrong?"

"Alex's shunt became blocked tonight and she had a seizure. Dr. Lee said a small blood clot had clogged the drain tube and the buildup of toxins caused the seizure. He is preparing Alex for a procedure where he will go in and unclog the tube and hopefully be able to drain some of the fluid off her brain to relieve the pressure," Bet managed to say in one long breath.

"Say no more, sweetie, I will be there in fifteen minutes. How is Kylie?"

"She was sleeping with Alex when the seizure began and was terrified by the ordeal, but she is resting well at the moment. I would appreciate it if you could take her to your place tonight and keep her until Alex stabilizes again."

"That won't be any problem at all. I was thinking just this afternoon how lonesome it was without Kylie around. Just let me change clothes and I will be right there."

"Thank you so much, Sandy," Bet said once again with tears in her voice.

"Try to relax, Bet. You know Alex is a strong woman, and because of you and Kylie she has so much to fight for in her life. I will be there shortly." Sandy hung up the phone.

The dam holding back Bet's tears burst and she collapsed. Bet allowed the tears to flow for several minutes and then fought to control her emotions. She needed to be strong for Kylie as she explained what was going on with Alex.

Bet wiped her eyes and splashed her face with cool water before leaving the nurses' lounge to return to the hospital room where her daughter was sleeping fitfully. Bet carefully sat on the edge of the bed and watched as Kylie grimaced in her sleep. Her body was curled tightly in a fetal ball, giving away the trauma the young child felt. She could imagine Kylie's dreams, probably filled with images of Alex's body as she convulsed on the bed and struggled to breathe. Bet could only imagine the horror Kylie felt waking to that scene at five years old. She softly stroked her daughter's tear-stained cheek.

"Kylie, sweetie," Bet softly whispered to her daughter. "I need you to wake up for me, baby." Bet added another soft stroke on her cheek.

Kylie slowly stirred and turned onto her back before she opened her sleepy eyes to find her mom sitting beside her. Kylie smiled briefly then her smile faded into a look of panic as she suddenly remembered the events that had taken place. Kylie flew up from the bed and hugged Bet tightly. "I love you, Mommy," Kylie said with a quivering voice.

"I love you too, my sweet daughter," Bet said as she held her close.

"How is Alex?" Kylie asked as she sat back in Bet's lap.

"Alex was very, very sick for a while, baby, but she is doing much better now."

"What happened to her, Mommy?"

"The tube Dr. Lee placed in Alex's head got clogged and the fluid that was supposed to be draining off her brain got stuck. When it couldn't leave Alex's body like it was supposed to, it put pressure on her brain and caused her to have the seizure that woke you up."

"That was very scary," Kylie said with a look of fear still in her eyes.

"I know it was, baby, but you did a very good job in getting help for Alex."

Bet's statement seemed to ease Kylie's worry and she could feel her body start to relax. "Dr. Lee had to take her in to clear the tube, but he felt sure she would be much better after that. Alex will be back in ICU tonight to be monitored closely and she may be in the hospital a few more days than expected, but Dr. Lee wants to make sure she doesn't have any more problems."

"So you really think Alex will be okay, Mommy?"

"Yes, baby, I do. You know how strong Alex is and how badly she wants to go home. It will just be a few days later than planned. I have called Miss Sandy and asked her to watch you for a few more days so she is on her way to pick you up, sweetie."

Kylie began to say something and then thought better of it, knowing that while Alex was in ICU she couldn't see her. "Okay, Mom." Kylie hugged her mother tight. "Just be sure to tell Alex that I love her when she wakes up, please."

"You have my promise, honey." Bet kissed her daughter's forehead.

Sandy tapped lightly on the door and walked in.

"Thank you for coming so quickly, Sandy," Bet said. "Dr. Lee is performing the procedure now and will let me know as soon as he is finished."

"If you will call me, I will go ahead and take Kylie to the house and get her all tucked in," Sandy said with a quick hug to Kylie.

"I promise," Bet said. She walked with them to the elevator and hugged Kylie and Sandy before making her way to the ICU unit.

The nurses were busy setting up monitors, in preparation for Alex's return to the unit. "Is there anything I can do to help out?"

"You can sit back and relax," Susan instructed her. "Tonight has been a busy night for you already and you need to relax a bit before she arrives."

Bet felt exhaustion setting in. She accepted a blanket and pillow from Susan and crept into the recliner sitting in the vacant ICU cubicle. "You will probably hear us coming, but if you don't I will wake you when she arrives," Susan promised.

Settling back into the chair, Bet snuggled into the warm blanket and allowed her tired eyes to close. She dozed for thirty minutes until the metal clattering of the surgical gurney woke her as it journeyed down the hall, followed closely by Dr. Lee.

Bet watched as Alex was pushed into the room and was relieved to see a healthy color in her cheeks.

"We were able to remove the clot safely and drained nearly a pint of fluid during the procedure," Dr. Lee said. "Another day or two in ICU for closer monitoring and we can consider moving her back into a private room again."

"That's excellent news. Do you think there was any permanent damage done during the seizure?"

"There was no evidence of it in the CAT scan and hopefully now that the shunt is functioning properly again the last of the fluid will drain and she can get on with her recuperation. We will do a few more CAT scans over the next few days to make sure there are no further clots and when her pressure returns to normal we can remove the shunt completely."

"So you feel like the seizure was a one-time event?"

"Most definitely. The buildup of toxins was fairly extreme and triggered the body's natural response to a rapid change in electrical stimulation in the brain. Now that she is draining once again, I feel the chance of additional seizures is very minimal. She will probably sleep through the rest of the night so I would suggest you do the same. Remind Alex when she awakens to let the nurses know immediately if she has any pain so we can prevent further problems."

"I will definitely make sure of that," Bet said as Dr. Lee reached for her hand.

"Get some rest tonight. I have a feeling Alex will be wide open when she wakes up again and we will need your help to ensure she relaxes and takes it easy for a few more days."

"I will be sure to eat my Wheaties in the morning then," Bet teased. With a soft chuckle, Dr. Lee left the room.

Susan had finished setting up all the monitors and turned to her. "You know the drill, get some rest, and let us know if there is anything we can get for you. I will try to be as quiet as possible when I perform my checks and will wake you if for some reason Alex wakes before morning."

Bet walked with Susan back to the nurses' station and quickly called Sandy to give her the promised update and to check on Kylie. Sandy let her know that Kylie was once again asleep and would look forward to a call in the morning hopefully after Alex had awakened.

Bet slipped back inside Alex's room. She moved her chair as close to the bed as possible, and placed her hand over Alex's hand. Her skin felt warm and dry and her facial features were relaxed as she slept deeply. Bet once again curled up into the chair and allowed her body to relax again into a restful sleep of her own.

Chapter Sixteen

The night passed quietly and quickly. Bet awoke to Alex's hand twitching under hers as she began to stir. Bet sat patiently and watched Alex's eyes flutter and finally open, trying to focus through the blur of drugs from the previous night. When she did focus, it was on Bet's concerned face.

"What's wrong, baby?" Alex asked as she looked up into Bet's face.

"You had a bit of a rough night last night, sweetie, and they had to bring you back up to ICU," Bet explained.

"Rough night what happened? The last thing I remember was falling asleep with Kylie tucked under my arm," Alex said with a look of confusion on her face.

"The shunt drain got clogged and triggered a seizure. Dr. Lee had to go back in and clear the fluid off of your brain," Bet said as calmly as she could.

"A seizure, oh my God, did I hurt Kylie?" She tried to sit up quickly.

Bet jumped up and eased Alex back onto the bed. "No, darling, you didn't. You gave her quite a scare, but she is all right and is staying with Sandy again."

Alex's eyes were beginning to focus better and she could see the monitors and equipment surrounding the bed. The heart monitor peaked wildly as Alex struggled with the news Bet had just relayed to her. "Is everything okay now?"

"Dr. Lee wants you to stay in ICU for a few days of monitoring, just as a precaution, to closely watch the shunt before he takes you back to a private room, but he does not foresee any additional problems. But you must relax and let the nursing staff know immediately if you have any pain at all."

Bet was comforted by the smile that crossed Alex's face when she softly replied, "Yes ma'am."

"Please tell me I don't have to start back on a liquid diet though?" Alex implored.

"I don't think so." Bet chuckled. "If you are hungry that's a good sign you are back to normal."

"I'm starved. I feel like it has been days since I have eaten even though I know it hasn't. It is Sunday after all isn't it?"

"Yes, it's Sunday morning, darling. If you will give me a minute I will go check your diet order. If Dr. Lee hasn't placed any restrictions on you I will go downstairs and get you some breakfast."

Susan was still on duty and checked Alex's chart. "Nope she can have anything she wants to eat."

"No limitations, honey, so what would you like?" Bet said, returning to the room.

"A couple pounds of bacon, French toast, and scrambled eggs," Alex said with a grin.

Bet laughed. "I will be back in a couple of hours then." She bent down to kiss Alex softly on the lips.

"Hurry back," Alex said, smiling.

Bet went downstairs to the cafeteria, and ordered up a large breakfast for Alex and then found a pay phone to call Sandy. When she answered the phone Bet said, "She is wide awake and starving."

Sandy couldn't help but laugh. "Well, that is certainly good news. How are you feeling this morning?"

"Very relieved."

"I know she gave us all a good scare last night."

"Yes, she did indeed."

"Would you feel better about leaving today if I promised to ask Glen to watch Kylie at night while I stayed with Alex?" Sandy asked.

"Oh, my goodness, I hadn't even thought about the trip to Alabama. I know she is stable enough this morning, but I don't want to leave her side."

"Well, she's in the best place should could be if she would have any further trouble. I know Alex would want you to go now to take care of the business you need to. And better now while she is under a watchful eye than once she gets home," Sandy added.

"You have a good point, Sandy. We will see how things go this morning and I will call you again at lunchtime." Bet ended the call just as the food arrived on the counter.

"Thanks," Bet said as she picked up the bags and headed back into ICU.

"Ah, there you are. I was beginning to get worried about you," Alex teased as she re-entered the room.

Bet watched Alex devour the food she had placed in front of her and was pleased with the strength she demonstrated. Alex caught Bet's stare and asked, "What's on your mind, babe?"

"I was just thinking of how adorable you look," Bet replied, not quite truthful, but close enough.

"I feel good, much better after that breakfast," Alex said to ease Bet's obvious worries.

"I am glad you enjoyed it." Bet sat back on her chair.

"So what time are you planning on leaving for Alabama today?"

"I am not sure if I am going."

"Yes, you are, dear. I will be fine, and I am sure these nice nurses will take very good care of me. You need to go ahead with your trip and take care of your business."

"I just don't want to leave you."

"I don't want you to go either but there are things that need your attention. Like I said, I am in very good hands here and I promise not to run any marathons while you are gone."

Bet chuckled at Alex's comment. "If I leave at lunchtime I can be there just after nine or so and can hopefully wrap up things by early Tuesday."

"I should be back in a private room by then, so please go ahead and get the trip over."

"Yes, dear," Bet teased. "Do you want Sandy to sit up here at night with you while Kylie stays with Glen?"

"No, let Kylie stay with Sandy. I will be fine, I promise."

"You must also promise to notify the nurses if you have any signs of pain."

"I promise," Alex said solemnly.

"Fine, I will leave today and get back as quickly as I can then," Bet said eager to get this trip over.

"Please don't get me wrong, I do love your company, but I wish you would leave earlier so you aren't so late getting there."

"Are you kicking me out?"

"No, but I would rest easier knowing that you are off the road before nightfall."

"All right, but not for another hour or so." Bet covered Alex's hand with her own.

The next hour flew by and Alex finally had to prompt Bet to leave. "You need to get moving, darling," she said and pulled Bet down for a soft, tender kiss.

Bet moaned lightly as Alex's lips brushed hers. "There are lots more of those waiting for you when you get back."

Bet said goodbye and turned away from Alex with tears in her eyes. She picked up her bag and Kylie's backpack and hurried from the ICU unit. She drove the short distance to Sandy's house to drop off the backpack and to check on Kylie before making the long drive to Alabama. Sandy assured her that she would take good care of both her women, again bringing tears to Bet's eyes. With a hug and kiss to both of them, she was gone.

†

The hours on the road flew by as Bet replayed the last week of her life and how beautiful and crazy it had gotten. She surveyed her memory of her life in Alabama, which seemed to be quickly fading away, and decided upon what items to pack to return to Georgia and her new life and what items would be sold or donated. As she drove she dialed up an old friend who volunteered to come over the next day to help her make arrangements to sell the house and to pack up their belongings.

Not until she finally pulled up in front of her house and killed the engine did the reality of the monumental tasks ahead of her set in. Bet would attend the memorial service for the man she was married to for five years and close out a chapter in her life that she would rather forget.

The house was deadly silent as she turned her key and stepped inside the place they had called home. Her steps echoed on the hardwood floors as she walked deeper into the house. She had poured her heart and soul into making it a home for Kylie. There were remnants of Brian's final rage scattered across the kitchen in the form of broken bottles, and bits of furniture. Bet shivered at the memory of those drunken rages. She quickly cleaned up the mess then walked into their bedroom. Brian had ripped most of her remaining clothes to pieces. Shocked by the evidence of his anger she bagged the ruined items, and carried them to the curb placing them with the rest of the garbage. She packed the remaining items in small suitcases and filled boxes with items to donate to charity, which she left stacked neatly by the door. With the most painful room complete, Bet moved into her daughter's room. The room was alive with her young child's spirit; the walls covered with her artwork and pictures of the two of them together at the park, the beach or at birthday parties. Bet could no longer hold the tears back as she packed away Kylie's stuff. Finally, physically and emotionally exhausted, Bet lay down on Kylie's bed and snuggled into the soft pillow and collapsed in a deep, restful sleep.

When she awoke the next morning to the ringing of her phone, Bet was startled briefly until she realized where she was. When she answered, Sue, her friend, was calling to invite her to breakfast before they started preparing the house for showing. It was good to see her old friend and over coffee and mounds of fresh pancakes, Bet told her friend of her life since escaping Brian and leaving Alabama.

Sue listened patiently as Bet retold the story of how Brian had tracked them down, stalking Alex and nearly killing her. She could see Sue cringe as she described the first few harrowing days in the hospital with Alex.

"This Alex sounds like a terrific person," Sue said, smiling at her friend.

"She is truly fantastic." The smile on Bet's face as she talked about Alex told Sue just how happy both she and Kylie had become.

Totally sated with pancakes and coffee, Bet and Sue returned to the house to continue emptying the house, packing up items that would return to Georgia and those to donate.

Late afternoon passed quickly and Bet showered and dressed for the memorial for Brian. She steeled herself for the flood of memories that would surely engulf her at his service. On the way to the chapel, she drove by the cemetery to locate Brian's final resting place. Bet sat in the car and shed a river of tears for the man she once loved but had grown to hate over the past few years. No one person should inflict so much pain and suffering, and to have forced Alex to endure what she was growing through because of her kindness toward her and Kylie was just inexcusable.

Bet slowly drove to the chapel and spoke with Brian's parents. She felt horrible for their loss, but at least no one else would have to face the rage Brian harbored inside himself. Bet gave them the number to Alex's home and promised that Kylie would come down for visits so she could stay in touch with her grandparents. They sat together as the minister spoke kind words about a man he obviously knew little about. Out of kindness to Brian's parents Bet stayed mute during the service.

Afterward, Bet invited his parents to the house to take whatever pictures of Brian or personal possessions of his that they were interested in having. She was surprised at the few items of Brian's that they wanted. When they left, Bet sat down on the couch with an audible sigh, relieved that at least that part of her journey was over. Sue returned a short time later and they finished packing up the house. Bet had an appointment with a Realtor the next morning to list the house, and with luck, she would be well on her way home by noon. She was so eager to see Kylie and Alex again that it lifted her spirits and made the task of shutting down the house much easier. With Sue's help she packed the Outback and set the remainder of the boxes to the curb for pick up before they went out to dinner. Bet had decided to spend her last night in Alabama in a hotel, unable to stand the thought of spending the night in a house where she had suffered so much pain and anguish.

†

She parted with Sue around eight and checked into the hotel. She called Sandy's house to check on Kylie. Kylie was so excited about her first day of school that she could barely get a word in between her excited chatter.

"I sure hope she can sleep tonight," Bet said when Sandy came back on the line.

"She has been this excited all day," Sandy said with a chuckle.

"How is Alex today?"

"She is missing you terribly, but looks really good. Dr. Lee told her she could move back into a private room Wednesday if she continues to rest so she is behaving herself very nicely." Sandy laughed.

"That is excellent news. I hope to leave here shortly after lunchtime tomorrow which will put me in late, but at least I will be home."

"We are all eager for your return, but do drive careful tomorrow."

"I will," Bet promised and hung up the phone.

After a hot shower, she lay down on the bed and drifted into sleep filled with sweet dreams of Kylie and Alex fishing out on the lake with Max. When she awoke the next morning, she showered quickly and went out to the house, eager to get on with the morning. She stopped at the mailbox to check the mail and placed the change of address card inside. She found several envelopes marked to her attention. Bet carried the envelopes inside and laid them on the table as she jotted notes to call to disconnect the phone service, utilities, and other scheduled deliveries. When she finally got around to opening the envelopes, she found a check from Brian's auto insurance to cover the destruction of his truck, and another huge sum from his life insurance that was unexpected. There was also a third envelope. Brian's parents had reported his death to Social Security and the letter stated both she and Kylie would begin receiving checks as survivor benefits in the next few months.

Bet was taken aback for a moment with the large sum of money she held in her hand. No amount of money could compensate for what she and Kylie had endured, but at least she had the money now to make sure Kylie would not lack for anything for many years to come. Bet decided she would use the insurance money from Brian's truck as a down payment on a new truck for Alex and the rest invest somehow for Kylie's future.

Bet had just finished her calls when the Realtor rang the doorbell. She was surprised to learn that Bet wanted to sell the house furnished and promised to get her the most she could for the home. Bet gave the Realtor her contact information and walked her to the door, giving her the set of house keys she no longer had a need to keep. With one final look, Bet walked to the Outback and closed the chapter on her life in Alabama.

✝

The miles couldn't pass quickly enough heading north. She barely stopped for anything besides gas and rolled into Sandy's driveway near eight thirty. Kylie nearly knocked her down at the door and talked nonstop until Bet told her it was time for her to go to bed. She tucked Kylie under the covers and kissed her forehead softly. "I love you, baby girl," she softly said and with heavy eyes Kylie said, "I love you too, Mom."

Bet chatted with Sandy for a few minutes until Sandy just couldn't stand her fidgeting anymore. "You need to head on up to the hospital now, dear," Sandy finally said, much to Bet's relief.

"Thanks for everything, Sandy," Bet said as she headed toward the door and disappeared into the dark night.

Chapter Seventeen

When Bet arrived at the hospital she sat behind the wheel of the Outback for a few minutes to collect her thoughts. She finally felt free. Free to begin a new life with Alex, and raise Kylie in a manner she felt a child should be, surrounded only by love. Free to be with the woman she loved so dearly without fear of repercussions from the father of her child, and free to love the way she always dreamed. With a renewed bounce in her step, Bet walked into the hospital eager to see the woman she loved.

She stopped at the nurses' station long enough to get a status report on Alex, which left her glowing. Dr. Lee had left orders to move her back to a private room first thing the next morning and within a few days she would be home. Home, what a beautiful sounding word. It echoed in her mind as she walked to Alex's room, and when she pulled back the curtain to step into the room she knew for the first time in her life, she had truly found home with the woman lying asleep on the bed. Bet stood at the foot of the bed for several minutes watching Alex sleep. There was absolutely no doubt that Alex loved both she and Kylie, and Bet knew that she would go to her grave to protect them. Ironic thought, as Alex had just about done that already. Bet moved around the edge of the bed, bent down and softly placed her lips on Alex's. "I love you so much, Alex," she whispered.

"I love you too, Bet," Alex whispered back and Bet looked up to see her sparkling eyes watching her. Alex raised her arm to drape around Bet's neck and pulled her face down for a long, sensual kiss that left them both a little breathless.

"Welcome home, baby. Did everything go as planned in Alabama?" she asked.

"Things went very well and I am so very happy to be home."

She took Alex's hand in hers as she sat on the edge of the bed. "How are you feeling?"

"Like a brand-new woman," Alex answered with a huge smile.

"You look fantastic, darling." Bet was unable to take her eyes off Alex. "I can't wait until you go back downstairs so I can snuggle in beside you on the bed. I missed you so badly these last two days."

"I missed you too, honey. I'm glad you are home safe and sound. You do look so very tired though, so why don't you spend the night at the house in a nice comfortable bed."

"There is no way I am leaving your side again. I have every intention of spending the rest of my life right beside you every night starting with tonight, Ms. Graves," she said with a smile.

Alex chuckled with Bet's response. "Very well then, my dear, there is no way I can argue with that."

They chatted deep into the night about Bet's trip to Alabama until Alex's eyes started to grow heavy. Bet kissed Alex once again and then stretched out in the reclining chair, her hand covering Alex's, and fell into a deep exhausted sleep.

✝

The next morning Bet woke to find Alex propped up in her bed watching her sleep. "Good morning, sunshine," she said when Bet's eyes fluttered open.

"What time is it?"

"It's almost nine, darling."

"Nine. Why did you let me sleep so late?"

"Because you obviously needed the rest."

"I guess you are right." Bet stretched her arms and yawned. "Have you already had breakfast?"

"A big one, as a matter of fact," Alex said with a smile. "The nurses say they are kicking me out of here this morning too. Why don't you go home and shower and check on Kylie while they get me all set up downstairs."

"That is a very good idea," Bet said. "Would you mind if I brought Kylie back with me? I know she is dying to see you and tell you about school."

"I would be disappointed if you returned without her. I bet she is going ninety to nothing about school."

"Oh, Alex. She is so happy and loves school so much. She hates to leave at lunchtime and wishes she could stay all day."

"Well, I certainly hope her hunger for knowledge will stay with her the rest of her life. You know, if she really wants to go to school all day, we could consider the private school. They have all-day classes."

"We can certainly bring that up to Kylie and let her decide."

"So kiss me and hit the road so these ladies can spring me from this place," Alex said with a smile playing in her eyes. "I need to see some sunlight soon. These windowless rooms up here are killing me."

Bet kissed her deeply. "We will be back soon then, love." As she walked out of the hospital, Bet planned her morning. She would drive out to the house and unload the Outback and then shower and dress before returning to town. She planned a stop at the bank to open an account for Kylie and to cash the auto insurance check. She would take that money to Sandy and ask Glen to buy Alex's new truck with it. By then she could take Kylie up to the hospital after school. Smiling to herself, Bet drove to the house to begin a beautiful day.

Unpacking the Outback was much easier than packing it up. After several trips into the house, she had the car unloaded and the bags settled in various rooms of the house. She showered, dressed, and stopped downstairs where Alex's bed was set up. She held her pillow to her face, breathing in the scent of Alex that lingered there. She locked the door and headed off to the bank to open her accounts and made it to Alex's office just before lunch. She handed Sandy the envelope of cash to give to Glen, and asked her to have him arrange for Alex's new truck.

"Glen will be like a kid in a candy store getting to pick out a new truck for Alex. So don't be surprised if there is a new truck sitting in the yard tomorrow," Sandy teased.

"Well, I certainly don't have a clue about buying her a truck All I know is it has to be green, according to Kylie."

"Speaking of which, I believe your little angel is about to arrive," Sandy said, pointing to the school bus that was entering the parking lot.

Sure enough, seconds later Kylie came bouncing through the door. She ran up to Bet and hugged her tightly. "I love you, Mom."

"I love you too, baby. How was school today?"

"It was fantastic, Mom, I got to read in front of the class today."

"That is fabulous news, Kylie, I am so proud of you." Bet hugged her daughter again.

"How is Alex?" Kylie asked.

"She is doing great, and was moved back into a private room this morning."

Kylie's eyes lit up. "So I can go see her again?"

"Yes, ma'am, I was waiting to take you back to the hospital for a visit."

"Tell Alex I will stop by after work this afternoon," Sandy said as she walked them to the door. "Maybe you and I will hit the diner tonight if that's okay with you Kylie?"

"Sounds yummy to me," Kylie answered as she slipped her hand inside Bet's. "See you later Miss Sandy."

†

Kylie all but dragged Bet across the hospital parking lot in her excitement to see Alex. When Bet opened the door to the room, Kylie flew across the floor to climb up on the bed next to Alex, giving her a huge hug. "I have missed you so, Alex."

Alex hugged her tightly. "I have missed you too, Kylie. I'm sorry if I scared you the other night."

"It's okay, Alex, I am just happy to see you again."

"So tell me about school," Alex said as Kylie snuggled in beside her.

Bet sat back in the recliner and watched as Kylie and Alex chatted about her first week in school, both of them excited about the events taking place. When Kylie slowed down enough to take a breath, Bet asked her a question. "Kylie, would you like to go to school all-day?"

Bet and Alex watched as Kylie thought carefully about her answer. "No, Mom, I like school a lot, but if I went to school all day then I wouldn't get to work with Alex and Miss Sandy."

Alex chuckled. "Well, I guess that issue is settled."

Bet, Kylie, and Alex talked the afternoon away. Late in the day, they heard a knock on the door. When it opened, Glen walked in carrying a large container of flowers and followed by Sandy. "Hey, boss," Glen said, setting the flowers down on a nightstand. "The boys wanted to send you these to cheer you up."

"That is very sweet of them, Glen, be sure to thank them for me."

"How are you feeling, Alex?"

"I feel terrific except for the itching going on under these casts. Two more days and I'm home free. Bet tells me you and the boys have me all set up at the house with a ramp and have moved my bed downstairs. Thank you so much for doing that."

Glen shuffled his feet with a blush rising. "That's the least we could do for you, Alex."

"The final inspection on the house is being done on Friday. If all goes well I plan on giving the crew two weeks off, if that's okay with you, boss."

"That will be fine, Glen. After that, we can begin clearing for the next two homes and maybe by the time that is finished I will have the plans finished up for both."

"Mark called again today and asked when his clients could see the house," Sandy said.

"Call him back tomorrow and tell him he can schedule a tour for his clients for Friday afternoon, and tell him the price will be firm at four hundred fifty thousand," Alex said.

"Will do, boss," Sandy said with a smile. It was so good to see the old Alex back making decisions and excited to be back to work.

Glen still shuffled around the end of the bed. "I was wondering if I could borrow Kylie for a little while? I need your help with something, if you wouldn't mind Kylie?"

Kylie looked at Alex first and she nodded her head "Can I go, Mom?" she asked, proud that Glen needed her.

"Sure thing, honey." Bet guessed Glen was going truck shopping for Alex.

"Cool." Kylie crawled down from the bed. "Let's go, Glen."

The adults broke out in laughter at Kylie's excitement, knowing she had no clue what Glen was planning. "Well, I guess we will see you later tonight then."

"I wonder what that is all about," Alex said.

"There's no telling," Sandy said with a wink to Bet.

"I just hope Glen knows what he's gotten himself into," Bet said with a chuckle.

"I am sure he can handle anything Kylie comes up with," Sandy said confidently. "Is there anything you need me to do, Alex?"

"You can go ahead and type up a contract for Mark's clients. I feel confident that once they have seen the finished project, they will jump on the offering price."

"I will have it ready by Friday morning," Sandy said. "I think I will head off to the house. Will you ask Glen to drop Kylie by when they return?"

"Sure will, Sandy, and thanks again for everything," Bet said.

"It has been a pleasure. I hadn't realized how much fun it could be having a child in my home. I hope Kylie will still visit after Alex goes home."

"I'm sure she will," Alex said as she smiled at the woman who was as much a friend as a mother figure to Alex.

"Well, just call if you need anything," Sandy said.

"Honey, would you mind if I sketched a bit?" Alex asked after Sandy left.

"Not at all, Alex." Bet stood to retrieve her sketchpad and pencils. When Bet opened up the sketchpad to hand it to Alex, her eyes fell upon the words "Our Place" written across the top of the page. She handed the pad to Alex and waited for her explanation.

"Would you mind if we had a larger home for our new family?" Alex asked.

"I had plans to ask you what one of the new homes you were planning would cost me," Bet said. "I wanted to use Brian's life insurance to invest in a home for Kylie."

"This one will be ours," Alex said. "I would rather you set up a trust for Kylie with the insurance money for her college fund and to give her a good start in life once she gets older."

"Oh Alex," Bet said with tears in her eyes, "I do love you so."

"Besides, Glen has wanted my house for years and would jump at the opportunity to buy it for his family. So in a sense it would stay in the family as well. Kylie, Max, and I can still go fishing whenever we wanted and the new home will have everything else we need."

"I would love that." Bet leaned over to kiss Alex.

"So tell me then, miss, what do you think of our home so far?" Alex asked as she turned page after page, showing her the design of their new home.

"It looks perfect," Bet said as she watched Alex draw in more and more detail. Bet sat beside Alex and watched as the new home came to life before her eyes, adding to the fairy tale feeling of her new life.

Hours later Kylie and Glen returned from the truck dealership and Kylie bounced onto the bed holding a brochure, which had a picture of Alex's new truck. "We did it, Mom," Kylie said excitedly.

"Did what, honey?"

"We bought Alex's new truck and it looks just like this." She unfolded the brochure across Alex's lap.

"Holy cow, it's even green," Alex said as she hugged Kylie's neck.

"I remembered it was your favorite color."

"Paid in full and will be delivered tomorrow," Glen said as he handed the paperwork to Bet.

"Thanks, Glen," Bet said. "I wouldn't have had a clue of what to get."

"Oh, it was a pleasure, Bet. Kylie and I had a blast picking it out and my brother-in-law appreciated the business."

"Glen, will you stay for a minute?"

"Sure, Alex, what's up?"

"I have something to ask Kylie and, depending on her answer, we have something to discuss."

Kylie looked up, awaiting her question. "Kylie, how would you like to live in the new house I am planning for the top of the mountain? I would like to make it our new home, if you wouldn't mind."

"Could we still go fishing and swimming?"

"That will depend on the new owner," Alex said. "Would it be all right with you, Glen?"

"Oh, heck yeah! You mean you will really sell me your house, Alex?"

"I think that decision has been made. Yes, Glen, if you are still interested."

"Of course you could swim and fish as much as you would like, Kylie," Glen said with a smile that threatened to be a permanent fixture on his face. "I can't wait to tell the wife and kids." He jumped up from his seat.

"I should have the plan ready by the time the boys have the lot cleared in a few weeks, so we can get started." Alex was almost as excited as Glen.

"Oh, Alex," Glen said, "you have made my dreams come true again. You know how badly I have wanted that house." He had tears in his eyes as he leaned down to kiss Alex on the cheek. "We will build you the best house ever," he promised as he stood beside his boss and friend.

"I know you will, and I will be there every step of the way to make sure it's the best it can be."

Glen sat back, still in shock at the news and just grinned at Alex, Bet, and Kylie. "This is the best news ever."

"I have one more favor to ask tonight," Alex said.

"Anything you want, Alex."

"Sandy asked if you would drop Kylie by her house on your way home tonight. Seems the two of them have dinner plans down at the diner tonight."

Glen grinned again. "Sure thing. Are you ready, Kylie?"

Kylie kissed Alex and her mom goodnight and walked toward the door with Glen. She stopped midway across the room and turned back to look at Alex. "Thank you for building us a home, Alex," she said sweetly.

"You are very welcome, Kylie," Alex said with tears in her eyes.

"See you at lunch tomorrow, honey," Bet said as Glen and Kylie left the room.

Tears of joy slid down Alex's cheek as Kylie's words struck deep in her heart. Bet crept onto the bed beside her and reached over to softly brush the tears away. "It looks like you are stuck with us for good now," she teased her lover.

Alex wrapped her arm around Bet's shoulder and embraced her body with all her might. Bet snuggled into the warmth of Alex's body and together they drifted off to sleep. A nurse turned down the lights when she came in to check on Alex and wrapped together they slept the night away dreaming of their new home together.

Chapter Eighteen

The next morning they woke to the clanging of the breakfast cart coming down the hallway. Bet looked at Alex. "I can't believe we slept through the dinner trays," she said with a chuckle.

"I can," Alex said. "I'm starved."

"Well, let me wake up and go down to the cafeteria then because I know that whatever is going to be on that breakfast tray is only going to tease you."

"Hurry back," Alex said with a wicked grin on her face and watched as Bet left the room.

Bet was right. The breakfast tray held oatmeal, toast, and two small strips of bacon that Alex had devoured by the time Bet returned. Dr. Lee was sitting beside Alex's bed when Bet walked in and the smile on Alex's face told her that he was bringing good news. "Good morning, Dr. Lee."

"Good morning, Bet. I was just telling Alex that I want to do one more CAT scan this morning. Then, if she's ready, I thought we might send her home today."

"That is great news!"

"Finish your breakfast and I will schedule the test with the nurses. Then we will get you out of here, probably around lunchtime," Dr. Lee said and left the room.

"Oh, honey, that is such wonderful news!"

"I can't wait to get home. It seems like forever since we have spent a night in our bed," Alex added, a gleam of mischief in her eyes.

"Breakfast first, Romeo," Bet teased, "then we will get you ready to go home.

Together they ate a hearty breakfast of scrambled eggs, toasted English muffins with jelly and bacon slices. Bet had just finished clearing the bedside table when the nurse came in to wheel Alex down for her CAT scan.

Bet picked up the phone and called Sandy at the office.

"Is everything all right?" Sandy asked worriedly after hearing Bet's voice on the phone.

"It's wonderful, Sandy. Alex will be released to go home today at lunch and I wondered if you could bring Kylie home and help me get Alex settled in at the house?"

"We will meet you at the house just as soon as we can get there. How about Kylie and I pick up some burgers from the diner for lunch?"

"That will be fantastic. Could you also ask Glen to bring Max home as well?"

"Sure thing. I know he will be so excited to see Alex and Kylie."

"Great, I will see you at lunchtime," Bet said and hung up.

It took Bet two trips down to the car to get all of their belongings packed into the back of the Outback. As she packed the car, she realized she wouldn't be able to get Alex and a wheelchair in the car. She called Sandy back once she returned to the room and asked that she stop by the medical supply store and pick up a folding wheelchair before meeting her out at the house.

Bet paced anxiously in the room until Alex returned from the test. "Crank up the car, baby," she said as the nurse wheeled her back into the room. "We are going home!"

"Hold on, hotshot," the nurse teased, "there is still paperwork to be done yet. It won't take too long though." She winked at Bet.

"I will keep her from bolting until you get back," Bet promised as the nurse left to finish the paperwork.

"I am so ready to be outside," Alex said.

"Well, let's see if I can take you downstairs to wait for the paperwork then." She left the room and received approval from the nurse to take Alex downstairs.

Once outside, Alex lifted her face to the sun and sighed as the warm rays caressed her face. "This feels so good, Bet, you just don't know."

They only had to wait a few more minutes for the nurse to join them with the discharge paperwork. Bet went to the parking lot and got the Outback. Carefully she and the nurse were able to place Alex across the backseat and propped her with a hospital pillow against the door. "Don't take any turns too tight and sling her out of the car," the nurse teased as she closed the door. "I would hate to have her as a patient again so soon."

"I promise to be careful." Bet crawled into the driver's seat. "Are we all set, babe?"

"Let's do it before they change their mind and decide to keep me longer." Alex grinned.

✝

Bet carefully pulled away from the hospital and they were on their way home at last. She glanced in the rearview mirror to find Alex looking out the window at the passing countryside, a huge smile on her face. When they finally reached the turn to the drive, Bet heard a sigh come from the backseat. As Bet made the turn, they saw a small crowd in their front yard to welcome Alex home. Max ran to meet them halfway up the drive, his excited barks ringing through the hollow. When they pulled up at the house, Alex opened the door and Max immediately covered her face with kisses. Bet heard Kylie's voice call Max and the obedient dog ran over to sit beside Kylie while Glen, Sandy, and Bet helped Alex out of the Outback and into the wheelchair Sandy had picked up. Alex caught sight of the beautiful green Chevy truck parked in her drive and smiled at Kylie and Glen. "She's beautiful," she said as Bet rolled her over to the truck. "You two did an excellent job of picking her out." Kylie and Glen grinned wildly.

"She runs like a charm."

"I bet she does. I can't wait to give her a test drive."

"Well, that will be a few weeks yet, sweetie," Bet said. "But at least you can sit out on the porch and admire her for a while."

Bet rolled the wheelchair up the ramp and turned the chair so Alex could look across the yard. Max sat in front of her and laid his head in her lap to welcome her home. "Is anyone hungry besides me?" Sandy asked.

She and Bet arranged a small table in front of them and they all feasted on burgers and fries from the diner and drank a gallon of sweet tea. After the meal, Kylie and Max played in the yard as the four adults sat on the porch and talked.

"It is so good to be home," Alex said.

"It's good to see you up and moving about," Glen said. "Just don't overdo it on your first day home."

"Yes, mother." Alex punched him in the arm.

"Well, just don't make us have to load you up in the back of your new truck and haul you back to the hospital."

"All right, enough already." Alex laughed. "I promise to be good."

Sandy asked Bet, "Do you need any help getting her in the bed?"

"No, I think I can handle it from here, but thanks."

"Well, let's get a move on then, Glen, and let these folks relax for the rest of the day."

"Call me tomorrow after the inspection, Glen, and Sandy please let me know what Mark says after his ladies visit the house."

"Will do," they said in unison. Both hugged and kissed Alex before Sandy took Glen back to get his truck.

✝

Bet and Alex watched Max and Kylie play, the silence between them comfortable as the shining sun warmed them. After another half hour, Kylie and Max walked onto the porch and fell down, exhausted from playing. "You know what?" Alex said. "I think we could all use a nap."

"That does sound good. Then later maybe Kylie will help me make some spaghetti."

"Yummy, Mom," came Kylie's response as she stood to hold the door open for Alex and Bet.

Bet managed to place Alex on the bed comfortably while Kylie washed her hands in the bathroom. Kylie crawled in beside Alex, Bet joined them and Max took his spot beside the bed.

"It's good to be home," Kylie said as she snuggled in between Alex and her mom.

"Yes, it is," Alex said as she smiled at Kylie.

The quiet of the house and the comfort of their bodies snuggled together quickly had Alex and Kylie snoozing away. Bet watched as the two most important people in her life napped. With love swelling her heart she closed her eyes and napped with her family.

Several hours later, Kylie began stretching in her sleep as her body began to wake. Alex and Bet watched as she slowly opened her eyes and smiled up at them. "Did you have a good nap, baby?" Bet asked.

"Yes, Mom, I did." She stretched one last time before sitting up on the bed between them.

"Why don't you take Max outside for a few minutes while I help Alex to the bathroom and then we can get started on supper."

"Okay, Mom." Kylie bounded off the bed with Max hot on her heels.

"Are you ready?" she asked Alex.

"My kidneys are about to burst," Alex said with a grin.

"So why didn't you wake me?"

"Because I was enjoying watching you more."

"Silly woman," Bet said as she sat Alex up on the bed and then eased her into the wheelchair.

"After dinner, if you would like, I can give you a light bath and change you into some shorts and a T-shirt. That might make you more comfortable."

"That would be wonderful," Alex said as Bet left her in the bathroom for some privacy.

"Just call me when you are finished." Bet closed the door and walked over to look out at Max and Kylie playing down by the lake. "Pure heaven," Bet whispered to herself.

"Bet," Alex called from the bathroom.

Bet stood Alex up and turned her in her arms to place her back in the wheelchair, but Alex had a different plan. She took Bet in her arms and kissed her deeply as she leaned against the wall for support. "I want you so badly," Alex whispered as they broke the kiss.

"Tonight, I promise." Bet sealed the promise with steamy kiss then lowered Alex into the wheelchair and wheeled her to the kitchen. "Do you feel like sitting up while we cook?"

"Yes, ma'am, I do."

"Why don't you gather up our children and we'll start cooking," Bet said before she kissed Alex softly.

"Will do." Alex rolled over to the front door. "Kylie, Max, it's time to come in," she yelled out to the yard and both kids came running onto the porch. "Wash your hands while your mom gets started," Alex instructed Kylie.

"Yes, ma'am." Kylie disappeared into the bathroom and then joined Bet in the kitchen.

Alex sat back in her chair and watched as mother and daughter toiled happily together in the kitchen to make a spaghetti dinner complete with salad and garlic toast. Kylie set the table and then poured dog food in Max's bowl while Bet served up the food.

Alex wheeled up to the table and took Bet's and Kylie's hands as Kylie began her nightly prayer.

"Dear God. Thank you for this wonderful meal we are about to eat and thank you for bringing Alex and Max home to our family again. Amen."

"Amen," Alex and Bet repeated.

Bet and Kylie giggled as they watched Alex try to eat spaghetti with one hand, but with a little practice, she finally got the hang of it and quickly caught up with the two of them, and even had a plate of seconds before they were all stuffed. Bet and Kylie cleaned up the kitchen and then went upstairs to pick out clothes for her to wear to school tomorrow.

"Why don't you take Max out for a few minutes and then it's time for a bath and bed for you, honey."

"Okay, Mom." Kylie ran down the stairs to take Max outside for a few minutes.

Bet went into Alex's bedroom and picked out a shirt and pair of shorts for Alex to wear after her bath and then went downstairs. "As soon as I get Kylie tucked away, I will come down and give you your bath," she said as her fingers played in Alex's hair.

"Will you tuck me in as well?"

"After I wear you out first," Bet replied with a wicked grin.

"Mmm, I do like the sound of that." Alex smiled up at Bet.

Kylie and Max came bounding through the door at that moment. "Hold onto that thought for a little while and I will be back. Are you ready for your bath, Kylie?" Bet asked.

"Yes, ma'am," Kylie said as she headed up the stairs.

"I'll be back for you next."

"I'll be waiting."

†

Bet followed Kylie up to the bathroom and drew her daughter's bathwater as they chatted. "I do believe Max really missed you, honey," she said as Kylie stepped in the tub.

"I missed him too, Mom. He is so much fun to play with."

Bet helped Kylie bathe and wash her hair, amazed at how quickly it was growing. "You are getting to be such a big girl," Bet said as she realized just how fast Kylie was growing up.

"Aww, Mom, I will always be your little girl," Kylie said in a tone that warmed Bet to the bone.

"Yes, you will, honey, no matter how old you get," Bet said with a laugh.

Bet helped Kylie dress in her pajamas then watched as her daughter used the blow-dryer to dry her hair. It wouldn't be much longer until Kylie didn't need her help, so Bet cherished every moment of her daughter's growing up. Kylie brushed her teeth and then looked to Bet for her approval.

"All set, sweetie?"

"Yes, ma'am. I'm going to go down and say goodnight to Alex and then I will be ready for you to tuck me into bed."

Kylie crawled into Alex's lap once she went downstairs and hugged the tall woman close. "Goodnight, Alex," she said sweetly and kissed her on the cheek. "It is so good to have you home again." With another hug, she was on her way back upstairs.

"Goodnight, Kylie," was all a shocked Alex could manage to say, but for the young child climbing the stairs, they were the only words needed.

Kylie crawled under the covers and Bet tucked them around her body. "I hope you have very sweet dreams tonight, honey. I love you, baby."

"I love you too, Mom."

Bet kissed Kylie on the forehead and turned to leave the room. "Please tell Alex and Max I love them too," she said as Bet turned off the light.

"I sure will, Kylie," Bet said as she quietly closed the bedroom door.

Walking up behind Alex, Bet whispered in her ear, "Are you ready for your bath?"

"Yes, ma'am, I am," Alex purred.

Bet pushed the wheelchair into the downstairs bath and drew some water in the tub while she stripped Alex's body. Bet carefully bathed her body, softly caressing the bruised areas that were still healing from the trauma and softly patting her body dry with a thick towel. She covered her body with silky lotion and helped her into the shorts and shirt she had brought down for her. "If you can tilt your head over the sink I can wash your hair for you," she told Alex. With a few awkward attempts, Alex managed to do just that.

The feel of the warm water on her head and the soft massage of Bet's hands were a wonderful combination and Alex felt her whole body relax under her touches. Bet rinsed and then towel dried and brushed Alex's hair.

"Do you feel better now?" she asked.

"Almost human again," Alex said as she reached for Bet. "Thank you for taking such good care of me."

"I am not done with you yet," Bet said and rolled the wheelchair over to the side of the bed. She helped Alex onto the bed and sat down beside her. "Give me a few minutes to shower and I will be back. Is there anything you need before I go?"

"A kiss, to hold me until you get back." Alex pulled Bet down to the bed and kissed her deeply. "Hurry back," she said when they broke the kiss.

†

Alex lay back on the bed and gazed out the window. She could hear the water running as Bet showered, and she watched the moon as it slowly began to rise. She was very relaxed and almost to the point of sleepiness when she felt Bet slip onto the bed beside her.

"Welcome back," she said in a husky voice.

"Did you miss me?" Bet teased.

"Oh, how I have missed you." Alex pulled Bet down for a kiss.

Bet's hand slid beneath the soft fabric of Alex's T-shirt and her fingertips grazed Alex's nipples as they swelled under her touch. Alex moaned into Bet's mouth as her hands softly caressed her sensitive breasts causing her heart rate to double. Bet's hand slid farther down Alex's body and disappeared under the waistband of her shorts to cover the warm mound that was becoming wetter by the minute. Her fingers teased the soft curls surrounding Alex's lips. Bet moved down the bed to remove the shorts from Alex's body.

Alex felt Bet's warm breath on her bare skin as she bent her head down to breathe in the scent of her excitement. Her body shivered with anticipation of Bet's touch. Bet kissed her way up Alex's body leaving a trail of gooseflesh in her wake and slowly lifted the shirt above Alex's head. Alex could feel the heat in Bet's skin as she lowered her naked body on top of her. Her right hand circled Bet's waist, caressing the soft skin of her back as Bet parted her lips with an urgent tongue.

They kissed deeply as their bodies moved together in a lover's dance, moving and flowing together with a growing need. Bet kissed her way down Alex's neck and covered a breast with her heated kisses. Her fingers parted Alex's swollen lips and entered her body, slowly stroking the liquid velvet with soft touches. Bet's mouth and fingers teased her body into a frenzy of desire and soon Alex's eyes were begging her for relief. Carefully, Bet moved down between Alex's thighs and spread her lips gently with her fingertips as the tip of her tongue lapped gently at the wetness, moving deeper with each stroke, until her tongue was deep inside Alex. Alex's fingers tangled in Bet's hair and soon she was convulsing in pleasure with each stroke of Bet's tongue.

Bet could feel Alex's hand on the back of her head, urging her on. Turning her body to allow Alex to touch her, she continued to give her lover pleasure. Alex parted Bet's lips with her fingers and plunged deeper into her wetness with each new stroke of her fingers. She could feel Bet's hips as they thrust down to meet her fingers, pressing her deeper inside as Bet's mouth moved onto her clit and she slipped two fingers into Alex's wetness.

"I want to taste you," Alex groaned as Bet's tongue circled her clit. Bet moved her hips carefully, straddling Alex's face.

Alex's tongue sank into Bet's wetness greedily drinking from her body as Bet's teeth grazed across her clit and her fingers dove faster and faster between Alex's quivering thighs. Bet could feel Alex's muscles tighten around her fingers and knew she was close to climax. She began grinding her hips onto Alex's face, coating her with wetness as her body began to quake with the beginnings of her own orgasm. Alex feasted on the rush of juices flowing from Bet as her body exploded. Alex could no longer hold back the flood of desire she had bottled up inside her and she came hard against Bet's face and fingers. Bet rode the wave of Alex's pleasure until she could no longer feel the pulsing of her muscles against her fingers then slowly turned to face her lover. Alex held out her hand and placed Bet's head on her shoulder as they both recovered from the heated lovemaking.

Bet could hear the strong beating of Alex's heart as her head lay on her shoulder and could feel the vibrations from her body become more distant as her orgasm faded away. The softness of Alex's hand on her body invited her to look up into the face and dark eyes of the woman she loved so much. The fire burning there she knew was hers alone and would never again be matched by any other. She smiled at Alex and lowered her mouth onto hers for a long, sensual kiss that seemed to last an eternity.

"I love you, Alex," Bet breathed into the skin of her face as her fingertips traced the outline of her jaw.

"I love you too, Bet," Alex breathed in response. She raised her eyes from Bet's face to look out the window again to see the full moon smiling down upon them.

The End

About the Author

Ali Spooner

Ali Spooner is a native of Florida, currently living and working in Memphis, TN. Home for Ali is Pensacola, Florida where she has a partner of twenty years, one son and a grandchild that has her wrapped completely around her little finger. Her other children are all four legged, three dogs and two cats, and my dearest companion in Memphis, Rascal, a rescued tiger kitten named after my favorite country group.

A true daughter of the South, Ali enjoy spinning stories about the South, the strong, but gentle women and creatures that make it a wondrous place to live.

As an "Indie" author, Ali has been writing for many years as a hobby, and after a cancer diagnosis in 2010, she decided to take a leap and start self-publishing and has published over a dozen stories. Ali's characters range from cowgirls and psychics, to a healthy dose of supernatural beings. She has written stand-alone titles and series. Ali frequently writes several stories at a time, depending on which characters are bouncing around loudest in her head.

Ali is an avid reader and her other hobbies include photography, outdoor activities and watching college sports.

Other Books from Affinity eBook Press

My Fair Maiden—Del Robertson

What's a hero to do?

Bodhi arrives at a so small, it's barely on the map village with only three things in mind: getting out of the heat, having a decent meal, and a better drink. She's managed one of the three at the local tavern before she's approached by a gorgeous maiden. That, in itself isn't so unusual. Women are attracted to her on a regular basis.

What's odd is the behavior of the locals. Everyone is acting strangely, including the beautiful Gwen. It doesn't take Bodhi long to figure out something is terribly wrong in this seemingly peaceful, isolated village. The question is…what?

She's a hero, a woman with a sword, and she knows how to use it. But, what's a hero to do when no one will admit there's anything amiss, much less ask for help, not even the maiden in distress…

What's a virgin to do?

Gwendolyn is a proper, chaste maiden living in a small, remote village. Hers is a simple life, filled with back-breaking, mind-numbing chores.

That is, until an ogre appears, demanding a virgin offering by the next full moon. It's her bad luck that she's just the tender, young morsel the villagers are willing to serve up on a platter.

She tries everything she can to escape her fate, but finds herself out of options and out of time, doomed to be an offering for an ogre.

Then, along comes a stranger. She's tall, she's blonde, and she's a professional swordswoman. She's also stunning enough to make many a maiden swoon. Problem is, she's not at all the hero Gwendolyn imagined. She's cocky, brazen, and rude. She's also Gwen's last, best hope.

Desert Blooms—Dannie Marsden

Luce's story continues in DESERT BLOOMS…

When we last met Luce Velazquez in Desert Heat, she went through hell and back to salvage her soul and reputation. Hoping to get her life back on track with lover Beth Ryan, a woman who understands her pain and can relate on every level. Instead, Luce is in the hospital, and Beth in protective custody.

Jessica Sullivan, Luce's friend and ex, has big doubts about the sincerity of Beth's love, and is in no hurry to release her from custody.

Can Luce's new found happiness last, or is Jessica correct in her doubts?

A heart stopping romance that will fill you with the wonder of friendship, anger of betrayal, and the everlasting vision of love.

Finding Her Way—Riley Jefferson

Is it love or just great sex?

After ending an abusive marriage, Jerrica Kerrison is finally alive and she's apologizing for nothing! She has a job with a financial firm in Boston, a townhouse in Newburyport, and a sports car she drives way too fast. Jerrica has everything except that indefinable emotion called love.

Madison Jeffrey is a lost soul. A PR job in the south has always protected Madison from the pressures of her family. But one day, fate brings her back to New England, forcing Madison to face her long buried demons, and a sister who despises her.

When a chance meeting brings Jerrica and Madison's separate worlds crashing together, the attraction is instantaneous. After one passionate night together, Jerrica retreats into the safety of her world, leaving Madison to figure out what happened.

Will Jerrica open up her heart to the idea of love? Can Madison finally believe that she is worthy of unconditional love? Or will a devil hiding in the shadows tear them apart?

HER—Lisa Ron

Fox has been looking for that one person who will make her feel complete-her perfect match.

Together with her friends, Megan and Tree, Fox continues her quest while dodging exes and clingers, laughing a lot along the way.

When she meets Madelino, she instantly knows that she finds HER.

Madeline has her own problems-notably a domineering husband.

Can Fox win her heart? Can they make a life together?

This story will make you laugh, cry, and hold your breath as the story unfolds.

With the right person love can conquer all.

Bayou Justice—Ali Spooner

Hell hath no fury like a woman scorned. When Kara, Sasha's, new lover is taken hostage as a diversionary tactic to allow the drug dealing Bellfontaine brothers to escape justice, Sasha springs into action.

Kara is released physically unharmed, however, her emotions, and budding career in the District Attorney's office are left in shambles when she is held blame for their release,

Appalled, by the failure of the criminal justice system, Sasha exacts her own brand of justice for the acts committed against her lover. From the Bayou's of Louisiana to the jungles of South America,

Sasha plots her revenge.

Beginning of the End—Alane Hotchkin

What happens when life doesn't go exactly as you planned and you must protect others from your own fate? Escaping a horrific childhood, Nikki longed to find happily ever after in adulthood. What she found was Hell. Or did it find her? Finding the courage to break the cycle of betrayal, she opens her heart one last time. Alex lived a childhood others dreamed of. Her father never once denied the young rebel a thing. All her life she dreamed of protecting others; to follow in her father's footsteps. Soon though she learned sex and fists made the most powerful of weapons. Alex controls the women in her life through fear and sex, will breaking the cycle be too much to overcome? Will loving Nikki be enough to change her, or is Alex beyond help?

Alex would give Nikki the world, but at what price? When a person's tightly controlled reality snaps what then…? This is the Beginning of the End for one of them and the ultimate sacrifice for the other. But who is who in this game of life?

Out of Retirement—Erica Lawson

Melanie Stokes was a doctor—a very good one, or so she hoped. She was calm and cool under pressure, and very little fazed her. Until…

Caitlin Joseph ran a small retirement home for older women in need. The fact that everyone in the house was gay was a coincidence, although it did cut down the number of women agreeing to live there.

Mel took up an offer to do some relief work for a local community center when their regular doctor was away on holidays. As soon as she arrived at the home she knew something was different about the place. Was it the little old lady chasing the paper boy down the street or the sign saying "Dykes Retirement Home"?

But there was something about the place that also appealed to her. Sure, Caitlin was cute as a button, but it was more the fact that she took very good care of her charges, despite their rather bizarre behavior.

The older women seized the opportunity to introduce a woman into Caitlin's lonely life, using any means possible to keep Mel coming back. Their plans were boosted by the introduction of another woman into the house, who set hearts a fluttering and blood pressure rising. Now if she was a lesbian it would have been perfect…

Letting Go— JM Dragon

A failed relationship puts Stella Hawke's life on the brink of chaos.

When her grandmother falls gravely ill in Ashville, Stella ends her army career to take care of the woman during her last weeks. Little does she know that an old army comrade, socialite Reggie Stockton, whose family owns the local newspaper, also lives in Ashville.

Will she allow herself to accept Reggie's help to turn her life around and let go of the past?

This is a journey where both women re-evaluate what they want out of life.

Will that path lead to happiness or to a parting of the ways?

Through the Darkness—Erin O'Reilly

Becca Cameron is a loner— by choice. She lives in a hundred year old farmhouse built by her great grandfather. A tragic accident in her home a year earlier drove away her lover, and Becca tries to accept what she cannot change and hang on to the belief that love can conquer all.

Chase Hunter, had a meteoric rise in the Eastman Corporation and was, at thirty-four, the youngest vice-president. To Chase, her work was all consuming leaving little time for friends or lovers. There was simply no place in her life for anything but her job.

When Becca and Chase meet at their work place, the attraction is spontaneous. Life begins to look brighter for both women as work takes a second seat to romance.

Unknown to either woman, someone is watching their every move…

Will passion outweigh doubt? Can love conqueror fear?

Galveston 1900: Swept Away—Linda Crist

On September 7-8, 1900, the island of Galveston, Texas, was destroyed by a hurricane, or 'tropical cyclone', as it was called in those days. This story is a fictional account of Mattie and Rachel, two women who lived there, and their lives during the time of the 'great storm'. Forced to flee from her family at a young age, Rachel Travis finds a home and livelihood on the island of Galveston. Independent, friendly, and yet often lonely, only one other person knows the dark secret that haunts her. Madeline "Mattie" Crockett is trapped in a loveless marriage, convinced that her fate is sealed. She never dares to dream of true happiness, until Rachel Travis comes walking into her life. As emotions come to light, the storm of Mattie's marriage converges with the very real hurricane. Can they survive, and build the life they both dream of?

This second edition of one of Linda Crist's best-loved novels maintains the original story, while incorporating some reader-pleasing passages that were cut from the first edition. As an added bonus, the short story "Something to Celebrate" is included at the end of the novel, detailing further adventures of Rachel and Mattie.

Rapture: Sins of the Sinners—A. C. Henley & Fran Heckrotte

A serial killer is targeting young lesbians throughout the state of Texas. Texas Ranger Cochetta Lovejoy is assigned to the case. Convinced she knows who is committing the murders, Ranger Lovejoy is willing to do whatever it takes to put the perpetrator behind bars--even if it means stretching the limits of the law by manipulating the judicial system. Detective Agnes Kelly-Elliott is one of Ft. Worth Police Department's finest investigators. When Ranger Lovejoy appears on the crime scene of a recent murder, Agnes fears a dark secret that, if revealed, could destroy her family ties, and end her career. This is a dark, gritty, graphic tale of desire gone awry, and flawed characters looking for redemption in all the wrong places.

Absolution—S. Anne Gardner

Games of the rich and famous, love, lust, and forbidden passions weave this tale that play out through decades and the world. The close ties the Alcalas have to the royal house of Spain provide them with an unspoken untouchable policy. Their passions and their secrets are about to come to light with a force that cannot be stopped. In this whirlwind is Cristina Uraca Alacala who is searching for a truth that has been denied to her most of her life and she must find. She is not unlike her family; Cristina does not stop until she gets what she wants. In the fog lies the truth that she must travel through to find.

In this tale wealthy socialite Annais Francesca D'Autremond is a pivotal person of interest in Cristina's search for the truth. When these two women meet they find themselves drawn together by something greater than themselves. As the truth of a hidden past becomes clearer their passions grow beyond the realm of the no return instead of a status quo. Both tied together by destiny; will both survive the onslaught of past and present passions?

Denial—Jackie Kennedy

Time spent in Somalia has Doctor Celeste Cameron accustomed to living and working in a war zone. Coming back home to America, Celeste is glad to see the end of the peril she has been in—or so she thinks. Danger seems to follow Celeste and she finds it in the shape of Amy. What Celeste feels for Amy scares her more than anything she has faced in war zones. Amy has the same feelings, but is in denial and vows to marry Josh, Celeste's twin brother, no matter what. When fate brings them together again, will they give in to their mutual attraction or will they once again deny what they feel.

Private Dancer—TJ Vertigo

Reece Corbett grew up on the mean streets on New York City, abused, used and in trouble with the law. Faith Ashford grew up wealthy, with all the creature comforts that money provides. When they meet fireworks begin.

Miriam and Esther—Sherry Barker

Miriam thought her life would play out in the bustling metropolis of Dallas, but after a life-changing accident, she moves to the small town of Cool Lake, Texas to get her head on straight and regain her senses.

McKee—A.C. Henley

Private Investigator Quinlan McKee has returned to Los Angeles after a three-year absence, only to find herself embroiled in a world of child slavery and police corruption.

Taming the Wolff—Del Robertson

ONLY ONE WOMAN...

As devastatingly beautiful as she is headstrong, noble-born Alexis DeVale abruptly finds her preordained life in upheaval. Abducted at sword-point, held for ransom, thrust into a maelstrom of lawlessness and piracy...

HAS THE POWER...

The strength of her passion, the depth of her love...

TO TAME THE WOLFF...

Mayhem. Brutality. Murder. These are the tools of the trade - and Kris Wolff is the master of her profession. Captain of the high seas, a roguish pirate, her heart hardened by life, her passion tightly controlled by the secret she's forced to keep. Faced with a new danger, The Wolff finds herself unable to guard her heart from the tumultuous desires that Alexis DeVale has awakened.

Caution Under Construction—TJ Vertigo

"Caution: Under Construction" is a story about learning, growth and happiness, and the pains it can take to achieve it. Mostly, it is about love, in all its aspects, from blinding passion for another, to love of family, and children of the four legged variety. Sheridan Landers needs to learn that love includes unexpected patience and basic human empathy.

Keefer Gibson has to learn to listen to her heart, and trust in someone whose womanizing reputation precedes her. Through it all, they both have to learn how to deal with a stalking, dangerous ex-girlfriend, who will not take 'no' for an answer.

E-Books, Print, Free e-books

Visit our website for more publications available online.

www.affinityebooks.com

Published by Affinity E-Book Press NZ LTD
Canterbury, New Zealand

Registered Company 2517228